A MIDLIFE GAMBLE

THE MIDLIFE TRILOGY
BOOK 3

CARY J HANSSON

ABOUT THE AUTHOR

Cary grew up in the UK, but now lives in Sweden. After a varied career that saw her tap-dancing in musicals and selling towels on shopping channels, she settled down to write contemporary fiction. She swims in the Baltic sea all year round, stands on her head once a day and prefers Merlot over Shiraz.

Please do consider joining my mailing list through my website: www.caryjhansson.com This is where you'll hear about new releases, limited print editions, box sets and extras such as themed bookmarks/stationary.

For 5 minute reads, follow my blog https://postcardsfrom midlife.blog/

Cover design and art direction by Berenice Howard-Smith, Hello Lovely.
Illustration by Amy Lane, Beehive Illustration Ltd.

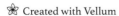 Created with Vellum

TITLE

A MIDLIFE GAMBLE

by

Cary J Hansson

PART I

1

So now you know the full truth of it. And that makes a grand total of five. I haven't told Helen. I've left that with Caro because it means they'll have to talk to each other. Things haven't been good between them since we got back from Cyprus, but that's a long story. My worry is that they're both Alex's godmothers, and if they're not even talking to each other, I don't know how they're going to be able to help him when...

Kay paused. Lips pressed tight together she tapped out the rest of the sentence... *I'm gone.* Her hand wavered over the keyboard as she read the words back.

I hope you're well! Send my love to Cyprus. How I'd love to go back one more time.

Kay

She pressed send, closed her laptop and looked across at the clock on the mantle.

Three am.

Too far from midnight, not close enough to morning, and the only time that hadn't mattered was when she had her baby pressed to her chest, him all wide-eyed and warm, her all exhausted and happy. Those days when the world still tilted at an angle that was scalable. When everyone she loved was alive and well and healthy. Which was all she'd ever needed but the truth of which, like oxygen, was only really evident when it had stretched too thin to be viable.

Her grandparents were gone. Her mother didn't recognise her. Her marriage had ended in divorce and her son... Ah, her son.

She spread her hands on the arms of the chair and eased herself upright, picked up her still-warm cup of tea, and walked across to the window. Outside a silver web of frost had cloaked parked cars, creeping across the road like sparkling lava. She loved these early morning hours. The few occasions she'd been awake to see them, it had always felt to Kay as if she was looking at a map marked *terra incognita*. A wide-open space and time in which anything and everything was possible. Because these hours contained both the optimism of list-making, and the quiet of reflection, a time to slip your skin and press pause on life. A raft on an ocean, a clearing in a forest that offered welcome, but vague possibilities. These were the moments in which she gave serious thought to the idea of giving up teaching, and picking up... tap dancing? Of selling the house and moving to Scotland? Or more lately, Cyprus. It just wasn't possible to entertain these ideas at three pm. Squashed in from all sides by the weight of commitment, three pm would have tossed her ideas aside as so much silly confetti. Its early morning cousin had always remained kinder, a more thoughtful listener to the internal workings of her mind.

Until now.

Her fingertips met around the cup, padding softly together as she sighed. What could this time of the new day reveal to her now that *terra incognita* really was full of dragons? What possibilities remained, that she couldn't glimpse at any other minute, of any other hour? A new land in which her mother did not have dementia? A country in which Alex wasn't destined for the lonely and financially difficult life she felt sure awaited him? A place where she did not have stage four skin cancer? Stage four being incurable. Stage four being, at some point in the not too distant future, terminal.

As if to banish her own thoughts, Kay shook her head. What was the point of hurting herself over and over with them? Dipping her chin she took a sip of tea and when she looked back up was almost surprised to see, within the darkened glaze of her front-room window, her reflection. *Still here,* she murmured, *still standing*, and her exhausted, haunted reflection looked back at her with sad eyes, and she thought, it's wrong. Wrong how people always talk about the days: *Those were the days! The days of our lives.* Because what about the nights? All those nights she'd slept so easy, with Alex in the room next door and her parents along the road. What a gift they had been. What a precious gift! Even those nights when she hadn't slept easy, she'd had nothing more troublesome to do than watch stars and consider a still benign *terra incognita*. Yes, those were the nights!

Now?

Now the terrain was mapped, nothing was unknown and all roads – every road – led back to cancer. The fact that it existed, was alive and growing inside her. The fact that it would take her away from Alex, who needed her. The fact that it would break her poor father's heart. The fact that the day after tomorrow, the first stage of what was going to be an aggressive treatment process would start for real. An overnight stay in hospital following lymph node dissection, which should reduce the burden of the disease. *Burden of disease.* She was learning a whole new vocabulary. Bio markers, LDH Levels, laser imaging, imaging tests, dissection, systemic therapies, combination therapies, T-cell transfer therapies… all of which, at some point in time, would end up spelling the same word: death. Hers.

Her mug felt suddenly heavy. Either that, or her hands had become suddenly weak. She managed to get it back onto the table and, as she straightened up, she pushed her hands into the pockets of her dressing gown searching for the scrap of tissue that always lived there. When she found it, she used it to blot silent tears. Silent, because upstairs, through the thin ceiling layers of gypsum and artex, she could hear the low rumble of Alex's snores and she would not wake him one moment before she had to. Not today. The day she was going to tell him she was dying. And where was the manual for that? The pages in the book of motherhood, no one had thought to write. On the mantle the clock ticked away sibilant minutes, and from somewhere far far away she thought she heard the crunch of wheels on the early morning frost. Life went on.

As the tissue fell apart in her hands, she used the last threads to blow her nose, shaking her head at the question that had unfurled, banner like, in her head the day she was diagnosed and had not folded since. How was she going to do it? How was she going to tell Alex?

And because she was no closer to finding the answer now than she had been at the beginning, she picked up her cup again and turned to the window, sipping tea, looking out at the street she had lived upon for so long. At old Mrs Newall's driveway, at the 30 mph speed sign, at the pothole that she'd probably never live to see repaired. The thought made her smile. Well, as long as her sense of humour was still intact. And now she was turning, scanning the room. What to do? What to do? Her eyes lit upon the TV cabinet.

She walked over and, using an armchair for support, lowered herself to the floor, knees creaking so loud the sound echoed. Five minutes later, she'd pulled out every last CD and VHS tape that had ever taken refuge in the rarely opened bottom drawer. Her wedding tape, its pencilled label almost as erased as the marriage. *Alex: first year.* Kay held the tape up. How long had she been meaning to get someone to transfer this onto something more modern? And this one: her mother's retirement party. Ditto. On she went, box sets of *Friends* and *Columbo*, piling up beside her.

By the time she'd finished, the blackness of night had begun to break apart. Streaks of grey and deep violet reaching from the east. On the kitchen shelf were stacked two piles of VHS tapes and DVDs, notes beside them: *Get sorted* and *Charity*. So, what to do now? Hands on hips Kay looked around. There was nothing to do. Last weekend, she'd sorted the cupboard under the stairs. Saturday night/Sunday morning it was her cleaning cupboard under the sink, all sorts of wire-wool and opened packets of Wash-it-White thrown away. The week before she'd done the shoe polishes. Worry equalled insomnia. The only upside being that, when the time came, she'd be leaving a house ruthlessly in order. More so, she thought wryly, than it had ever been. She picked up the top DVD from the charity pile. *Think Yourself Thin*; it was still in its cellophane. Then, dropping it back down, she moved to the sink, rinsed her cup, left it on the drainer and went upstairs. Her wardrobe. She would start on her wardrobe, eighty per cent of which hadn't fitted her since 1995.

The surge of enthusiasm carried her easily through a swathe of misshaped, worn out navy and black. Everyday stuff that was easy to sling, because every day was every day and there were still everyday days left. It was her silver jacket that threw the sucker punch. Her Vegas jacket. Bought for a honeymoon trip that had been promised by a man who had, in the end, disappointed. Wheeled out from then on for various special occasions, the last being Helen's fiftieth. She reached for the sleeve, holding the fabric as tenderly as she'd once held Alex's hand. Was that it then? Was Helen's fiftieth destined to be the *last,* last time? And then how many other *last* times had she already missed? How many had passed without her even noticing? The *last,* last time she swam in the ocean? Got soaked in the rain? Laughed until she cried? And for the second time since three am, Kay smiled. Because this, thank goodness, she could remember. It had been in Cyprus, with Caro. The afternoon Lawrence had turned up and they'd set about trying to warn Helen. Laughing, like schoolgirls, yes until she'd cried.

Slowly she slipped the jacket off its hanger and onto her shoulders, and as outside her window dawn stretched itself into neon orange rays, Kay turned to look at herself in the wardrobe mirror. A hundred years ago, as a bride-to-be, an irresistible impulse had carried her from street, to shop, to changing room, where she'd stood in the reflected light of a thousand silver sequins, listening to their whispered possibilities... Which had all come to nothing. Despite all the talk, first as a child with her father as they'd played Sunday afternoon card games, then with Martin her ex-husband, she never had made it to Vegas, and now she never would. She had, after all, only been playing dress-up.

A shrill bleep cut across her thoughts, sharp as a knife. Before she could catch a sense of where it had come from, the sound repeated. And again.

Alex's alarm. Dazed, Kay turned to her own bedside

8

clock. The digits flashed 07:00. It was time. She could put it off no longer.

IN THE KITCHEN, Kay filled the teapot, pulled on a knitted tea-cosy and waited for Alex to come downstairs. Running her fingers over the bumpy wool, she was thinking of her mother who had knitted the cosy especially for Alex. Blue and yellow he'd asked for, his favourite colours of the time. Like the sun and the sky. He wouldn't touch it now. Over the years it had stained, which Alex equated with dirty, saying as much to his grandmother. Her mother's thin-lipped smile, Kay had known, had hidden the hurt. But this was Alex. Unable to follow, let alone forge, the delicate web of everyday conversation. The distortions and dissembling, economies of truth, exaggerations. All of which, she feared, was going to make what she had to say so much harder. Not for Alex, for her. Because, where much of the world was obligingly content to have difficult truths fudged, Alex, she knew, wouldn't be. Everyone she'd told, for example – and here she meant the bare necessities of the situation – had nodded seriously and said nothing at all... until she'd offered them the escape route they'd been desperately looking for from the moment she'd started talking. Without fail, as she had shown them the door with vague statements such as *well, the treatments these days,* or *we just don't know at the moment,* they had grabbed that nebulous thread, as if it were steel cable. But Alex? The irony was that the person it was going to hurt her the most to tell was the person best equipped to take it. She could have laughed, or cried, but whatever she did, she *had* to tell him.

. . .

9

A MINUTE LATER, he came into the kitchen, his head buried in the work sweatshirt he was still pulling on. Kay had an urge to step forward and run her hand through his mop of unbrushed hair, as his head popped clear, but those days were long gone. The closest she got now was an awkward standing to attention, if she dared to give him a hug. If she was lucky she might get an awkward pat on the back in return.

'Cup of tea?'

Alex picked up his keys. 'I have to go.'

'Oh.' She glanced at the clock. He didn't start until eight. 'You have time, don't you?'

'I wanted to get in early today. We're clearing space for the first delivery of Christmas trees. They're coming next week.'

'Christmas trees?' Kay murmured, vaguely aware that this was the first time Christmas had come into a focus clear enough to be seen. Cancer had destroyed so much, not least her peripheral vision. For weeks now, she'd been living in a tunnel, at the end of which was a sign: dissection. And after that, another narrow space in which again, there would be no room for turning: radiotherapy. Every day for four weeks. Where, in all that, was Christmas supposed to fit? 'Will you sit down a moment, love?' she said. 'I need to tell you something.'

Standing by the back door, Alex paused.

'It won't take long. And it is important.' She opened the cupboard and took out his cup.

When, a moment later, she turned around and saw, her heart filled with emotion. Swelled in fact, so much that she had time to think how true it was that hearts can and do swell. What she was looking at, was her small kitchen table, framed in a square of sunshine as it always was on sunny winter mornings... and Alex, bumping his chair forward, so that he fitted inside that square of sunshine... as he always had, on sunny winter mornings. To anyone else watching, it would have appeared as if he couldn't get comfortable. But Kay knew. Alex was shuffling himself into the square of light. He remembered. Just like she did. A memory opened, of an ordinary morning, in her ordinary kitchen. Alex, maybe five years old, insisting they both bump their chairs in, so close their slippered feet met, toe to toe, she giggling as she'd ducked forward to comply with his wishes; him waiting to start his toast until she was 'fully' in the sunshine. Her eyes filled with warm tears. She was dying. She didn't feel like she was, but apparently she was, and the moment had come to tell him. She took the cosy off the teapot, placed it in the middle of the table and took her seat. Then without speaking she bumped her chair in, closer and closer. 'Am I in?' she said, leaning over her shoulder to check.

'You're in, mum,' he answered.

Kay leaned forward. 'I have to tell you something.'

'Fifty percent?'

Kay nodded.

Barely ten minutes had passed since she'd begun the most difficult conversation of her life. Knowing the way her son's mind worked, she'd come prepared, going through her diagnosis and treatment, stage by stage, always staying truthful. She had explained the procedure she would be undergoing in just a couple of days and the outcome that everyone was hoping for. She'd talked through the effects of radiotherapy and gone into detached details about the course of combination therapy it was likely she would be offered afterward. How she would be taking tablets and receiving monthly infusions. How regular scans would show the progress, or the remission of her cancer, but how realistically the best she could hope, the very best, was a fifty percent chance she'd still be alive in five years.

Spoken out loud, said simply and directly, had made it sound so harsh to Kay she was frightened anew, for both of them. She had just explained her illness in hard and non-negotiable terms, like shining the white light of a microscope upon the brush strokes of an impressionist painting. Where, she thought now, were the nuances and the shadows? Where had they gone, the softened corners from which something hopeful might emerge? She picked up her cup and sipped her tea and as the quiet minutes slipped by, a measure of calm returned. There had never been another way. If she'd hidden any part of this under *ifs* and *maybes,* Alex would have gone away and set those undefinable terms into concrete moulds of his choosing. And later, when reality had refused to fit, he'd have returned wildly angry, accusing her of lying to him. *You said it worked!* When what she had always said was, *Sometimes, it worked.* No, she had had to keep it real. 'Fifty percent,' she said softly.

Alex looked out of the window.

Kay didn't speak. He wasn't avoiding her, he just couldn't look her in the eye, not as he was trying to process it. In times of extreme emotion, he needed space, lots of it.

'Ok.' He stood up and put his cup in the dishwasher. 'I have to go,' he said.

Kay nodded, her lips pressed tight together, just like her mother before her, sealing shut the hurt. 'Ok,' she managed, her voice tight. 'Have a good day.'

And then there was nothing to do but sit and wait for the sound of the back door closing, for the moment in which she could drop her head to her hands and let out a grief that was becoming unbearably heavy. But the sound didn't come, instead there was a sudden warmth, very close to her face, and Alex's head, dropped on her shoulder, his hair brushing her cheek, one hand patting her shoulder in that stiff and childish way of his.

And without turning, Kay reached back and grabbed his hand. She could trace the child. Could still sense the way his small palm would grip her own. Hanging on for reassurance and comfort, for life itself, those times he'd been terrified – of noisy cars, or loud strangers. How was she ever going to be able to let go? How would it work? When the time came, would her fingers release his? Or would the grip remain, after life itself had left? Please, she thought, please let it be like that.

'It'll be alright, mum,' Alex said. 'It'll be alright.'

Kay gulped back what she couldn't allow to escape. 'Make sure you save a good tree for us,' she managed

2

'**A**re you kidding me?'

Helen stared at the face on the flier in front of her that her daughter Libby had just handed over. An infant face stared back, cheeks and forehead covered in thick black swirls, like a Māori warrior painted for war. Or a baby left alone with a marker pen.

'Why,' she gasped, 'would anyone give a baby a marker pen?'

'It's not marker pen!' Libby huffed. 'It's plant-based paint. *Organic* plants. Completely harmless! In fact,' she said as she took the flier back and hammered it on the fridge door, with a loud clunk of magnet, 'it's edible!'

'Edible?' Helen watched as the aftershock of Libby's thump sent her kingfisher notepad sliding from the fridge to the floor. She bent to pick it up.

'If you don't want to go, I'll ring Leanne and cancel,' Libby muttered.

'I didn't say that.' But they both knew; she might as well have.

'I could take him to the park?' she tried. 'Or the library...'

'Fine, mum.' Libby picked up her phone. 'I told Leanne I'd meet her there afterwards. We were going for lunch, but never mind. Arthur will be disappointed, that's all.'

Watching, Helen folded her arms. Arthur was Leanne's eight-month-old son, and Leanne was Libby's new friend and although Helen didn't give two hoots about the imaginary hurt feelings of an eight-month-old, she did care very much about the tender and easily bruised feelings of her daughter.

At twenty, Leanne was six months younger than Libby, and had, in the last few weeks, brought a burst of fresh air and energy into her daughter's life. The two of them had met at a mother and baby group, forming an immediate bond, Helen had guessed, upon the fact they were so much younger than all the other women. It had been a lifeline for Libby and, in some ways, Helen. Chattering away on the one occasion they had met, Helen had seen what light and easy company Leanne was, wholly unencumbered by all those lost expectations that so weighed Libby (and herself) down. Leanne, it had been clear, didn't think it a disaster to have a baby at twenty. On the contrary, Helen had realised, she thought it was exactly what she should be doing, and was having the time of her life whilst at it. A breath of fresh air indeed. In fact, there had been times when listening to her daughter make plans on the phone with her new friend, Helen had had moments of lonely pause in which the loss of both Caro and Kay's company had overwhelmed her. Many times.

She hadn't seen Caro since the night she'd taken Libby's baby and stayed out too long... *far* too long. And recently, Kay's calls had become less frequent. Thinking all this,

Helen sighed. Kay, she suspected, had run out of patience. Had, after all these years, finally tired of playing go-between, between herself and Caro. And who could blame her? She'd relayed the message to Helen more than once. Caro was desperately sorry, distraught that she'd caused Libby such anguish, but no, she still couldn't explain what had happened. She understood that Helen didn't want to meet, but hoped that once the dust had settled...

'She's not answering,' Libby said, looking up from her phone. 'I'll send a text.'

Helen turned, the sound of Libby's voice calling her back into the room. 'Put it down.' She nodded at Libby's phone, and bent low to her grandson, strapped in his bouncy chair. 'We'll go to Messy Play won't we?' she cooed. 'Mummy can come along after her exam.' And as she straightened up she added, 'It'll be nice for you to have lunch with Leanne.'

Libby stood with the phone in her hands. 'Are you ok, mum?'

'Fine.'

Helen turned to busy herself with tidying the table. It was too complicated. Firstly, she wouldn't bring up that night again in front of Libby for anything. And beyond that... How could she explain? Friends, getting them, keeping them – easy as breathing when you're five years old and you invite the whole class to your party, and the whole class wants nothing more than to come to your party. So much harder as adults. And it wasn't as if the need diminished in proportion. In fact, as her children had needed her less, she had, she knew, needed her friends more. So where did it go? The simplicity of childhood friendship? Helen closed her eyes. She understood where. It got stamped down by life. Experience making strangers of people you thought you knew inside out. And how could she possibly explain that?

'So you're sure about going to Messy Play?' Libby asked.

'A hundred per cent,' she said with a jollity she didn't feel. She fixed her notebook back in place, opened the freezer and stood staring at it. 'What time does it start?' she said, pulling out a packet of fish fillets. 'We'll have fish for dinner.'

'Eleven.' Libby was moving to and fro along the length of the table, jamming bottles and nappies, spit-bibs, wipes, rattles, spare clothing, books that squeaked, and a change-mat into the baby bag. The baby bag that came with more pockets and clips and pouches than Lawrence's cargo pants. In went a towel, and a thermometer, and a dummy, and a spare dummy, spoons and spare spoons, one jar of baby food, one pouch of yogurt, one enormous packet of what looked like the polystyrene bits used to pad out fragile packages but were apparently edible corn.

Helen stared. Was that it? The amount of baby paraphernalia required seemed to double with each generation. She didn't know, and she wasn't going to ask, because anything she might say like, *How long are we going for?* Or *How many babies are you packing for?* Or *Goodness, I wonder how mums in the Gobi Desert manage,* would, she knew, be met with the titanium resolve of the brand-new mother that Libby had evolved into.

Because starting from the night Caro had taken her baby, something had awoken in Libby. She had undergone a metamorphosis. Out had gone the shell-shocked pyjama clad sleep-walking youngster of before, and in had blown this most formidable of creatures – the new mother: determined on providing the best possible start, in thrall to the latest fad and blissfully oblivious to the fact that women had been keeping babies alive for millennia, long before books, let alone those that squeaked, had been invented. A sleek and energetic lioness, perpetually on guard.

Not that Helen was complaining. Libby *had* needed to step up. It was just that she understood how unsustainable it all was. Libby, despite her youth, wouldn't be able to juggle all these plates for long. She was about to re-sit the first of her final exams. The exams she should have taken several months ago. After that, she had a future mapped out, which sounded great on paper but which exhausted Helen just to look at. But what could she say? What could she possibly advise? *It's a marathon, Libby, not a sprint. You don't have to be perfect every day Libby. Even if you get it all right there will still be times when you will want to just walk away...*

Ah, what was the point? Libby would learn chopping her own path through the jungle. It was Helen's job to walk behind, not forge the way ahead.

And of course today, exam day, Libby was extra-wired. As if the first real test of her ability to get herself out of the mess she had created had arrived. Not that anyone could consider Ben a mess... Helen bent low, took hold of Ben's chin and waggled it between thumb and forefinger. He responded with a deep-throated gurgle of joy. She smiled at him. That was the problem with babies, wasn't it? No matter what went before, they swept it all away once they arrived, cleared the decks with their cat-clean mouths and their other-worldly smell... and their other, all-too-worldly smell. 'Umm, I think he might...'

'Not again!' Libby cried.

Helen nodded. She unstrapped Ben and lifted him up, her nose wrinkling. 'He's going to need new trousers,' she said, looking at an ominous brown stain across Ben's bottom.

Libby closed the bag and turned for Ben. Just as she did, the doorbell rang.

'Go and change him,' Helen said. 'I'll get the door and then we'll be off.'

LESS THAN HALF A MINUTE LATER, one hand still on the doorhandle, it took Helen a long moment for her mind to catch up with her eyes.

She'd answered the door to Caro. There she was, on the doorstep, looking smaller than Helen had ever seen her. Looking so diminished, so drawn, that instantly Helen understood something was wrong. She opened her mouth, but then and forever after, would have no idea of what she might have been about to say.

'It's Kay,' Caro managed, in a timbre Helen had never heard before. 'She has cancer. She's dying, Helen, and there's nothing we can do. Nothing.' The words were forced, as if Caro was struggling to let them live, as if she would rather strangle them. And then her head wobbled, and she took a step sideways, swayed and began to fall backward.

Helen grabbed her arm. 'Kay's...' But her own voice was mostly air. 'She's—' Sounds would not take shape.

Caro nodded. She'd managed to straighten herself so that her face was now very close to Helen, her free hand pressed against the brickwork of the house.

With arms of tingling lead, Helen manoeuvred her over the threshold and closed the door, watching as Caro leaned against the wall.

'I'm sorry,' Caro whispered. 'The last thing I meant was to blurt it out on the doorstep.'

Nodding, Helen brought her hands to her chin, knitting her fingers, and all the time three little words snaked around her feet like a cold mist. *Kay has cancer. Kay has cancer. Kay has...*

'She's going in for an operation tomorrow.'

'An operation?'

'Lymph node dissection.'

'When—' Helen stopped talking. The recent longer periods of silence between herself and Kay had been real. A widening gap, that Helen had thought she'd understood. Which she hadn't, because this she hadn't seen coming. And looking at Caro's shattered features, Helen remembered her mother, *Now then, Helen. It'll be alright. Everything will be alright.* The day she had broken the news of her own cancer, what a shock it had been, how despite the fact her mother had known for weeks, neither Helen nor her brother had had any suspicions something was wrong, terminally wrong. So how long, she thought now, had Kay known? How long had she been struggling with it, unable to get them all in the same room together, to break the news. 'How long have you known?' she said, her voice hoarse.

'Yesterday,' Caro whispered. 'She told me yesterday.'

'And that's why you're here?'

Caro nodded.

Neither of them spoke. Eventually, after a minute, or maybe five, Helen said, 'Kitchen?' And with this, Caro nodded, turned and made her way along the hallway.

Helen stood looking at nothing. Then she turned to the hall mirror and saw how her mouth had turned down in a long sad curve. Kay would have needed them. Should have been able to turn to them, using the long-established ropes of their friendship to guide. But how could she have done that, when those ropes were such a tangled mess?

'I can't believe it.'

Caro didn't answer. She stood at the far side of the table.

'I just can't believe it,' Helen said again and looked down at the crumpled packet of fish on the table. The packet she'd taken out a minute earlier, which was a different lifetime ago. The lifetime in which Kay didn't have cancer.

'Helen.'

'It can't be true!' The veins in her neck tensed like rope.

This time Caro didn't say *Helen*. This time she just looked down at her hands.

A rock rose in Helen's throat, so brutally hard she couldn't swallow. 'Where's your car?' she croaked and it seemed very strange that she should think of this now, but she hadn't seen a car. There hadn't been a car in the driveway when she'd opened the door. Not like the last time Caro had been at her house, when she'd left her car and her phone and taken Ben.

'Around the corner,' Caro said quietly. 'I...' She didn't finish the sentence.

She didn't need to, they both understood why Caro would have approached the house with caution, would have made as quiet an entrance as possible. And now, as if for the first time, Helen saw how she had also positioned herself, upright and tense and as far away as possible. The sight weakened her. Once upon a time Caro would have swept into this kitchen as easy as a breeze. She would have pulled out a chair without asking, without waiting for Helen to finish whatever domestic chore she was in the middle of. She would have sat herself down and poured the wine, sliding Helen's glass across, watching as Helen flittered around tidying up. All those evenings they'd laughed and cried over life, and how rubbish and wonderful it was, and over what they'd expected as opposed to what had been delivered. Evenings that had ended with the world tilted right again. How she'd missed that! In these last few months, how much she had missed all that! She looked at Caro and the solidity of shock crumbled. Kay had cancer and Caro was at the other end of the table. How were they going to put this right? How on earth were they going to put the world back on course again?

'Sit down,' she whispered. 'Will you? *Please.*'

Slowly, Caro pulled out the nearest chair and slowly, Helen did the same. Neither of them spoke and with every moment the silence became heavier. It dropped like leaden snow on Helen's head, rounded her shoulders and her spine. 'I should have called,' she whispered. 'I didn't know how.'

'I didn't know either,' Caro whispered back.

The house was silent. Across the room, on the fridge, her notepad clung on at a lopsided angle. *Bread, milk, cheese,* written in her own hand.

Bread, milk, cheese.

'I never...' Caro's voice was tiny. 'I... I never meant to...'

'I know, Caro,' Helen said flatly. 'I know.' And with the pad of her thumb, she pressed down, through the fine wool of her sweater to her wrist, feeling the bone roll and move. She went to press again, as if it might ground her, but now her hand was loose as water. She couldn't make a shape of it, couldn't feel it. *Kay has cancer* dissolved every thought she was attempting to think. Opening her fingers she looked at her hand as if it was something she'd never seen before in her life.

'It's skin cancer,' Caro murmured.

Helen looked up. 'But that's treatable,' she said and found her voice strong. 'It's treatable these days. It's—'

Caro was shaking her head. 'It's spread, Helen. She

22

found out a couple of weeks ago. Tomorrow she's going in for a dissection.'

'And then chemo? There's such a lot...'

'Not chemo. Radiation. And then targeted therapy to... to buy time I suppose.' Caro looked down at the table. 'I'm going to see her afterwards and she wanted me to tell you. She wants you there... She wants both of us there.'

A wave of nausea swept up Helen's chest. A couple of weeks! Kay had known for a couple of weeks! She put the back of her hand to her mouth and looked at Caro, tears streaming down her face. No one needed to explain to her the details of a cancer that had metastasised. No matter how much time passed, some moments retained their clarity, and always would. One of which was the day her mother had explained her own diagnosis. The gently emphatic way she had closed down every entreaty Helen had made, because... well because there was no way out of the maze. 'I don't understand,' she said now, shaking her head. 'She looked so well.' But even as she said the words Helen knew they weren't true. Kay had looked exhausted for months now. Every time they had seen each other, Helen had urged her to go to the doctor. Get a little HRT, she'd badgered, as if it were the cure-all for everything. Kay who had urged her to pick up the phone to Caro. Kay who was wiser than the two of them put together. Kay who had known for two weeks. Who was dying. Who couldn't possibly be dying. 'I'm sorry, Caro,' she whispered. 'I hope you know that I mean that. I wasn't big enough to make the first move.'

'It doesn't matter.' Caro tipped her head to the ceiling and pinched the bridge of her nose. 'Nothing matters now, except Kay.'

Helen nodded. She looked up the clock and then she looked across at the packet of defrosting fish.

'What are we going to do?'

The sound of feet on stairs, of Libby's voice, of Caro's chair scraping the stone floor as she stood, all of this silenced Helen. She turned first to the hallway, then back to Caro.

'I'll go,' Caro said.

'No.' That wasn't what she wanted! She pushed her own chair back, rose to her feet.

'Mum?' And then Libby was in the doorway, holding Ben, staring at Caro. 'Hello, Caro,' she said, almost shy. 'It's... it's nice to see you.'

'Hello, Libby,' Caro managed. 'It's... it's nice to see you too.'

And turning to look at Caro, Helen burst into tears. If she had appeared diminished on the doorstep, she was almost vanished now. Swaying in the brutally gentle force of this most difficult of meetings, she was a reed, her face hollowed and pale.

'Caro.' Helen put her hand to her mouth. 'Oh, Caro.' She moved across and threw her arms around Caro's shoulders. 'It's ok,' she sobbed, a geyser of emotion releasing. That Caro should be reduced to a ghost in a house that had once been a refuge was unbearable. That Kay was dying was unbearable. That life had pushed them so far apart, Kay had been unable to confide in them was unbearable. If they didn't have each other, who did they have? No one. That was who. *No one.* Squeezing Caro tighter, she felt the embrace returned and heard the small hiccup of sobs, regular and restrained, as Caro too wept.

Libby stood in the doorway.

'Are you ok?' Helen mouthed, over Caro's shoulder.

'Yes,' Libby mouthed back. 'What's happening?'

'Kay has cancer,' Helen whispered and watched as her daughter's face drained.

'Cancer?' Libby's eyes filled with tears. 'What about Alex?'

'I don't know,' Helen said. She pulled back from Caro. 'I don't know.'

'She's telling him today,' Caro said quietly.

'Oh God.' Closing her eyes, Helen took a deep breath. Alex. Her godson. Kay's entire world. By the time she opened her eyes again Caro had moved away, her hand pushing deep into her pocket, pulling out car keys.

'Sit down. I'll make tea.'

'No, no.' Caro's brow knitted. She turned to look at the table, as if she'd left something there. 'I'll go... I should go.'

'Please stay.'

Helen turned.

'Mum has missed you,' Libby continued, looking directly at Helen. 'Haven't you, mum?'

And flushing, Helen brought her hand to her forehead to rub it. She felt dizzy with emotion. That Libby had noticed... was capable of such a breadth of compassion, there was no room left for pride. 'I have,' she managed. 'I've really missed you, Caro.'

'Me too,' Caro whispered. 'And I'm—'

Helen nodded. 'Me too. I'm sorry too.'

No one spoke. In the doorway, safe in his mother's arms, Ben gurgled.

Helen looked at him. How beautiful he was, and Libby too. This new generation. Blinking back a thousand tears, she turned to Caro. 'Tea then?'

'I...' Caro's head bobbed in confusion. 'I ...Yes. Tea.' And very slowly, she lowered herself back into her chair.

As Helen moved across to put the kettle on, Libby

looked down at Ben and took hold of his fingers. 'I'll take Ben to Messy Play,' she said. She was still in the doorway.

'You can't!' Helen had the kettle in her hand. 'You can't, Libby.'

'Why not?'

'Your exam?'

Libby shrugged. Her smile as swift as it was small. 'I'm not sure that matters much now, mum.'

Helen turned to the tap. Did it still matter? It didn't feel as if it did. What had been so important just a few minutes before seemed as muted and distant now as a yellowed photograph. Past. Swept out of existence by the news that had blown into her life. Either way, she wasn't going to argue it. She hadn't the energy. Suddenly she hadn't the energy for anything.

'Unless...' Taking hold of Ben's little finger Libby lifted it with her own little finger. He gurgled with pleasure and she smiled. 'Unless I leave him here? He'll probably sleep if...'

'Do that,' Helen said. Because something had to be salvaged. Something *always* had to be salvaged. She went to take Ben. 'You've prepared, and it is important.'

Meeting her eye, Libby gave Helen a tiny nod, then without saying a word she turned and walked over to Caro, and placed her baby into Caro's lap.

'Libby,' Caro gasped, instinctively drawing the baby to her, holding him safe.

'It's ok,' Libby smiled. 'I know you'll look after him.'

'I...' Caro couldn't finish. Her lips pressed together as she shook her head and blinked away tears. 'I will, of course I will.'

'I'll leave you to talk,' she said and barely a minute later, the sound of the front door closing had ushered a new silence into Helen's house.

She was still standing by the counter, next to the kettle. Caro was still sitting holding Ben. In much the same way, Helen thought as she watched, Caro had once held Libby, or Jack, twenty odd years ago. Where did it go? All that time? Caro would have held the baby Alex too. Alex who, more than any of them, still needed protective arms around him. Turning back to her window, she leaned her hands on the counter, dipped her head and wept. She had just seen a depth of maturity from her daughter that she hadn't witnessed before. Even so, Libby was wrong. This was not a time for talking. She'd been here before with her mother. There would be no talking, because there were no words.

3

The A5 wipe-clean board, propped up against the window-ledge of her mother's room, read:

Today is Wednesday
The weather is sunny
The next meal is lunch.

Kay looked out of the window. It was a Thursday and it was pouring down.

'I know.' The woman clearing her mother's dinner tray looked across at the sign and then at Kay. 'I'm sorry. I must change it.'

'I'm sure she doesn't mind.' Kay smiled. I don't either, she felt like saying. I'm more than happy for mum to be living in a never-ending, always sunny Wednesday morning. She sat and watched as the woman eased the tray-table to the end of the bed and leaned across to smooth the sheets, as carefully as if she were smoothing a silk gown.

'Thank you... Lisa,' she said, noting the name badge. Most of the staff at Ashdown House, the nursing home her mother had been living in since the summer, she knew by name now. But this lady had been away recently. Lisa =

large, she noted. It was a memory trick. A mnemonic that helped her remember names, because from the beginning it had felt important to Kay that she knew the names of everyone involved in caring for her mother. From Fiona the cook (F= food = cook) to Hollie the perpetually h = happy manager. It reinforced the idea that Ashdown House really was a home, her mother's home, a place where everyone knew everyone else's name. And this lady, Lisa, was quite large.

Smiling, Lisa straightened up. She poured a fresh glass of water and placed it on the bedside table. Turning back to the bed, she picked up the dinner tray and went to the door. With a hand on the handle, she turned, stretched out a leg and used her foot to nudge the wastepaper bin back against the skirting board. 'Your mum thinks it's a cat,' she said. 'Wants it up on the bed with her. *Not always.*' Lisa smiled, emphasising the words.

Kay looked from the bin to the bed. Moving it, as Lisa had, meant it was now hidden from her mother's view.

'Are you coming to hear The Purple Irises?' Lisa said. 'They're really fun.'

'I'll be out in a few minutes,' she managed.

And the door brushed shut.

Kay turned back to the bed. Lisa wouldn't know of course, but her mother didn't like cats. She wouldn't go within touching distance, let alone have one up on the bed. They'd never had one in the house, and she collapsed in a fit of sneezing if she ever came into contact with them. But it was exactly as Lisa had said. The shrunken woman in the bed before her, this fragile knit of wasted muscle and hollowed skin, plucking at the bed sheets, *wasn't always* her mother anymore. Like now. All through her lunch, spoon-fed by Lisa, this bird of a woman had been kept upright by a nest of feathered pillows. But that wasn't *her* mother. *Her* mother had been a straight-spined, formidable presence in the corridors of the school where she had been headmistress. *Her* mother had worn Debenhams jackets with softly padded shoulders, tan-coloured tights and court shoes. And throughout her childhood and most of her adulthood, Kay had never seen so much as a bare shoulder from *her* mother. But the woman that lay before her now was dressed in a thin and oddly childish nightie, her bare, wasted arms and speckled chest on show to the world. And, the woman who lay before her now, was a widow. Hadn't she just told Kay and Lisa all about the funeral? How she'd buried her husband on a Monday afternoon, after a terrible battle with pneumonia. It had been snowing. Snowing! Which was all so wrong, because *her* mother's husband, Kay's own, dear father, was right now in the lounge, with a cup of tea and a slice of fruit cake, settling himself into a ringside seat to hear The Purple Irises, whose monthly cabarets were a highlight of Ashdown House.

No, the woman before her, either in body or in mind, was *not always* her mother. Dementia had gouged away so much. The fathomless hurt came from the fact that sometimes she still was. Sometimes there were lucid moments in which they knew each other as profoundly as they ever had. Moments that were wide and open as the prairie, clear as raindrops. Moments Kay knew she would never poison with the vocabulary of cancer, dissections, radiotherapy, burdens of disease, but in which the child inside her yearned to lay her head on her mother's chest and weep. *Mum, I'm sick, I'm very sick and I'm very scared.*

The reality was, lucid or not, in the manner that mattered the most, she was now motherless. Disease, both her own and her mother's, had separated them as effectively as the grave.

She stretched a hand out, placed it on top of her mother's and pressed down, seeking to quiet the constant plucking. 'There,' she said. But as soon as she withdrew, the clawing of the sheets began again. One more agony to witness.

'The Purple Irises are here,' she tried. The first month her mother had been at the home, she'd enjoyed a wonderfully lucid afternoon, singing along with the songs from her younger days. Frank Sinatra, The Carpenters, Barry Manilow. It was always worth mentioning them.

But the woman in the bed looked up at her and with clear eyes said, 'Kay's gone.'

'I'm Kay,' Kay said calmly.

Her mother shook her head, a film of spittle leaking from her lips. 'She took the children. I drove her to the station. We didn't have time to pack the kiddies' wellies.'

Bumping her chair closer, Kay took her mother's hand and pressed it between her own. 'I'm Kay,' she repeated, but again her mother shook her head.

'She won't come back this time. I told her not to come back.'

'No? I don't think she will then.'

'I hope she's going to be ok.'

'She'll be fine,' Kay said and squeezed her mother's hand with a conviction made strong by hindsight. Back in 1974, Kay's mother had driven their next-door-neighbour, Marion, to the railway station, Marion's two tiny children alongside. There hadn't indeed been time to pack the kids' wellies and Marion never did go back. Not to the house next door, or the abusive husband with whom she had lived. So yes, she was fine. Living in Dorset and a grandmother of five. Her mother had all the details of the story correct. It was just the characters she mixed up.

She released her mother's hand and leaned back in her chair. Out of the window she could see the garden. The lawn that sloped upward to open farmland and the twiggy shrub border, bare now save for the glossy evergreen of rhododendrons. It was a beautiful garden. Her mother had arrived in August, just in time for the late summer bloom, and they had already spent many hours sitting on the patio, surrounded by rich golden dahlias and slender lupins. Ashdown House was a lovely place and after the difficulties of the summer, it had become very clear, very quickly, that with her mother settled into full-time care everyone's quality of life had improved. Her father visited every day, reassured to see his wife in such kind and compassionate hands and quietly accepting of the new empty spaces in his house. And a huge slab of responsibility had fallen off Kay's shoulders. So it was ironic, beyond ironic really, that just as she had successfully negotiated her way across this bleak territory, as she should have been coming out of the woods and into the sunlight, the thunderbolt of cancer had struck, pinning her as sure as a butterfly to a collector's board, checkmating her every move.

She let the thought float away, over the grass, disappearing into the darkly furrowed soil of the farmland beyond. 'So mum,' she sighed and turned back to the bed. 'Can you hear that?' Behind the door, the sound of singing, faint and tremulous, could be heard. It was coming from the lounge.

But the bird-like creature in the bed had closed her eyes, and already a whistle of sleepy breath escaped her lips. Kay stood. She eased her mother's pillows out, and cradling her head, laid her down to sleep.

'See you next week,' she whispered as she stood in the doorway. 'I can't come for a few days. I'm having a little operation.' And she eased the door shut.

Outside in the corridor the singing felt both closer and further away, and for a moment Kay felt marooned between worlds. Ahead, the large drawing room called to her with the clatter of teacups and the chatter of voices; behind, on the other side of the door which she now leaned against, lay a silence akin to death.

And where then did she belong?

Taking a rag of tissue from her pocket she blew her nose, surprised to discover again the wetness of tears. Then she took a deep breath and steadying herself, followed the call of a world she was still a part of.

THE DRAWING ROOM of Ashdown House had been built for another age. It was elegant and well proportioned, with detailed cornices and huge bay windows that overlooked a sweeping driveway. Positioned now, within the curve of the bay, stood a group of ladies, none of whom were a day under fifty and all of whom were dressed, head to toe, in shades of purple. From imperial magenta to pastel lilac. Two wore feather fascinators, another three had deely bobbers, all of them singing their hearts out. The Purple Irises were going through their well-practised routine. They were colourful and good natured, as enthusiastic as their headgear, that bounced and jiggled regardless, making no distinction between the upbeat rhythms of Frank Sinatra, or the mournful tones of The Carpenters. One of them wore a sequinned vest and it had Kay thinking of her Vegas jacket. She hadn't been able to throw it away, and it was back in her wardrobe.

Across the room, her father waved. He was sitting in a winged armchair, close to the sideboard. Craig stood next to him, wearing – Kay squinted – a set of purple deely bobbers he'd obviously commandeered from one of the Irises. Next to Craig stood Hollie, the manager; both of them were scoffing cake and swaying to the music. Kay smiled. Craig and Hollie were peas in a pod. The kind of effortlessly cheerful people, whom it was as impossible to dislike as it was to emulate. Rare as hens' teeth. So it was more than good fortune she'd managed to find two in her life, and thinking this gave her comfort. Because if the worst happened, if both her mother *and* her father outlived her, at least they would be in good and kind hands. Which of course, still left Alex.

Martin, Alex's father and her ex, had just become a father for the third time. He had a whole new family, which in theory should also have given Alex a whole new family. Only it wasn't working like that, and in a way Kay understood. Martin's young wife had neither the time nor the energy to accommodate a six-foot man, with the emotional vocabulary of a child. And Martin? Men compartmentalised. That was a fact. And right now, the compartment Martin had popped his first son in seemed so far out of his view that Kay sometimes wondered if he'd forgotten about it completely. Closing down an avenue of thought that led nowhere satisfactory, she made her way across and sat down next to her father. The day had drained her, she needed the bonhomie of fruitcake and tea and Barry Manilow's 'Can't Smile Without You'.

'How was she?' Hollie mouthed.

Kay shook her head.

'I'll get you a cup of tea.' Code for, *I understand. I'll make it as right as I can.*

Kay mouthed a thank you, leaned her head back in her chair, closed her eyes and allowed the music to wash over her. She didn't actually notice it had come to an end until she felt a hand on her arm. Dazed, she opened her eyes to see her father. She must have dozed off. One of those micro-sleeps that are supposed to be so beneficial. The Irises, she saw, were taking a break.

'Are you getting enough sleep?' her father frowned.

'I'm fine.'

'You need another holiday,' he said. 'You should get yourself back to Cyprus.'

'That would be nice.' Cyprus? Kay smiled. That week at the beginning of the summer when the itch at her neck had been just an itch, when her teaching career remained unblemished... It felt as far out of reach to her now as the moon.

'I'll just pop along and look in at your mum,' her father said, easing himself out of his chair.

Kay nodded. She watched as he walked across the room. He was still spritely, still steady on his feet. How on earth was she going to tell him?

Telling Alex today had made the total number of people who now knew the real extent of her diagnosis, six. Nick her headteacher had been obvious, explanations were necessary, practicalities had to be addressed. Ditto with Martin. Marianne, whom she had met at the hotel in Cyprus, not so much obvious as completely unexpected. She hadn't intended it this way, but exchanging emails with her, which they had been doing since the holiday ended, had become an exercise in self-care for Kay. Alone, in front of her laptop, she'd found herself spilling the kinds of hopes and fears and dreams that once she would have shared with Caro and Helen.

Craig slid into the now vacant chair beside her, his deely bobbers bouncing wildly. 'I'm going to join them for the next one,' he grinned. 'I can sing you know.'

Her smile was too weak, she knew this by the way his face changed.

'Kay, are you—'

'I'm fine,' she interrupted.

'Are you ok?'

'I will be.' And Craig, who also knew. Well, he offered the ease of confidence she'd found with Marianne, with the practical arrangements of Nick. Plus, he was impossible not to talk to. He had become her partner, if not in crime, then certainly in subterfuge. It was Craig that would be handling the domestic arrangements for her father while she was in hospital. Craig whom she had sworn to secrecy these last few weeks, as she came to terms with first the diagnosis and second the treatment necessary.

And then finally, just yesterday, she had told Caro. Who had immediately asked if Helen knew, and when Kay had answered *No,* had understood what wasn't being said. *I'll tell her,* she'd said and Kay had nodded.

Thinking all this, she tipped her head back and looked at the ceiling. It didn't matter. It could have been either of them. What mattered was that they would have to be in the same room, they would have to talk.

1

---

1. If you'd like to read more about Lisa, The Purple Irises and life at Ashdown House, you can do so by clicking here to order True Book Two of *The Gen X Series*

4

THE NEXT DAY

lat on her back in bed, encased in white cotton, Kay stared at the ceiling, at the lattice of sunlight that rippled across, accompanied by a stream of bubbling voices that sounded so very much like children's chatter and that seemed to come from the window? Or further? Turning her head, she squinted as she struggled to make sense of what she was looking at. It was a park. Well, a sad square of grass, lined with a perimeter of ash trees that had been stripped bare by winter. A view that should have been a unilaterally bleak one, but wasn't because something very bright and very lively was flashing. Winking silver at her, from across the grass. In her mind, she attempted to sit up, but whether she achieved any actual movement, she didn't know, because a deeply embedded stiffness began throbbing from her left shoulder, spreading across her chest and all thoughts of changing position fell away. If she stayed just as she was, she was, she decided, just about comfortable… and actually very sleepy… and that winking light might be a star. Her lids, heavy as water, began to close, but in the humming silence of the white room, the voices remained. With great effort, she peeled her eyes open again and this time she saw them. A crocodile of children, winding a path across the grass, every one of them wearing a yellow safety vest, with winking, silver stripes. The corners of Kay's mouth turned up to a lazy, dozy smile. All that flashing was making her think of the sequinned jacket she'd seen one of The Purple Irises wearing many years ago. Or even yesterday. She couldn't decide. And then she was thinking of her own silver jacket, hanging in her wardrobe, and then she was twenty-four, with a waist... Trying on that jacket in the changing room of Topshop, turning around, as a thousand sequinned eyes winked at her, *Kay's going to Vegas...* And then she was asleep.

THE NEXT TIME she opened her eyes, the ceiling was a dull-eyed grey. The park was empty and the children, with their flashing vests, had gone. *Why didn't you wait for me?* she whispered. *I have one too. A silver jacket.* A tear leaked from her eye. If they had just waited, she would have put her jacket on and followed them. What had happened? Where was the sun? A rising tide of soreness lapped at the edge of her consciousness. With effort she twisted her neck and looked down at her left arm. A small clear tube seemed to run down the length of it, connecting to a bulb-shaped container half filled with pink liquid, like strawberry juice. She stared at it, from the liquid to the tube and back again, unable to join the dots that would have spelt traumatic wound, fluid collection, drain. All down her arm, across her shoulder, her chest and along the top of her back a lumpen stiffness had dug in. She thought about shifting her weight, but knew she wouldn't be able to. From outside came the high-pitched yell of a child. They're back, she thought, and the relief closed her eyes. The children were back.

THE NEXT TIME she opened her eyes, the room was bathed in warm yellow and the park had vanished completely, the window view now was that of a room, with white walls and a bed with white sheets. She strained to raise her chin. Oh there she was! She was in that reflected bed! And there was a table at the end of it. How odd. She turned and the scene became even odder. On the table was a vase of chrysanthemums. Kay frowned, made a mental note to sit up, attempted to do so and as she did a wave of pain roared along her arm, twisting her into submission.

'Don't try and move.'

There was a hand on her arm and a figure looming above the bed.

She looked up. 'Caro?'

Caro nodded. 'How are you feeling?'

Again Kay thrust her chin forward, as if she was trying to sit.

'No... don't try and move by yourself.'

Her head fell back on the pillow. It was all too odd. Caro's lips hadn't moved, and her voice seemed to be coming from the other side of the bed.

'You mustn't try and move,' the disembodied voice said again and with titanic effort, Kay strained to look the other way. And there was Helen! It was Helen who had spoken. Helen on the other side of the bed.

'The nurse said we were to help. That you shouldn't move yourself.' Helen smiled.

'Ok.' Her voice was a whisper and her lips were dry as sandpaper. Helen on one side, Caro on the other. I'm dead,

Kay thought; it was, she considered, the only explanation for the fact that they were both in the same room. She closed her eyes and began to wonder, about the wonder of it all. How calm being dead was! How much like being alive, in that you could close and open your eyes. How much space to think through what had happened! The operation would have gone wrong, of course. That would have been what happened. She was probably still on the operating table. How nice of them then, to let Caro and Helen in to say goodbye. A tear leaked from her eye and slid down her cheek into her ear. She'd only got enough dinner in for Alex for the next three days. An overnight stay, the surgeon had said, so erring on the safe side she'd shopped for three nights. She hadn't erred on the dead side. Another tear leaked, very cold, and again it was amazing to Kay how much space there was to wonder at the visceral reality of death. She had time for one more thought. They'd better not be arguing, Helen and Caro. They'd better not be standing there bickering over her dead body... If they were, she'd float above them and bang their heads together and...

'*Kay.*'

Kay peeled her eyes open. There was Caro and there, still, was Helen. She was weighted as an anchor and lighter than a feather. She was not whole. Her consciousness spilled over the edge of her skin like water overflowing a bottle, like candles in the wind. Those lovely ship's candles, forged in metal cradles, designed to sway with the tide but never go out. Candles on a tide, or *in a wind.* Like Elton John and Princess Diana who was so young and... and... An explosion of sobs escaped her, the most frighteningly guttural sound she thought she'd ever heard. It sounded like a bear! Had it actually come from her? Then, as if she'd been punched, her chin dropped and her chest heaved as she gasped for air and sobbed with a life force that was as reassuring as it was uncontrollable. She wasn't dead! She knew this now. But she was in hospital. And she was in hospital because she had cancer. Cancer that had spread, that they were trying to cut out. '*Ouch.*' Another wave of pain shot across her shoulder.

'Are you in pain?'

The question came from her right-hand side. Caro.

'Sore,' she managed.

Helen was on her feet, moving towards the door. 'I'll get the nurse, to keep on top of the pain.'

And within a space of time that Kay couldn't have attempted to estimate, a nurse had been in, administered a shot of morphine and left again. And sure enough, the pain began to retreat as quietly as a wounded animal. In its place a tremendous feeling of wellbeing flooded her veins, filling every cell, imbuing her soul with bliss. Yes, bliss! She looked from Helen to Caro, and Caro to Helen, a huge lop-sided smile on her face. 'My friends,' she beamed, 'my beautiful friends. How young you both look... Oh, I'm thirsty. I've never been so thirsty.'

Suppressing a smile, Helen moved to collect a carafe of water from a side table. She poured a cup, and the next thing Kay was aware of, was hands supporting, and easing her up. Hands pushing the clump of hair back from her brow, and hands positioning the cup in her own hands, which shook with the effort of holding it. She put her cracked lips to the straw and the first sip slipped down her throat. The coolest, most delicious water that had ever existed. Within moments she had drained the glass, a sharp reality drawing the room and its contents, Helen's face and Caro, the vertical frame of the window, into a solid mass. She was no swaying candle, and there was no metal cradle to keep her flame from going out. She took a deep breath in and although the pain was still there, the padded wall of the morphine kept it at a manageable distance.

'Here.'

A warmth cupped her hands. Helen's hands, over her own, easing the cup away because, she could see now, her hands were shaking badly. 'I thought,' she said, watching Helen place the cup back on the table, 'that I was dead.'

'You're not dead.' Helen turned to her.

Kay nodded. 'I thought that it was going to be over someone's dead body before you two were ever in the same room again. I assumed it was mine.'

'No one,' Caro said firmly, 'is dead.'

'You were dreaming.' Helen smiled. 'About a silver jacket.'

'Was I?'

'Your Vegas jacket?' Helen said and sat down on the edge of the bed.

'Ouch!' Kay recoiled in pain.

'Oh God! I'm sorry!' Helen stood again. 'I need to lose some weight,' she muttered. 'Sorry, Kay...'

Kay smiled. 'I can recommend a good diet,' she said, and with a wave of her hand that exhausted her, indicated for Helen to sit again. She closed her eyes. So, they were back in the same room. She tried to imagine what had happened, what might have been said... But it was no good, all her thoughts were met by a fog as dense as night. She was muffled and swaddled and deeply content to see the two of them together again.

'Has Alex been in?' Caro said quietly.

Kay shook her head. 'I told him not to... He doesn't like hospitals... He... He...' Turning to Caro, her face collapsed. 'What's going to happen to him?' she sobbed, all the sweet

42

contentment of a moment ago, lost. 'How's he going to cope on his own? He can't live on his wage, my savings won't... I...' And then once again, hands were holding her, cradling her, easing her down to the pillow and she was floating, ever-so-gently persuaded into a chasm where she knew an immense rest waited. She heard a chair scrape and a voice, Helen.

'You're not to worry about anything, Kay. We're here. Caro and me, are here for you and Alex.'

'You need to sleep now.' It was Caro.

'Is there anything we can get you before we go?'

But Kay was already far away, dreaming in flashes of silver, sequins that winked.

PART II

5

EARLY MARCH

Sammy's list to live for!
1. Be blonde!
2. Scatter mum's ashes
3. Buy Versace jeans and wear them
4. Renew passport
5. Ride in a DeLorean
6. See George Might-be

'Can you see it?' Stretching her arm out, Kay held her phone up to show them the photo displayed on the screen. 'I met her at this cancer workshop I went to. We all had to write a *List to Live For,* and Sammy wrote this. It was so funny I had to take a photo. She didn't mind.'

Sitting on the opposite couch, both Helen and Caro leaned forward.

'Versace jeans,' Helen murmured. 'I wouldn't mind a pair myself.'

'George Might-Be?' Caro peered at Kay's phone. 'If that's meant to be George Michael, she's a little late.'

Turning the screen to re-read, Kay laughed. 'No, she means George Might-Be. Her husband had already made her write a similar list a while back, and she couldn't think of anything to put on it, so to keep him quiet, she put George Michael. He went straight off and found an Eighties Weekend, Butlins, I think, with a look-alike. George Might-Be!'

'Great name.' Helen smiled. 'He sounds like a good man,' she added, a little wistfully. 'The husband.'

'Yes, he does.'

'And the workshop sounds as if it was... fun? Is that the right word?'

Kay smiled. She'd been persuaded into the workshop by her doctor. It had been in a pleasant room of the hospital she now visited every three weeks for immunotherapy infusion. The chairs were big and padded, in cheery greens and orange, and across one wall, in a mosaic of bright colours, a mural had spelled out *Please Believe*. A far too young woman by the name of Jennie had been the leader. She'd come complete with a stylish dress that confirmed her efficiency, and a portable easel, upon which she'd written in painstakingly slow handwriting the title of the session. *A List to Live For!* By the time she'd gotten to the exclamation mark, Kay had switched off. A *Please Believe* mural? How much had that cost? She was a middle-aged woman, facing a terminal diagnosis, not an animated cartoon in a Disney movie. If she hadn't turned and seen the nearly completed list of the woman next to her, she would have made her excuses... *Not feeling up to it... Not for me...* and left. But she *had* turned, and before she'd been able to stop herself had read a list that had struck her as one definitely worth living for. *Be blonde?* Why not? *They're supposed to have more fun,* Sammy had winked. Why not indeed. It was an idea she'd contemplated herself. Hadn't every woman? Still, Sammy's speed in completing her list hadn't helped Kay get past number one with her own.

1. Make sure Alex is ok.

It was all she could think of. Nothing else mattered and ideas of how to raise money, earn more money, consumed her night and day... Along with the more deeply wounding, slower burn of, why hadn't she saved? Been better prepared? More pro-active about the future... Or more to the point, why had she assumed there would be a future? She put her phone on the table. 'It was interesting,' she said quietly. 'I understood how Sammy felt.'

'About George Michael?' Caro's eyebrows arched. 'I thought you were always more into The Specials.'

'About not knowing what to put on the list.' Kay shrugged. 'I couldn't think of anything either.'

Caro nodded. She leaned back, nursing her coffee cup in her hands, an inscrutable expression on her face. Beside her, Helen looked equally distant.

Picking up her cup, Kay too leaned back in her seat. On the far side of the coffee shop, two women had caught her eye. They were of a similar age, engaged in an animated conversation, their gestures uninhibited, their laughter arriving often and easily, in a way, Kay knew, that had been lost between herself, and Helen and Caro. She understood why and it saddened her. Six months since her diagnosis, and despite the fact that her treatment was going as well as anyone could have expected, still the cancer shadowed everything. Once a month she visited the hospital for immunotherapy treatment, which was a bit like giving blood. Cold, but she got a blanket and a cup of tea and a nice chat with the nurses. Of course, even a partially responsive result to the treatment she was on did not mean she was cured and did not mean she would live the length of time that, until a few months ago, she had fully expected to, but, she felt great! Really quite well. And ironically, because she was still on sick leave from teaching, she had more time on her hands than she could ever remember. Long morning walks and lazy relaxed afternoons in front of *Real Housewives* had benefits. If someone could have come along and waved a magic wand to produce the kind of nest-egg that would leave Alex not rich, but comfortable, she would, she thought, have more peace of mind than she'd had in years.

But even Caro, with all her financial acumen, couldn't conjure up a miracle. The one and only time they had met to discuss starting a fund for Alex had left them both flat. She didn't have anything to invest, her pension wasn't transferrable, Alex wasn't considered a dependent and it had become very clear, very quickly, that with the time she might have left, she wasn't going to be able to do much at all. *Even five thousand?* Caro had asked. *I know a young man who can probably double that within a year, and then you'll be off the starting blocks.* But she didn't have it and Caro's assurance, that she wasn't to worry, that she would personally look after Alex, well meant as it was, missed the target. He was her son, and the need to make sure he was provided for wasn't something she would ever be able to switch off, or pass on.

Shadows. It was a beautiful spring morning, the kind of day when hope is bountiful and seemingly achievable. 'So,' she said resolutely cheerful. This was the first time they'd all seen each other since her operation. Radiotherapy had proved exhausting, and Caro had been mostly down in

Salisbury visiting her mother, who had passed away last month... Shadows again. Her smile was as small as it was wry. Weren't they supposed to be shortest at noon? Try telling that to a group of midlife women. 'So, what would you two put on your list to live for?' she said, a very conscious desire to let in light steering her thoughts.

'Me?' Helen startled.

'Or, Caro.' Kay shrugged. Now that it was out, the idea grew legs, was already warming up, she could see it in the way the two of them sat thinking.

'Umm, I don't know,' Helen started. She glanced at Caro. 'I can't think of anything, can you?'

Caro frowned.

And then Helen frowned and the two of them sat for so long, with such pained expressions on their faces, that Kay tipped her head back and laughed.

'What?' Caro said, half-smiling. 'What's so funny?'

'You two, between the two of you, you can't think of a single thing to live for!'

'It's hard,' Helen said.

Kay nodded. 'I told you so. Swim with dolphins?'

'I don't like getting my hair wet,' Caro muttered.

'See the Northern Lights?'

'Freezing,' Helen said. Then, 'Let's go around the table! At least one thing each. No, two! We all have to think of two things.'

Kay let out a long breath. 'Well one is easy for me. But two?'

'What's number one?' Caro asked.

Kay looked at her. 'Make sure Alex is ok,' she said simply.

'Of course.' Caro nodded.

'Your turn, Helen,' Kay urged. They had to keep moving;

if they didn't want to get swallowed up by all that life had become, they had to keep moving past number one, forward to sunnier climes.

'Umm.' Helen shuffled to the edge of her seat and put her cup down. 'It's hard, isn't it.'

'Sleep under the stars?' Caro offered. 'Not me, you. You always wanted to sleep under the stars.'

'I did!' Helen laughed. 'I still do! You're right, that's my first.'

And watching them, sitting close together, Kay felt a sense of peace. Back in August, this was something she was sure she would never experience again. The three of them, comfortable in each other's company.

'Mine is do something spontaneous,' Caro said seriously.

Both Helen and Kay laughed.

'I mean it!' Caro smiled. 'Do something that I hadn't expected to do.'

'Or planned?' Helen said.

'Or planned, yes.'

'I have a number two,' Helen said excitedly. 'I want to throw another dinner party!'

'I thought you never wanted to do that again!' Kay said.

'I know, but it feels different now. And wouldn't it be fun? One last time before the house is sold?'

'Is it definitely happening?' Caro asked.

'Lawrence is dragging his feet, but he is repaying the money he took for Everest and when it's back, yes, the intention is to put the house on the market.'

'Good, Helen.' Caro nodded. 'That's good.'

'What about Libby?' Kay asked.

'Well, it's not going to happen tomorrow, and I hope by the time it does happen, Libby will be ready. I mean, she's going to need to stand on her own two feet... I can't... I can't *not* live my life, can I?' Helen said, every word sounding less assured than the word before.

'No.' Kay sighed.

Helen looked at her. 'So what's your number two?'

She winced. 'This is where it gets hard,' she said and turned to Caro. 'What's yours?'

Again, Caro frowned.

'Go backpacking?' Helen joked.

'Stay in a Premier Inn?' Kay said.

'God forbid!' Caro laughed. She folded her hands together and rested her chin on them. 'Grow my own tomatoes.'

'What!' Helen fell forward, her hand over her mouth to cover the fountain of coffee that had exploded.

'Tomatoes!' Kay too was laughing, so hard that a tear escaped from each eye. She wiped them away.

'Why not?' Caro said looking from one to the other, as she waited for them to recover themselves. 'I've never had the time before.'

Helen picked up a napkin and stretched out the neck of her jumper, blotting coffee. 'You haven't changed your mind about quitting then?'

'No. I have two more clients to see through their IPOs, and then I'm leaving.'

'IPO?' Kay asked.

'Initial Public Offering,' Caro said. 'When a company first goes public with shares.'

'Gosh, I wish I'd taken more notice of all that,' Helen said. 'Did you know Amazon shares were something like eighteen dollars in the beginning, they're nearly a hundred now.'

'True.' Caro nodded.

'I wish I had too,' Kay said.

'Anyway,' Caro continued. 'I would like to grow my own tomatoes... From seed... And then eat them. And...' She paused. 'I'm going down to my mother's house tomorrow. There's bound to be pots and trays in the shed. My father used to grow stuff.'

'Tomorrow?' Helen asked, her voice full of quiet compassion.

Caro nodded. 'I can't say I'm looking forward to it. But it sold so quickly, we have to get on with things.'

'It's hard,' Helen said, 'going through everything.' Her eyes were glassy as she added, 'But I think that's a good number two.' And she turned to Kay.

'I still don't know,' Kay said. She pressed her lips together. She was trying not to think about what might happen when the time came for someone to go through all her things, her old pot plants, her wardrobe, her odd socks. 'It's too late for The Specials as well,' she joked. 'Although I suppose there's probably also a tribute band for them.'

'Is there anywhere you would go?' Helen persisted. 'If you could.'

'Money no object,' Caro added.

Kay looked at her. 'Where would I go?' In her mind the wardrobe doors had already opened. In her mind, someone else was pulling out her Vegas jacket, dumping it onto a pile marked *Charity*.

'Yes, Kay!' Opening her arms, Helen threw the words out. 'If you had your chance, where in the world would you go?'

'Vegas.'

'Vegas!'

'Yes.' Kay nodded. She drew her shoulders to her ears and smiled. Because she hadn't seen this bullet coming, she'd hadn't been able to dodge it and now that she'd been hit, it felt sublime. The moment was sublime. This moment in which she, one hundred percent, believed that she could go to Las Vegas Nevada. 'I'd go to Vegas,' she said again.

'Well you have the jacket,' Caro smiled.

'I always wondered about that,' Helen said. 'Why Vegas?'

'I'm not sure.' Kay paused. 'My dad used to joke about it when I was a kid. We played a lot of cards together. He would joke about us winning a fortune there. And then Martin and I were supposed to go for our honeymoon.'

'Why didn't you?' Caro asked.

Kay shrugged. 'I don't know. I don't know why I never went.'

'There's still time,' Helen said gently.

Kay shook her head. 'No.' The seed of fantasy had already perished. Vegas? Blowing a fortune on a holiday like that was out of the question. Every resource she had would now be going into making sure Alex was left secure. 'No, that's never going to happen.'

[1]

---

1. If you would like to read more about Sammy and her 80s reunion weekend, you can do so by clicking here to order Back, to her future Book one of the *The Gen X Series*

55

6

THE NEXT DAY

All the way down to Salisbury, the man in the passenger seat beside her had been a calming influence that Caro knew she needed, today especially. It was why, riddled with doubt, she had sent the text.

> I have to collect some personal items from my mother's house. Would you come with me?

His response had been swift.

> Of course.

Shook, Kay's neighbour. The man who had found her that night in August last year, had driven her and Libby's baby back to Helen's house and had been there for her ever since. Always answering the calls she hadn't been able to stop herself making, the late-night, one-glass-of-wine-calls. And more recently the weekend walks, followed by quiet pub lunches, that had come to feel as necessary to Caro as sunlight. Silly texts, saying nothing and everything. *How are you today? Think I'm too old for New York.* Sometimes sending a photo of the fancy restaurant meal where she was about to eat, (Shook, it turned out, was a foodie. Even so. Photographs of food?). So much so that now, as she turned the key in the lock of her mother's house, and a familiar panic swept through, she found herself turning back to him for reassurance.

He was a couple of feet behind her on the path, hands in his pockets, watching.

'I'm nervous,' she laughed.

Shook looked at her.

He wasn't, she knew, fooled. Neither was she. She was so much more than nervous. She was eleven again, lingering at the door, afraid to open it. *Forty years ago*, *Caro* she murmured. She was fifty-one, her parents were gone and finally, there was nobody inside, snapping at her to go around the back, asking where she'd been, judging, criticising.

After the stroke, her mother never had come home. She hadn't in fact woken up. And the irony for Caro was, that it hadn't mattered. Through the last few weeks, she had spent many many hours by her mother's bedside, talking through the years of her life, talking through the years of her mother's life. She had said everything she'd wanted to say, including a few things she hadn't known she'd wanted to say and once, just once, was sure she had felt a squeeze of her hand. The doctor had said it was highly unlikely and the nurse had shaken her head and given Caro a sympathetic smile, but her faith, so new, had been untouchable. She knew she had felt her mother's touch, and that had been enough.

The moment had carried her through all the times she had taken a soft-bristled brush, the type designed for a baby, to untangle her mother's sparse hair, the afternoons she had helped change her mother's nightdress and, most frequently of all, the long hours she had sat, in silent company, shouldering winter shadows that threatened to swallow them both.

Leaning forward to press her forehead against the front door, she breathed in. *It's ok,* she whispered to the little girl that lived inside her, the child destined to remain forever on edge, nervously trying to second-guess the mood of the house. The key grated, metal against metal, one hard quarter turn and the door opened. She looked back at Shook. He nodded, and she turned and stepped inside.

Everything was as it had always been. The spotted mirror above the mantle, the bookcase and the unopened books, the ceramic cats waiting on the window ledge for an owner who would never return. The table and chairs which would never again be sat on, the sofa and the old-fashioned glass cabinet with its cheap crystal glasses, free gifts from a fuel campaign. A room as cold as a coffin. Arms crossed, Caro stood, an island, in the middle of an ocean of memory.

'Ok?' Shook said softly.

'Yes... I...' Helplessly, Caro waved at her surroundings, hot tears streaming down her face. The first time, in three weeks, that she had cried. 'I wasn't close to her,' she managed, the back of her hand pressed to her nose as she walked to the window and looked out at the street. Her tears had been sudden and warm, a heat of emotion that she hadn't been prepared for. Last summer, in the immediate aftermath of her mother's stroke, coming back to her childhood home had felt familiar, but manageably distant. As if the furnishings and fixings of the house were shrouded in nothing more permanent than imaginary dust sheets. A covering that could be removed, behind which she would still be able to hear the voices, sense the life she had once been a part of. But it did not feel like that now. It was very different, and watching the movement of the street outside, she felt the sense of finality inside. Those voices were no longer distant, they were gone. She pulled a tissue from her pocket and held it to her eyes. Death, as it is prone to do, had fundamentally changed things. Alienated what was once known. The gloves of her bereavement were off. She turned back to face the room. These weren't her books, or her chairs, or her crystal glasses. And now that her mother was dead, they weren't anyone's. *Now do you see?* they seemed to say. *Now do you understand? It's over.*

The house had sold within a week of going on the market. Which was exactly what everyone had expected. In less than a month, the sale would complete and the home she had grown up in, that had shaped such a large part of her psyche, would be unrecognisable. Walls gone, wallpaper stripped, cupboards ripped out. She could almost sense the violence coming, the annihilation of everything that had gone before, and the strength of her grief astonished her. Hadn't she spent half her life trying to escape these bonds? Why then was she so devastated to understand how finally and irrevocably they would now be broken? She was an orphan, taking her place with all the millions of other middle-aged orphans, and she hadn't understood, because even at the height of their estrangement, her mother had been more reachable than she was now, or ever would be again. She turned to Shook. 'When my mother was seven years old, her mother, *my* grandmother, pushed her into a bomb shelter. There wasn't room for both of them. That's always seemed odd to me, don't you think? I mean how could there *not* be room?'

Shook didn't answer. He dropped his head to one side and looked at her.

'And then she never came back.' Caro looked down at her sleeve, brushing away an invisible fleck. 'Caroline,' she said, as she looked back up. 'That's what her name was, and my mother spent the rest of the war at the garden gate waiting for her to come back. In fact,' and with this, Caro sighed and turned back to the window, 'I'd say she spent the rest of her life waiting for her to return.' Now that the words were out, now she'd finally given voice to an idea, nurtured and nourished for so long, they stunned her with their perfect sense. She stared outside. Across the street two small girls were standing on the pavement. They were pointing at something on the ground that she couldn't see, their heads touching, absorbed in a shared moment of concentration.

She took my hand, Caroline. I can still feel her doing it. She took my hand and pushed me in.

How many times, growing up, had she heard the story? And how many times, as a young girl, had she then watched as her mother stared into the eye of memory, as lost to her child as her own mother had been to her? The battle had lasted a lifetime. The battle for her mother's attention and affection, waged between her and her dead grandmother. A fight, she understood only now, she'd never had a chance of winning.

A dog barked and the two girls broke apart. Arms pressed against her chest, like a shield, Caro watched as, a few feet behind them, a man walking a Labrador came into view. He caught up with the girls and the group walked on, one child either side of him.

Were they friends, those little girls, or sisters? Her thoughts went to Helen, because, ever since yesterday, she hadn't been able to stop seeing the look on Helen's face when she'd mentioned that she was coming down to clear the house. The glassy tears Helen hadn't allowed to fall. How little she had understood of what Helen would have gone through when her mother died. Three years? Was it only three years? A hard lump formed at the back of Caro's throat. Was this shame? She'd offered platitudes of course, sent flowers, called... but she hadn't understood. She'd thought she had, but she hadn't. How could she? How could anyone, until they'd walked in the same shoes? Her eyes were hot again with unshed tears. Now it was Kay she was thinking of. Would it be Kay next? Flowers and platitudes? Condolence messages on social media? She put her hand to her nose and turned a half turn and no further, and then Shook was standing in front of her, with his hands on her shoulders, guiding her to the sofa, saying, *Sit down.* So she did. And then his face was level with hers and he was crouching in front of her.

'I'll make a cup of tea. Is there tea in the house?'

Dabbing at her eyes, a rash spreading up her throat, Caro nodded at the kitchen.

He put his hand on her knee. 'I'll make tea.'

'Is that what you call it?' Caro joked minutes later when she was holding a cup of milky-white hot water.

'Try it.' Shook smiled.

She did and it was so unexpectedly sweet it was like drinking warm honey. She took another sip and another, feeling it warm her blood. 'I don't...' she started and then stopped.

'You don't what?'

'I don't normally take sugar.'

'I know.'

'Do you?'

'Yes.' He nodded. 'When I first met you. At Kay's, remember?'

Caro stared at him. Of course she remembered. But she hadn't for a moment considered that he had. Confused, she looked down at her cup.

'You needed it.'

'Did I?' She stared at him. Decades of working with some of the world's wealthiest and most powerful men, and she'd never failed to be amused at the way their decision-making abilities evaporated whenever wives or girlfriends appeared. Guilt made idiots of them. Guilt at the long hours they worked, or over other women they'd slept with, or money siphoned off... She'd become shrewd at spotting it. The guiltier they were, the more inept they became. As if deferring to a wife over the choice of that evening's restaurant was atonement for sleeping with a secretary. Shook, it occurred to her now, hadn't a single thing to hide.

She watched him sip his own tea. Did he take sugar? And if he didn't, would she know the moment that he needed to take it? And then have the self-assurance to offer it to him? He was, she thought now, perhaps the most genuinely self-assured man she'd met. 'I hardly know anything about you,' she said, and looked down at the hand that now covered hers, the rough calloused joints and the clean short nails of this man.

'What do you want to know?' He smiled, his eyes that same unlikely shade of clear blue. Like little swimming pools; incapable of hiding even the smallest lie.

A feeling of anticipation rose in Caro. All these weeks, they really had been saying nothing to each other. She hadn't spoken of her miscarriage, or the pregnancy, or how she had come to be pregnant in the first place. And he hadn't spoken about his life. They had simply ambled along together, falling in step as easily as dance partners. Life left clues enough. And it simply hadn't felt necessary to insist upon the kind of unpacking that she might have gone through when she was younger. *What do you want? What do you do? Where do you see yourself?* What was the point of hurrying to unpack something that was so clearly damaged goods? Still... She took a deep breath. If they were going to see exactly how damaged, one of them was going to have to be brave and take a closer look. His real name was Tomasz, but she never used it. She loved the silliness of his nickname; the sound of it, but maybe she should start there. 'I remember,' she said now, 'Kay said, that before Shook, they called you Shaky. When did it change?'

But his response was not what she had expected. He withdrew his hand and lowered his chin, stretching his arms forward, so the heels of his hands came together around his cup. He didn't speak.

Anticipation turned to unease. 'I hope,' she whispered, 'you don't mind me asking?'

And still he didn't speak, and within the long moment of his silence a doubt that had never existed before began budding in Caro's mind, unfurling into technicoloured flowers. Had she touched on something raw? Overstepped a mark she hadn't been aware of? Or maybe – and this was the quintessential source of her doubt – he wasn't yet sure about the relationship? All this time she'd presumed it was her holding him at arm's length, because although there had been times when she had felt closer to him than any other man, ever, the reality was that walking and talking was the extent of their physical relationship. 'It doesn't matter,' she said, laughing to mask her discomfiture. This was why... this was why she'd kept her reserve. After the devastating blows last summer had brought, she was a fool to have risked exposing herself to the idea of love, of company, again. 'No, it really doesn't—'

'Coffee break,' Shook said, turning his head sideways and looking directly at her. 'Third week of February.'

'Oh.' A corner of Caro's mouth turned up. The tiniest outward sign of the river of relief that flowed. 'That's... exact?'

Shook nodded. 'There's a kid at work. I was drinking my coffee, and he said my hands weren't shaking. From then on, it was Shook. I didn't mind.'

'And were...' Now she was looking at his hands. His wonderful, strong, honest hands, feeling the warmth of sun in her world again. 'Were you really that shaky?'

'Yes.' He nodded. 'Yes, I was.'

'Oh.'

'Do you remember,' he said, 'when the Pope first came to Poland? 1979.'

Caro frowned. 'Vaguely. I was very young. 1979... that sounds such a long time—'

'That was the day I started drinking.'

She stared at him. 'How old were you?'

'Fourteen.'

'Oh. Well...' she started. 'Teenagers here—'

'But I didn't stop, Caro,' Shook interrupted, and amongst the crumple and ruddiness of his cheeks, his eyes remained that bright clear blue. 'It's ironic. Two million Poles got themselves sober to go and see the Pope. But me? That's when I started getting drunk.'

'Did you go and see him?' Caro's voice was soft, the question tentative. They were talking about something that had passed through her consciousness over forty years ago, as fleetingly as a comet. How strange, she was thinking, that this long-ago event might hold the key to getting to know him.

Shook nodded. 'I went with my family. With every relative I've ever known and more. And when we got back everyone fell asleep early, because they were sober, and I found the *bimber*.'

'Bimber?'

'You don't want to know.' He shrugged. 'Everyone drank. Every day. You wouldn't get through your shift at the factory otherwise. The cold and the noise. You had to drink.'

Caro stopped smiling. She was thinking about those two last words: the cold and the noise. She'd never worked in a factory in her life. How different they were. And if this thought had occurred to him, she would never know, because suddenly he said, 'So that's when my name changed. And I'm still here. And I can still handle a saw and those tiny screws, you know?'

Caro laughed. 'No I don't know. I don't think I've ever used a screwdriver.'

He took two of her fingers and made a quarter-inch space between them. 'They're this big,' he whispered, looking straight at her. 'Very hard to keep hold of.'

'That's good,' she managed. Grown-up Caro yearned to go with this moment, open herself up to all the messy, unpredictable highs and maybe lows it would facilitate. But she was sitting in her childhood home, on her mother's settee, and that Caro didn't stand a chance. The child inside did what it had learned over the course of so many rejections. Battened down the hatches, pulled up the drawbridge. Retreated before it was wounded. Releasing his hand, she stood up. 'We should get on,' she said. 'There's a lot to do.' Turning away from his bemusement, she went into the kitchen and rinsed her cup under the tap, unaware that he had followed her and was now standing in the doorway watching.

'Caro?' he said gently.

Caro turned the tap off. 'Is your mother still alive?' she said, staring at it.

'Very much so.'

'And... are you close?' Now she turned to him.

'Yes.'

The simpleness of his response was like a sting. Caro looked away. 'I think,' she whispered, 'I think, my mother was too damaged to be able to... She could never show me that she loved me.'

'No.' It was a very gentle *No*, but she couldn't turn to it. 'Caro,' he said. 'Look at me.'

'Shook... I don't think you understand. There's...'

'Sssh,' he said, stepped forward and cupped his hands against her cheeks. 'She gave you her mother's name. She must have loved you very much.' And then his lips were on hers, warm and forceful, and closing her eyes, Caro heard the voice in her head. *Please let this work, please let this work.*

HOURS LATER, with Shook driving, Caro sat in the passenger seat of her BMW, a bag full of empty seed trays on her lap, thinking about what Shook had said. Fifty-one years and she hadn't understood that her name had been an act of profound love. How smart she'd been in some ways, and how unbelievably stupid. It was so obvious now. If her mother had never been able to say it, she'd shown her love in the only way she could. Caroline. She leaned her elbow on the rim and looked out of the window.

Where, she was thinking, did that leave her? How had she shown her love to the people in her life that had mattered the most? It occurred to Caro now, as she looked out at the suburban spread that indicated the proximity of London, how stunted her empathy skills were. It was almost to be expected. She'd been handed a much-reduced example to begin with. She didn't belong to the Kays and Helens of this world, who had grown up wrapped around in demonstrated affection, who had understood, before they could talk, how to give and receive love, and for whom it was all natural as sunshine. And again she was thinking of three years back, when Helen's mother had died. How present had she been for Helen then? Or further back, during Kay's divorce? These were times when she'd barely been in the country. Business class flights and after-hours drinks filling her diary.

The thought had her leaning forward and reaching for her handbag, pulling out her phone and opening the calculator app. Her mother's house would raise a considerable sum. Fifty percent of which was hers. She didn't need any more money. She did need her friends, and one of them was dying and now that she too had had her feet held at the fire of bereavement, the loss of both her baby and her mother, she had come away wiser.

'Are you ok?' Shook glanced at her phone.

She reached across and took his hand. This afternoon with one wonderful kiss, they'd taken another step forward on the way to a lovely warm place she knew she'd never want to leave. It scared her. 'I'm fine,' she managed. 'I'm just thinking.'

He nodded. 'What are you thinking?'

Caro looked up. 'Vegas. I'm thinking about Vegas.'

7
———

mazing!' Caro nodded seriously.

'Wow... just, wow!' Kay added.

'Beats a trek up Box Hill,' Craig said.

'Lawrence, this is an incredible achievement.' Shook, who was standing beside the elegant inbuilt fireplace in Helen's living room, nodded at the now blank TV screen. 'Incredible,' he repeated.

Across the room Lawrence turned his palms to the ceiling, an almost genuine embarrassment creeping across his face. 'Well, getting up is only half the equation. There are as many climbers lost on the way down as on the way up.'

'Not you though,' Helen said brightly. 'So that's a relief.' And she turned to the light switch.

But Lawrence didn't seem to hear. He'd leaned over his laptop, reading glasses halfway down his nose. 'The descent,' he was saying, 'is a whole other story. It took us eight hours. The next video shows—'

'Which we'll have to save for another day!' Helen finished.

The overhead light burst on and the room jumped as if a lid had been lifted from a pan of live frogs.

Kay put her hand across to shield her eyes.

Sitting beside her, Craig frowned.

Caro blinked.

And at the light switch, Helen stood guilty as a child caught stealing sweets.

'Oh.' Lawrence straightened up. 'But the video isn't eight hours,' he smiled.

'Thank God for that,' Craig murmured.

Kay kicked him.

'*No*,' Helen said carefully, 'but pudding will be ready soon.'

'*And* we have the presents to do,' Caro added.

Helen looked down at her wine. She'd lost track of how many times Caro had mentioned presents now. Silly as it was, considering that it was now spring, they were doing a Secret Santa. A delayed Christmas meal, because back in December Kay wasn't in any fit state to eat more than half a rusk, let alone the three-course banquet Helen had planned and was currently enjoying serving. Dinner had been a triumph. Even the beetroot soup, a Polish tradition that Shook had brought along, had been a revelation. Never mind that Lawrence had managed to spill some down his white shirt and spent the best part of the meal looking as if he'd been shot in the chest. Her house was a cauldron of warmth and fragrance and voices and light, and there had been moments when Helen had thought that she'd never been happier in it. If Caro could just ease back from trying to organise the presents. The tiniest ripple of irritation stirred; she wished it hadn't.

'There's probably not enough time to do the descent justice?' Kay offered diplomatically.

'Not unless they all slid down,' Craig hissed.

Helen looked at him and pressed her lips together, thoughts of Lawrence sliding down Everest on a tin tray flitting through her head. He was funny, this young man Kay had bought along. Very funny. 'Anyway,' she managed. 'I'll get on.'

BACK IN THE KITCHEN, she leaned against the sink and raised her glass to her lips, savouring the last drops of wine while watching the microwave count down minutes on a luxury Marks and Spencer Christmas pudding no one had been able to face at Christmas. Libby had been trying to lose her baby weight; Jack was always hung over; Lawrence was perpetually in training and Helen was tied up in knots of worry for Kay. It was good to see it get used. With Jack back at university and Libby away, Craig and Shook she was sure would enjoy it. She turned to the window as she so often did, and stood staring out across the back garden.

Lawrence's Everest slideshow had been as spectacular this third time around as it had been the first. Kay and Caro, Shook and Craig, for whom it had been a first, had all been suitably impressed. Lawrence, thankfully, had been suitably falsely modest and she was now, in a funny sort of way, content. All of which was astonishing given the fact that it wasn't even a year ago she'd been bored to tears with the idea of dinner parties, vowing *never* to sit through another Lawrence video ever again. But this was what she did! She looked after people very well. It was a gift she knew how to curate and enjoyed dispensing. Her love of good food, good company, of beauty and order. The table had looked glorious, the meal had been delicious, and *if* this was going to be Kay's last Christmas...

Slicing the thought clean off, Helen twisted away from the window, the suddenness of the movement so momentarily disorientating that she stood, blank, but successful in having outrun the one thing she couldn't bear to think. It took a long silent moment for the sound of voices floating along the hallway to anchor her back into time and place. Here she was, Helen Winters. Making dinner for her friends. One of whom was dying.

She managed to get her glass down on the bench before her head dropped to her hands and she folded under the swing of an ever-present wrecking ball. It didn't last long. One heft forward, one blow back, a few chest-wracking gasps and she had wrested back control. She grabbed a beetroot-stained napkin from the table and blew her nose. The idea of losing Kay was a storm that would consume her if she allowed it free rein. And it would gather in every other loss she'd suffered, amalgamating them into a force she knew she wouldn't be able to withstand. And what was the use? It wouldn't bring anyone back. Screwing the napkin into a ball, Helen did what every woman in the world does with such grief. She picked it up and packed it away in a special place. A place where she would not stumble across it, but where it was safe, where she would always be able to find it, bring it out and hold it soft against her cheek in the sanctuary of a private moment. Daniel, her lost baby. Her mother. At some time in the future... Kay. Her chest heaved and as it did her bra strap slipped. She stuck a hand under her blouse and yanked the strap back up and stood staring across the room, eyes blank.

'Can I help with anything?'

The voice, clear and cheery, startled her. Craig was in the doorway.

You'll like him, Kay had said, when she'd asked if she

could invite him. He'd started, Helen knew, as Kay's mother's carer, but was now so much more. Plus, he was driving Kay to see her mother at Ashdown House afterwards, which meant that Kay could have a glass, or two, of champagne. *The more the merrier,* Helen had answered. Frankly, Kay could have brought Atilla the Hun if it had meant that Helen could keep topping her glass up.

'Yes,' she answered and didn't move.

'Are we doing pudding?'

'Yes,' she said again.

'Caro…' Craig turned and nodded back along the hallway. 'She wanted to know when we were doing the presents.'

'Ok.' Helen's nose wrinkled. Caro, she could see, was altered. The death of her mother, the miscarriage, had softened her. And then of course there was this new man, who seemed lovely and was unlike any other man Caro had ever been involved with. Twice she'd seen him place a hand on Caro's arm, a relax signal, which, to Helen's surprise, Caro had responded to. It was almost amusing to see. He was a calming presence and he seemed to be able to reach a part of Caro neither Kay nor she ever had.

'I think,' Craig laughed now, 'she's more excited than I am. She seems a bit worried about time.' He looked at the clock. 'We do have to leave by five.'

Helen nodded. And then again, in other ways, Caro hadn't altered at all. Here she was back in full micro-management control mode. The microwave pinged. 'It's ready now,' Helen said. How long did anyone need to open a five quid Secret Santa present?

.   .   .

WITH ONLY A FEW raisins left littering plates, and coffee cups filled, Craig knelt under the small artificial tree Helen had clambered up into the loft for. He was smiling like a Cheshire cat, one last package on his thin knees.

'I've been a bit naughty,' he said. 'I bought an extra one for Kay.' He blushed a deep red.

'But I've had mine.' Kay held up the bottle of bath oil she'd received. 'And whoever bought this was naughty as well.' She looked at Caro.

Caro smiled. Clarins was obviously more expensive than the five pounds allowed, but as soon as she had seen who she was buying for, the budget had gone out of the window. How many more occasions were there going to be when she could buy for Kay? She shifted her weight on the settee, allowing her thigh to rest alongside Shook's. Bath oil wasn't the half of it. She had been far far naughtier than anyone might guess, and right now all she could hear was the chorus of voices in her head, singing their doubts. *How presumptuous she'd been. How impetuous. How foolish.*

I'm thinking about Vegas, she'd told Shook, barely a week ago. And then as if it had been ordained, Helen's text had arrived that same evening.

> Consider yourself invited to a delayed and much needed Christmas dinner, Sunday, 3pm. No 2 ticked off my list, over to you ladies!

It had pushed her over the line. She'd opened her laptop and *Done Something Spontaneous.* Booked a seven-day, all-expenses-paid trip to Vegas for the three of them. Business class flights. Good idea? Terrible idea? She still didn't know. She'd woken the next day plagued by doubt, and more than once had gone to cancel. *Trust yourself,* Shook had said when she'd told him her doubts. And because she'd found herself able to trust him, she hadn't cancelled.

'As long as it's not a motivational fridge magnet,' Kay was saying now, laughing as Craig leaned across to deposit the last package in her lap.

'You'll see,' Craig smiled.

Kay pulled the wrapping open and the room, as a whole, drew forward. What was visible was a mound of white, the shape and volume of meringue, the texture of fur. A furry meringue.

'A wig!' Kay gasped and held it up.

'Not just any wig. It's a Roxette wig!' Craig winked.

Kay doubled over with laughter. 'You idiot! I knew I shouldn't have told you!'

'What's this?' Caro asked.

'"It must have been love". That Roxette?' Helen said.

Kay nodded. 'Remember Sammy's list? The workshop? Well I made the mistake of telling Craig.'

Caro nodded. Of course she remembered the list. The repercussions of it were burning a hole in her handbag right now. Three tickets, one travel itinerary, folded in a neat envelope.

'You said that if you were going to go blonde, you'd want to do it like Roxette,' Craig said. 'That's what you told me anyway, and as you don't have that much hair to start with, it should fit nicely.'

Kay wiped away a tear of laughter.

'But you also told me that this Sammy had *See George Michael* on her list, so I'm not sure I believe a word of what you say any more!' He finished with an exaggerated wink.

'Isn't he dead?' Arms folded, leaning against the fireplace, Lawrence frowned.

'As a Dodo,' Craig said.

With a sideways shuffle, Kay manoeuvred herself to the edge of her chair. 'It's a lookalike, Lawrence. George Might-be is performing at a Butlin's Eighties Weekend. And Sammy's husband has even hired a DeLorean car to travel in.'

'Oh, that sounds fun!' Helen clapped her hands together.

'Doesn't it,' Kay smiled. 'So.' She held the wig up. 'Shall I try it?'

'Yes,' Craig said.

'Yes,' Helen echoed. 'There's a mirror in the hall.'

And moving swiftly, the three of them swept out of the room, giggly with excitement.

Inching forward, Caro moved to join them, but was stopped by the sight of Lawrence raising his arm to point at Shook.

'Now that,' Lawrence boomed, 'is a great film! *Back to the Future!* Did you have that in Poland, Tomasz? I wouldn't have thought that kind of western influence was allowed back then!'

Caro flinched. For the first half of this evening, Lawrence hadn't been able to shape Shook's real name, Tomasz, and his reticence had functioned as a brake, limiting conversation. But now that he was at least one bottle of red wine down, his tongue had loosened so the name had begun to flow as freely from his tongue as the wine into his glass. And with every slurry extra *S or Z* Lawrence added, Caro could sense him moving closer. It made her uneasy. Twice now, slipping behind her to reach a glass, he'd rubbed up against her. If she could, she would have turned around and slapped him.

'Not at the cinema, Lawrence.' Shook smiled as he answered, and Caro felt his hand on her leg. Immediately she slipped her own hand over his. 'But I saw it on VHS,' he continued. 'I always remember, because it cost me a fortune. Eight thousand zloty.'

'Was that a lot?' She turned to him. There was still so much about his past that she had no idea of, she felt she could listen to him for days. Plus, it would steer the conversation away from Lawrence's control.

'Well... my father was making 25,000 a month.'

Her mind went through a tumble of arithmetic. 'Quite a lot then,' she settled for.

'Quite a lot of queueing,' he smiled. 'Yes.'

'Queueing?'

'Everyone queued, Caro.' He shrugged. 'For everything. Meat, butter, sugar, potatoes, rice, fruit, soap, washing powder. The kids started at five and the neighbours paid us. When they finished breakfast they came to take our place and we went to school. When we finished school, we got back in line for someone else. All the kids did it.'

Caro stared at him.

'It was worth it though,' Shook smiled. 'I mean a DeLorean? Even if it is only on the screen. The only cars I knew then were Fiat Polski. Excuse me,' he said squeezing her hand, 'I must go to the bathroom.'

'Fiat Polski! ' Lawrence rocked back on his heels, laughing as Shook passed.

And just like that, it was only the two of them in the room.

'He's a funny fella.' A corner of Lawrence's mouth turned up in a sly smile. He dropped his head to one side and from under bloodshot, eyes, said, 'Not really your type, I wouldn't have thought.'

Caro glared at him.

He didn't notice. He'd already crossed the room, was

already sitting down alongside her. Very close. Too close. Leg to leg close. From the hallway she could hear laughter. Craig's voice. *Pull it down a bit!* And then Lawrence's hand was on her knee. Time stopped. Caro looked down at it. She felt as if she was looking at a scene which she was not a part of. She couldn't move, and although her physical capacity had frozen, her mind raced. *Don't let Helen come in. Don't let Shook come in. Don't let Helen...*

'Caaro.' Lawrence's voice, dragging with alcohol, settled in her ear like a warm, heavy thing. 'You've haad a hard time,' he slurred. 'Yoou know you can doo better...' His hand inched higher up her thigh. 'We're the ssame, you and me. We're the go-getters of thiss world.'

'L—' The letter stuck on her tongue, the weak flabby shape of the first letter of his name.

'It'ss not too late,' Lawrence whispered. 'You sshhould have told me how you felt. I thought it was just a sshag between us, but ss'not too late.'

A peal of laughter rolled in from the hallway. And although Caro heard it, it was light years away from where she had been stranded. Another world.

'Helen...' Lawrence shrugged. 'Sshhe doesn't under-stand. It was a mistake. Twenty-five years ago, I made a mistake.'

Mistake. Now Caro looked at him, the word turning between them in slow wheels. Up it went. *Mistake.* Down and round again. *Mistake.* 'Your marriage,' she said and left a long icy gap before continuing, 'was a *mistake*?'

Almost confused, Lawrence drew back, his smile so flabby, Caro had a moment to wonder how it stayed on his face. He turned his palms to the ceiling and shrugged. 'Maybe.'

And although she knew that she should move away, that

every fibre in her body was screaming at her to stand up and leave the room, she couldn't. And she couldn't, because to do so would have been a betrayal. All these years, so many of them, for better or worse, she'd watched Helen sacrifice herself, her dreams and ambition, almost everything, to make this house a home, to build a nest for her family, to create what, from the outside looking in, had seemed perfect and would, for those on the inside, have felt perfect... *For this?* For this man to dismiss it as a *mistake.* Fury rose.

'Now, now...' Lawrence leaned in. 'I'm talking about uss now,' he slurred. 'Yoou and me, Caro.'

His hand was on her leg again, but this time, Caro peeled it back and placed it on his own leg, watching him as he stared at it, her lip curling in distaste. A movement caught her eye. A shadow passing across the front window. Exactly as if someone had been standing in the open door-way, and had now backed away.

'Caro.' And for the third time, Lawrence's hand was on her thigh.

This time she whipped it off. 'You're right,' she said leaning into him, using a voice perfected over years. The voice she'd reserved for the junior in the office who went over her head, the visitor who mistook her for the secretary, the taxi driver who asked her male colleague for the fare. 'All those years ago, one of us did make a mistake. But it wasn't you, Lawrence. It was me. It was me who made the mistake of sleeping with you in the first place.'

Lawrence frowned.

Caro looked at him. She could hear the blood running in her ears. That reflected movement had spooked her. She was as jittery as she was doubtful, but above all she was determined. This stopped. Today. His entitlement, her vulnerability. Leaning in closer, she whispered. 'I was never in love with you, Lawrence. Don't flatter yourself. I may have once thought I was, but honestly?' And reaching out, she patted his hand. 'I was a twenty-one-year-old virgin. I'd have convinced myself I was in love with Boy George, if there was a chance he'd have taken me to bed. Confidence,' she finished as she drew back, 'is such a precious resource, don't you think?'

He looked at her, his mouth slightly open, his right eye making an involuntary twitching movement.

Caro shook her head. 'I had none, you see, Lawrence. None at all! And I didn't know it, but I was looking in the wrong place thinking I'd find it by sleeping with you, especially when...' And suddenly she stopped talking, pausing to stare across the room, as if she was waiting for something to reveal itself.

'Especially when what?' Lawrence was sneering now.

'Especially when what I needed was what I already had. Friends,' she murmured. 'The only thing I needed, I've ever needed, was my friends.'

Lawrence stood up and went across to where he'd left his bottle. Filling his glass, he said, 'You'll be bored of him within a month. Face it.'

And at this, Caro allowed her head to drop to one side and smiled, as if she was looking at a lost sad puppy. 'You just don't get it do you? It doesn't matter if it doesn't work out with Tomasz. As long as I have my friends, I won't be unhappy.'

From across the room, he looked at her and she looked back at him, taking a long moment to do so. This athletic, well-educated, supremely confident man she'd once prized so highly. 'No,' she said again. 'I'll survive. But if I lose my friends, well that's another matter. That would make me very unhappy indeed.' And with that, Caro stood and went across to her handbag. It was time to commit. She needed them, Helen and Kay. They were staples, helping to hold together a Caro that had over this last year been beaten paper-thin.

'I WISH I had the balls to wear this out of the house!' Roxette wig in place, Kay sailed into the room. She stood, hands on hips, cheeks flushed, eyebrows bare, a huge puffball of platinum blonde on her head. It was as ridiculous as it was beautiful, as joyful as it was tragic.

'Oh my God, that's absolutely marvellous!' Caro gasped. It was. Kay looked marvellous!

Helen and Craig followed. Caro glanced nervously across at Lawrence. He was at the far end of the room, knocking back wine.

'I feel like a different person wearing it,' Kay smiled.

'You look like a different person,' Caro said. It was true. Kay looked more buoyant than she had done for months. She was afloat again. 'Well done, Craig! What a great present! It's brilliant to see Kay laughing.' Craig, it was true, seemed to bring out a side of Kay that Caro realised she hadn't seen much of in years. Certainly not since Alex had been born and Kay's life had settled within the parameters of his diagnosis. It emptied Caro a little. She'd taken up so much of Kay's time with her own problems, with all her unspoken but obvious comparing and complaining and dissatisfaction with life, and not nearly enough time with just laughing. Glancing across to Helen, she wondered if Helen was thinking the same, but it was hard to tell what Helen was thinking. She was busying herself now with tidying cups and glasses. A little too busy, Caro thought, and her confidence over what she was about to do wavered, thin as a soap bubble.

Then Shook came in, and looked at her and no... she didn't imagine it, he gave her the tiniest, almost invisible nod. It was time. If Shook thought the moment had arrived, it had. She trusted him in a way she had never trusted any other man.

She reached down for her handbag. As she straightened up she was aware that her stomach had liquefied and her legs were shaking. She was nervous. More nervous than she'd thought she'd ever been. Which was more than silly, because how many times had she stood in front of a board-room full of men without a trace of nerves? But those times didn't matter. No one was dying. The people were acquaintances, not friends whom she loved and relied upon and wanted only to be kind to and do the best by. That's where this gift was coming from, and the last thing she wanted was to get it wrong. Memories of Helen's fiftieth lunch surged. She'd gotten it wrong then, completely and horribly wrong. Her stomach flipped. Everyone, she realised, was looking at her.

'You alright?' Kay asked.

There was a hand on her back. Shook. He knew exactly what she was going to say. They'd even rehearsed it a few times. The objections that might need to be overcome. The protestations that it was too much, too extravagant an offer. But the sale of her mother's house was already going through, making a rich woman even richer, while Kay kept a jacket she'd hardly ever worn, and Helen kept the lid of her ambitions down.

'So,' she said and paused. She felt a pressure form Shook's hand. She thought she heard him say, *Go on.*

'Confession time from me as well,' she said, in a voice strangled by nerves. 'I also bought a couple of extra gifts.'

No one spoke. Everyone seemed to know that whatever was coming out of Caro's handbag wasn't a Roxette-style wig.

She swallowed hard, pulled the envelope out, and said, 'We're going to Vegas. Me, Helen and Kay.'

Helen's face was still.

'It's my treat. No arguments! You both know I've come into some money. And I—'

'Your mother's house?' Kay said.

Caro nodded.

'My jacket?' Kay whispered, her face under the mountain of wig breaking into a huge grin. 'I get to wear my jacket?'

And from Helen, came nothing.

8

Caro sat squashed into the corner of Starbucks, her suitcase jammed into the space between two chairs, her jacket piled on top, her brow sweaty and her ears ringing with the cacophony of sound. The café was chaos. Toddlers crying, pensioners jawing at huge muffins, sticky coffee spills, harassed staff. It was her idea of hell, and considering that on the other side of security the calm of the executive lounge waited, she had no idea why Shook had insisted on accompanying her into the terminal and then suggesting coffee. Then again, she had no idea why he'd insisted on leaving for the airport so early in the first place. So far he hadn't put a foot wrong, but arriving for a flight three hours before it was due to leave was provincial territory and if there was one thing Caro did not consider herself, it was provincial. But she hadn't objected, not least because she enjoyed his company so much that eking it out like this was actually a thrill. As if they were teenagers parting for the weekend. Watching his back now, as he stood at the counter, her worry subsided, replaced by warm contentment. Goodness, she was happy. Six months ago, if anyone could have told her how content this spring would find her, she wouldn't have believed it. But yes, content was the right word.

She settled back in her seat. Overhead the tannoy system called the names of missing passengers; closer by snippets of overheard phone conversations floated past. *Going through in five minutes. Let's meet at the gate. Don't forget the charger.* At some point in her recent past, every overheard conversation like this would have been a poignant reminder, another little flag that waved back her loneliness. She'd never had someone to send that last quick text to, no one to sign off with a kissing emoji. As she looked across at Shook again he turned and smiled, a coffee in each hand. Well, she did now.

He put the coffees on the table and manoeuvred Caro's case so he could sit down. Caro picked up her cup. She was thinking about the drive for profit that had coffee shops positioning tables far too close together, and then she was thinking about the fact they were flying business class, and how relived she was and how much she was looking forward to seeing Helen and Kay's faces when they saw the executive lounge. So much going on in her mind that she didn't notice until she was just about to take a sip that Shook had leaned forward to nod at her cup.

'What?' she said, looking down. Across the surface, the barista had swirled a heart shape. 'Oh.' She turned the cup so the heart was the right way up. 'Did you ask for that?'

'Of course.'

'You fool,' she said, feeling about fourteen. Then, 'You didn't have to come in with me, you know.'

'I know.'

Of course he knew.

'I would—'

But he'd lifted his forefinger and was now tapping it against his lip, as if in the gentlest possible way he was asking her to stop talking, saying to her, that they were good without words. Which they were. They were always good. He'd steered her through that awful evening last August, the shock of Kay's diagnosis, the coming to terms with the resignation from her job – which she hadn't rescinded and which she would have to face the reality of when her final client was handed over in a couple of weeks... and of course, the death of her mother. He'd become a fixture in her life, perhaps the only one that she'd never pursued, or coveted, or pinned a thousand impossible hopes upon. Quiet and welcome as a summer breeze, comfortable as an armchair, he'd entered discreetly from stage left, or right, and never left. She put her head to one side and smiled. How lucky she felt.

Once again, Shook smiled back at her, then he took a sip of his coffee, mopped the froth from his lip, reached into his pocket and pulled out a small, faded, bronze-coloured box.

Caro stared at it. She felt her stomach drop to her feet. Her hands, wrapped around her warm coffee, went icy cold. The box was a ring box. The box was a ring box... 'Shook,' she started, and again his finger was at his lip, tapping her silent. Good. Because she didn't know what she would have said. Anything and everything that was on her mind. That's what would have come out, that's what people tended to do when they weren't prepared. And she wasn't prepared. Weekend walks and late-night, one-glass-of-wine-calls were one thing. Ring boxes? She was terrified, nervous and excited. Was that even possible at her age?

'Of course I didn't have to come in with you,' Shook said. 'You're a big girl now.'

Caro pushed her hair back behind her ear. Her smile

was weak with fear. Not for herself. For him. She had no idea what she would say, and her uncertainty was like a terrible power that she knew she had to keep hidden. Exposed, it could hurt him. It could hurt them both. It could... it probably would... be fatal if she said it now... *I don't know,* when he so obviously did.

'And I understand this is not what you were expecting, ' he said and paused, his hand on the box. 'Which is why it isn't what you think it is.'

Caro didn't speak. She stared at the box. Across the bottom she could see a scroll of white, the jeweller's name. Hirsz, Watchmakers & Jewellers.

'This ring,' Shook continued, 'was my grandmother's. I bought it back from Poland with me the last time I visited. There is a story behind it that...' He smiled. 'That I would very much like to tell you.'

Caro nodded. She was scrabbling for information. The last time Shook had been to Poland was Christmas, barely a couple of months after they had met, which left this whole scene even more unanchored. A crowded airport coffee shop? For her first ever proposal of marriage? At fifty-one, from a man who'd *known* after barely a few weeks? With a ring that had a story, that she wasn't going to be told?

'I know what you're thinking.' He smiled.

'No you don't.'

'You're thinking, *Why now? Why here in this place?*' As if to emphasise the point, Shook offered his palm as he looked around the oh-so-ordinary scene surrounding them.

And because there was nothing else to do but laugh, Caro laughed. It was almost exactly what she'd been thinking.

And Shook laughed too. And for a moment they sat, looking at each other, laughing and shaking their heads.

Then, Shook stopped smiling and reached across and took her hand. 'The only question I'm asking you is if one day you think you will say yes to hearing the story?'

She didn't answer, watching in silence as Shook drew the box towards him and slipped it back in his pocket. 'I don't understand,' she said helplessly. Was this not a proposal of marriage then?

'I know you, Caro,' he answered quietly. 'Sometimes, I think I know you better than you know yourself. You will need time to think about your answer. When you have, you can let me know and if the answer is yes, you would like to hear the story, I promise I will find somewhere that is not Starbucks to tell you.' His mouth twitched at one corner and his eyes crinkled in amusement.

'And then?' she whispered.

'And then we will go from there.'

The only thing she could do was swallow down the swirl of emotion and nod in agreement. Perhaps he really did know her better than she knew herself. Mike had been the only man that she'd ever imagined progressing to this stage with. And every time she had entertained such imaginings, the one element she'd never accounted for was surprise. If it was coming, she'd already constructed the reality in which it would come with images of beaches or restaurants with sky-high views. And with so much else in place, she'd also known how she would answer. But this? Shook had blown every plan she'd never known she had into smithereens. And what's more, he understood this. So what was he really doing? Asking her to marry him? Or asking her if she wanted to hear a story? She thought she knew, she really did, but it was as if in layering the scene in such a deep fog of ambiguity he was giving them both time and space to escape. He'd shown her a door and eased it open just a crack so she could see what lay behind. He did know her. He knew she could never jump blind. Gambling wasn't her style. Staking her future on one impetuous decision? Not her style at all.

'I won't call you, or text while you're away.'

'You won't?'

'No. And that's a promise,' he said. 'You can trust me.'

'I know.'

1

---

1. If you'd also like to hear Shook's story, you can do so with the short story that accompanies this series. *The story of the ring*

PART III

9

Dear Kay! I can't thank you enough for inviting me on this trip. I'm so excited. I haven't been on holiday on my own like this since 1995! My son is telling me, Etekleri zil calıyor! This means all the bells on my skirt are ringing! It's true if I'm wearing a skirt, but I'm too fat for them, even though I have been on a diet since you invited me. Only olives. For breakfast, dinner, lunch. Like that footballer's wife. You know the footballer covered in tattoos? Never mind. The olives didn't work. I've gone to meet an old friend. I didn't want to disturb you, so I didn't ask them to ring your room. My room is so beautiful! The hotel is beautiful! I can tell you my manager, Sofia, you remember, the one with her know-all degree in tourism, the one who makes me stand behind that plank

91

of wood, she calls a desk? She could learn a thing or two about desks if she got her skinny backside over here! The only thing that is not good, is no chairs! Where are all the chairs?

I won't be long. I brought with me all the out of date Pringle minis from the hotel. I left them on the table by the mirror in my room if you need a snack.

Marianne.

F olding the note in two, Kay looked around. Marianne was right about the chairs! The foyer of the huge hotel they were staying in was a massive space under a dramatic dome boasting a frescoed ceiling. It was packed with a constant flow of people, faces grey with exhaustion, wheeling cases between rows of giant rope that looped between ostentatious gold posts. Exactly like the post office, Kay noted. Or Ryanair. With a marbled floor and a marbled desk, noise ricocheted relentlessly. It was like being stuck on a squash court in the middle of a particularly energetic game, she thought, though she didn't really know because she didn't actually play squash. And although the scenery was spectacular, with cascading boughs of delicate pastel flowers, a waterfall that flowed upwards and, most impressive of all, a great globe thingy, which, according to the plaque beside it, was a replica of a Renaissance instrument designed to watch the stars... the only thing that Kay saw now was, yes, Marianne was right, there were NO

SEATS. Not a single one! Not even a flip out pad to lean against!

Settling for the edge of the massive check-in desk, she frowned as she opened the note and read it again. Who on earth did Marianne know in Vegas? And how strange that she hadn't mentioned anything when, as casually as a chef might drop egg into a consommé, Kay had first dropped the idea of Marianne joining the trip into their WhatsApp chat. Which wasn't quite true. A chef would have had a much better idea of what was going to happen to his soup than Kay had when she'd typed.

> Fancy joining us?

> I'd love to!

Marianne's response had been instant, throwing Kay into a flurry of doubt. This was Caro's idea, for the three of them. And although Marianne was paying her own way, that wasn't the point. Turning the square of paper over in her hands, she stood amongst the jostle and noise. What she had to remember was why she had asked Marianne in the first place. Helen's stony silence when Caro had presented the tickets hadn't gone unnoticed. Something had happened at Helen's house. Something between Helen and Caro. *Again.* And this time, Kay had come to the almost instant decision that she wasn't going to let it affect her. She wasn't going to play piggy-in-the-middle for a moment longer. Her time was limited, precious beyond description, and once she had come to terms with the fact that she would be leaving Alex (*It's just a week,* as he kept saying. But a whole week, when weeks were rationed now?), she had been determined to enjoy every moment of the trip, which meant steadfastly ignoring any drama between Caro and Helen. Marianne, she knew, would provide a much needed buffer.

And she sensed that somehow Helen and Caro knew that her listening skills had dried up. In the short time between Caro presenting the tickets and them boarding the plane, neither of them had been in touch, not beyond practical arrangements. They hadn't responded either when she'd texted to say she was thinking of asking Marianne to join them. Expressions of surprise of course that the friendship had developed to this degree, but aside from that they had both kept their counsel, texting back encouragement.

Of course.

The more the merrier.

Something was going on, and so remembering the scene from Cyprus last year, when Helen and Caro had had a public row, she had gone ahead and dropped that egg, never really thinking that Marianne would grab the opportunity, wrap arms and legs and body around it like a drowning man to a life-raft. Text after text had pinged through.

Flight booked. What hotel?

Bought a bikini!

Been cooking all day. Six home-made moussakas in freezer for my son.

Why am I doing this? There's a McDonald's ten minutes away.

Took bikini back.

Every one of them producing a quiet chuckle as Kay read. She was bemused and pleased that Marianne was here, because although she hadn't been looking, it was true, Marianne had become a friend. Radiotherapy had been tiring. Caro had been tied up with her mother and Helen's new role as a grandmother encroached on her time more than Kay suspected Helen was entirely happy with. During long restful afternoons, laptop on knees, 'chatting' to Marianne had become easy and natural. And it was, Kay knew, the same for Marianne, because she'd reciprocated with emails full of woes and worries of her own. Hard for Kay to believe at first, living in the paradise of Cyprus as Marianne did. Then again not hard at all. Scratch the skin of any middle-aged woman, she knew, and what is revealed is a tapestry of joy and regret, happiness and grief. And it really wasn't too much of a stretch to say that this blossoming friendship with Marianne had been akin to falling in love again and just as unlikely. Ships tended to sail, and friends were like hair, plentiful at the beginning, prone to sparser patches later in life. At fifty there were things she'd thought she'd never experience again. Making a new friend had been one of them. She looked down at the note in her hands. Still, who on earth did Marianne know over here?

'Excuse me madam, would you mind?'

Startled, Kay looked up to see how she'd become surrounded by suitcases and sweaty, exhausted arrivals. Hard as it was to believe, given the enormous size of it, she'd been blocking access to the main desk. She moved across the foyer to an equally enormous side table where dozens of red roses had been arranged in a round vase, every flower head so similar in size and shade that, studying them, she became convinced they were fake. She put her nose to a petal and inhaled, but there was no scent. Which didn't mean there was no scent. In fact, as she put a fingertip to a petal, she could tell instantly that its cushioned softness was so perfect it could only have been formed through that unhurried and ancient alchemy of photosynthesis. The lack of scent simply meant that her sense of smell hadn't yet fully returned. It would. Everyone said so. The doctors and the nurses and all her fellow cancer warriors. It had her thinking about the scratchy Roxette wig Craig had bought her, which along with her jacket was upstairs in her hotel room... although hell, she was sure, would freeze over before she dared to wear it. She was still thinking this, wondering if she could or would dare, when a few feet away, the ping of the elevator doors broke the thread of thought. She turned to see first Helen step out, followed by Caro, who immediately twisted away and started sneezing.

'Every time she leaves the room,' Helen muttered.

Holding the back of her hand at her nose, Caro joined them. 'It's that scent,' she gasped before another sneeze swept her words away.

'I can't smell anything,' Kay said.

Helen wrinkled her nose. 'You're joking? I have to agree. It's really strong. Reminds me of my first school disco.'

'Really?'

'Brut. Can't remember the boy's name, but I do remember the aftershave.'

'Why on earth is it so strong?' Caro said.

'Every casino has its own scent,' Kay smiled. 'They do it to keep people gambling. To cover more unpleasant smells. I read it in my guidebook.'

'Like when smoking got banned in pubs?' Helen grimaced. 'And all you could smell was farts?'

'You mean it's even stronger in the casino?' Caro had her hand back at her nose. 'I'm not going to last five minutes.'

'I'll be fine,' Kay said. 'One of the very few benefits of my treatment, I suppose.'

The joke fell flat. Caro went pale and Helen took a deep breath in, her lips pursed. 'I'm sorry,' she said.

'What for? Not laughing at my joke?'

'No. I mean...'

'The smell,' Caro interjected. She glanced at Helen, who barely met her eye before turning away.

'Yes,' Helen said. 'It was insensitive of us.'

'We weren't thinking,' Caro murmured.

'No,' Helen echoed, still looking away, 'we weren't.'

Kay watched them. Who were they kidding? She could almost hear the donning of kid gloves as they stumbled over themselves in the hurry not to offend either her, or each other. When had Helen ever apologised for telling a joke? When had Caro ever even been aware of *not* thinking? A lack of smell she could cope with, but not this loss of the comfortable space between them all. The space that had accommodated their friendship perfectly, custom built as it had been. That had held so much. Humour, ribaldry, sympathy, support and, so recently, that most demanding of guests, forgiveness. It was fragile. And with every anxious apology and over-fussed explanation she could feel the foundations shake. Soon enough they would all be shying away from saying anything that might hold a seed of possible offence. And then what the hell would they talk about? The three of them, for whom nothing had ever been off-limits? Yes, she was dying – albeit slowly – but right now her sense of humour was still alive and kicking and would (she was determined) be the last bloody thing to go. She didn't have time for this. Unconsciously her fingers folded the note into a tinier square. Hopefully Marianne would turn up soon.

'Sooo.' Bridging the silence, Caro stretched the word out. 'Has Marianne arrived?'

Kay held the paper up. 'She's here, but she's gone out again. She left a note.'

'Gone out?' Helen said.

'To see a friend.'

'A friend?' Caro pushed her hair behind her ear as she looked around the foyer. 'Who does Marianne know in Vegas?'

'Good question,' Kay answered.

And then Helen yawned, stretched her arms to the ceiling and said, 'Breakfast?'

'Another good question,' Kay said, 'I've been here for five minutes, and the smell of the buffet is driving me crazy.'

And she didn't imagine it: Caro and Helen exchanged another small, uncomfortable glance.

'*Enough!*' Kay raised her hand. 'Can we get one thing straight? I've lost my sense of smell, not my sense of humour. Right,' she paused. 'Breakfast.'

10

—————

R ed hair, blue hair, no hair. Laced up, zipped in, spray-tanned. Off the shoulder, slashed at the stomach, backless, braless, strapless. Bride to Be, 21 Today, Last Night Of, First Time In. Burgers on trays, meat in mouths. Plastic cups, paper straws, cardboard trays... slurping, burping. Midnight shades. Angel wings. Knee-high boots, plastic boots, peep-toe boots. Wood chip soil. Crooked legs, one eye, no hope, one-dollar water...

HELEN STOOD on one of the many pedestrian bridges that crossed Las Vegas Boulevard and looked down at the human flow of the sidewalks below, at buildings that sprouted from buildings, towers that started parallel but arched toward different suns, at 3D digital billboards, so lifelike they had her ducking for cover. At a city as smooth as a smart phone. At shiny buses with fluorescent lighting. Neon walkways and canopied entrances. At surfaces that reflected and multiplied with almost as much frequency as the four words that had taken residence in her head the moment she'd heard them.

It was a mistake.

It was a mistake.

They were a kaleidoscope, every bit as colourful and vibrant as Vegas itself. They had set in motion a whirling wheel of images where she had been unable to find a north or a south, a way in or a way out. Scenes from the early days of her marriage when she'd been happy and she really thought Lawrence had. From further back, at university with Caro and Kay, when they all had definitely been happy. Scenes that had taken place in her home, occasional looks between Lawrence and Caro she'd intercepted and dismissed hours later at the kitchen sink, always reaching the same comfortable conclusion. Because although the fact that Caro had once had a thing for Lawrence was unspoken common knowledge between them, all of them had grown up and moved on. Lawrence had married her, and Caro had begun a thoroughly rewarding and exciting life that Helen had admired and envied and *loved* to hear about. Stunted in her own world, she'd been genuinely proud of Caro and her transformation from a debilitatingly shy student into a confident woman. And until so very recently, grateful to have her as a friend. The one who got away, who kept coming back to tell them what it was like on the other side of marriage, and motherhood.

She spread her elbows wide and, resting her head on her hand, leaned on the parapet and watched Vegas go about its business.

Happy Hour, All Day, Pre-dawn, After Sunset, One Day Only, As Much as U Like, Whenever-U-Like. Casual Dining, Late-Night, Patio-Side, Celebrity Chef, In-Room, Grab & Go.

Ice-cream, Frozen Yogurt. Fat Tuesdays, Best Buds, Shrimp Co, I Love Sugar, Burritos, Sushi Sliders.

The anger she'd felt that day had gone, replaced by something that was proving harder to live with. A terrible disappointment. A dreadful searing disappointment. Not with her husband. Helen had neither the will, nor the energy, to go rummaging through the past for answers to questions about their marriage she'd never thought to ask, and had no use for anyway. If Lawrence considered their twenty-five-year union a mistake, then so be it. This was the only sane approach she could take. No, the weight she carried now was bound up with Caro. How could she have behaved so deceitfully? What kind of person canoodles up to the soon-to-be-free husband of a friend one minute, and then presents an all-expenses-paid trip for the same friend the next? It almost took her breath away, this capacity Caro had to put her needs first. They had fallen out over it in Cyprus, with Caro, fifty years old, intent upon having a baby that wasn't genetically hers. And, although Helen still thought it was selfish, they had managed to get over it. They had even managed to get over what had happened in August. But this?

For Kay's sake, cancelling the trip had proved impossible. Every time she had picked up her phone to ring Kay to tell her she was sorry, she couldn't come, she'd ended the call before it had begun. Because what kind of an excuse was going to wash? She wasn't cancelling a dinner party, or a shopping trip; she would be cancelling the dream of a lifetime. Kay's dream. And what would she say anyway? *Let's go next year! Let's go without Caro!* Caro, who had arranged and paid for it all, who had, Helen knew, gone to huge efforts to make sure everything went smoothly. Who'd taken it upon herself to talk with Kay's doctors to check she could make the trip, crossing every *T* and dotting every *I* regarding Kay, whilst ignoring the great slashing mess she'd scrawled through their own friendship. No, for Kay's sake, and Kay's sake alone, she had determined she would go, papering over cracks with Caro that were actually chasms. But never had she been less enthusiastic about a holiday. And after... well, who knew how long Kay had left. A lot longer, Helen felt sure, than she and Caro had left. And that she really didn't want to think about, because the future looked very lonely without them.

Her feet, in foolhardy wedge sandals, throbbed like a frog's throat. Her diamante-studded t-shirt sagged hopelessly, as if in the face of Vegas-style bling it had given up even trying. The morning was as stuffy and warm as a twelve-tog duvet and sweat was already rippling down the ample padding of her back and under her arms. Pushing a sticky clump of hair back from her forehead, she looked down at the eight lanes of traffic below and whispered a prayer of thanks for the fact she was wearing leggings with an elasticated waist. Nearly twenty-four hours since they'd left home, and she'd done nothing but eat. It was, she supposed, what happened if you didn't sleep.

Because much to Helen's surprise, the flight had been too wonderful to sleep. The only thing that had been asked of her was that she kick back, watch TV, eat and drink. With *real* cutlery and *real* glasses. And ironically all her anxiety about facing Caro had been diluted by the bustle of the airport, the novelty of the executive lounge, where she was sure she'd spotted an actor from EastEnders, and by Caro herself, who had seemed distracted. So much so that, turning three hundred and sixty degrees through this new and exclusive world, a glass of champagne in one hand and a prawn cracker in the other, Helen had had plenty of time to think about the travelling she'd done over the years. The kids and dogs, the anoraks and holdalls, the sandwiches and thermos flasks, the tent poles, damp towels, stained car seats, and of course, the husband. All those journeys that had ended somewhere as damp and overcast as where they'd started. But business class! She hadn't wanted to get off! The whole experience had been such a revelation that, when the plane had taxied to a halt, she could have quite happily levered her seat back and stayed on. Like those people who spend all day on buses, just for something to do.

And now she was here and it was so much more than she could ever have imagined. The Great Pyramid of Giza, the Eiffel Tower, a New York skyline. Vegas was like something out of a storybook. She turned to look up at the peppermint- and emerald-green gridlines of the MGM hotel, then turned the other way to where the Disney turrets of the Excalibur rose corn-blue and peach. Yes, exactly like a storybook.

At Kay's suggestion, they'd walked along the strip for what had felt an age, aiming for landmarks that only seemed to recede as they got closer, the sidewalk constantly diverting them through a maze of walkways, and overhead bridges, and back into casino entrances and malls. As well as a storybook, Vegas was a hall of mirrors, an illusion, and looking at it now, Helen wasn't at all sure she'd be able to find her way back to the hotel even if she was wearing slippers. She turned to Kay standing beside her. 'Ready to walk back?' she said. What she really meant was, *Shall we take a cab?*

'Of course.' Kay didn't hesitate.

'We could,' Caro said carefully, 'do like the kids do.' She

was on the other side of Kay and, Helen noticed, was also shifting her weight from foot to foot. She looked down at Caro's shoes. Heels. 'Uber it back to the hotel?'

'Are you serious?' Kay turned first to Helen, and then to Caro.

'I just thought,' Caro said, 'if you were tired?'

'I'm not.'

'Are you sure?' Despite her initial impressions of Vegas being more positive than she had expected, Helen's feet were now burning lumps. She'd have done almost anything to get into a cab, anything but disappoint Kay.

'*I'm not tired*,' Kay snapped. She took a deep breath and shook her head, opened her mouth as if to speak and then closed it again. 'Shall we walk?' she said and before anyone could answer set off across the bridge.

'Ok.' Over the top of Kay's head, Helen caught Caro's eye, before looking away. It was too difficult. The only way she was going to get through was to keep interaction to a minimum. Smooth over silences, make sure that everything Kay wanted to see and do, she got to see and do.

STAIRS ALREADY BEING out of the question, she took the escalator that ran from the bridge down to the sidewalk. As she stepped off, something cool swept across her toes. It was such a contrast to the solid relentless burn that Helen squealed and looked up, straight into the eyes of a tiny dark woman dressed in a neon-yellow vest and holding a dustpan and brush.

'Sorry,' the woman smiled, white teeth against the hewn black leather of her cheeks, then her head dropped and she was moving backwards again, sweeping.

It took Helen a long moment to understand that the tickling sensation had come from the woman's brush, and that she was sweeping the sidewalk. Among a crowd of thousands, she was sweeping the pavement. There couldn't be a more pointless, or thankless, job. Straining to keep sight of the woman she stretched her neck forward, but it was hopeless. Within seconds Vegas had swallowed her, only a glimpse of the yellow square of her vest visible.

'*Helen!*' Kay waved from the other side of the sidewalk.

Helen turned and as she did a Target carrier bag slapped her on the shoulder.

'Ouch!'

But the woman swinging the bag didn't break stride.

'Watch where you're going!' Helen called, indignant now. It was one thing to be slapped by a plastic shopping bag, another thing to not receive an apology.

The woman turned.

She must have been six foot, wearing a sequinned bra and huge colourful wings that arched behind her like a couple of stained-glass windows. Helen stared.

'What?' the woman drawled. 'Never seen an angel shopping?'

'No,' she said. 'I have never seen an angel shopping.'

The woman gave a derisive snort. 'You haven't lived, girl,' she laughed and turned on six-inch glitter heels, her generous bottom wobbling along, encased as it was in fishnets and thong.

And still Helen stood, an island, around which the pavement crowd flowed like water from a tap. No one giving second glances to thong-wearing angels carrying shopping bags, or women sweeping pavements. How green she was. And how old she felt. She had turned up to the city-wide fancy-dress, let-it-all-hang-out vibe Vegas was, in jeans and t-shirt. The angel was right. She hadn't lived. Not at all.

11

Eventually, although she was never sure how, there came a point on the interminable walk when Caro looked up to see the now familiar row of gothic arches and imitation Rialto bridge over bright blue water that meant they were back at the hotel.

A quick walk after breakfast, Kay had suggested. And because there wasn't going to be a suggestion from Kay that she would disagree with, Caro had agreed. She simply hadn't been prepared for the temperature. Whatever volume she'd managed to coax into her hair that morning had collapsed, and it hung now thin and straggly as string. Her cheeks had broken out into blotchy pinks, and she'd lost count of the number of blisters she could feel forming. She was over-heated and over-stuffed because she hadn't been prepared for breakfast either. Neither the chaos of the moving lines of people carrying plates, like ants on sorties. Nor the stomach-churning quantities on display. Hash browns, bacon and sausage, breakfast ham and scrambled eggs. Maple syrup and waffles. Omelettes made to order, with onions and peppers, mushrooms, tomatoes, cheddar cheese... and back to breakfast ham. Pastries, croissants, muffins, cinnibons. Cereals, granola, frosted flakes and... breakfast ham. Toasted bagels. Strawberries, whipped cream, butter balls, melon, grapes, yogurts, breakfast ham... and finally, coffee.

Her stomach churned, her shins ached and her blouse, she feared, showed dark underarm patches. She didn't dare look. Unable to persuade Kay into a taxi, together with Helen she had been able to persuade her onto the hop-on/hop-off bus, where Kay had insisted they hop-off at Treasure Island, only to be told, by an angry woman, herding three crying kids, that the Pirate show Kay had wanted to see had ended a decade ago! *You'd think they'd let folk know!* she'd yelled, as if they had been personally responsible for the mix-up. Vegas, Caro feared, was fast turning into hell on earth. The trip was only seven days, but all this, along with Helen's perplexingly hostile attitude, she was already exhausted.

Following the others onto the escalator, Caro held the rail and with immeasurable gratitude allowed the moving stairway to bear her upward to the bustling mix of chain store coffee shops, oxygen bars, tattoo parlours, boutiques selling jewellery, luxury chocolate, sunglasses, scents and socks that led eventually to the hotel foyer, and hopefully (if there was any mercy left in the world) a place they could all sit down.

From her step on the escalator Caro could see, further down, only the top of Helen's shoulders and the back of her head, her cloud of thick blonde hair. And it seemed appropriate, this turning of Helen's back, because she wasn't imagining it. Ever since they had met at Heathrow, Helen had been cold and distant and, in the short spaces of time when she had thought about it, Caro could only put it down to one thing. Helen still hadn't really forgiven her for that night back in August. On the plane she had chosen to sit across the aisle and plugged herself into the movie. In the taxi, she'd used the other door to sit on Kay's far side. And when it had just been the two of them, in the elevator for example, the tension had been inescapable. Perhaps, she thought now, there was something else. Perhaps Helen even minded the fact that she had paid for it all, stuck as she was in the house with Lawrence. It occurred to Caro now that maybe Helen resented the financial freedom she had. The means to move her life forward. It wasn't a vibe she had ever picked up before from Helen, but then again Helen had never attempted financial independence before... She just didn't know. Here she was, doing something spontaneous, and it hadn't gone down well at all. Kay, on the other hand, had been and still was delighted, and it was this that Caro had chosen to focus on as she'd finalised the preparations. And then of course Shook had sprung his own surprise. Which she'd had no time at all to think about.

The first couple of hours of the flight had been spent going over figures with Kay, who was still intent upon setting up a fund for Alex. Caro understood why, of course, but any balance Kay might hope to achieve in the time-scale they discussed was never going to be enough. And it had been wounding, listening to the dispassionate manner in which Kay discussed her prognosis. A manner Caro knew she would never have used with Helen. Because if Helen was the emotional heart, and Kay was the wise soul of their friendship, it was down to her to be the hard-head of it. So she'd played that role. She'd stayed dry-eyed and steady-voiced as they had discussed wills, and lasting powers of attorney, the price of caskets and funerals, and how much she should set aside. Yes, wounding and draining. So much so that when she had managed to settle Kay's mind, and seen her ease back with a movie, Caro had ordered a bottle of wine and drunk herself to sleep.

On arrival they had disembarked into an airport terminal deafening with the bells and whistles, hoots and horns of numerous slot machines. In the taxi, the driver had delivered a non-stop monologue of recommendations they had neither asked for, nor since been able to remember. And at the hotel, in a foyer even busier than the airport, they'd been handed a book of vouchers and a room key. It hadn't actually been until the elevator doors had pinged shut, encasing her in a silence like the first silence on earth, that Caro had been able to hear herself think again. In her hotel room she had peeled off her jeans and crawled into bed more exhausted than she thought she'd ever felt in her life.

Twenty-four hours in, felt like twenty-four years. At some point the pace had to slow down.

As the escalator came to an end, Caro stepped off and looked up to see another Rialto bridge, overlooking another canal with bright blue water. Either side, murals of eighteenth-century Venice stretched away, offering dimensions and scenery that she knew did not exist, but appreciated the artistry of anyway. If her feet hadn't been hurting so much she might have taken more time to admire them. As it was, a huge cheer went up from the bridge and drawn by the sound and the general flow of people, they wandered along towards it. As they neared she saw, on the water below, a gondolier applauding his customers.

'What's happened?' she whispered.

'They survived the ride,' Kay laughed.

'Really?'

Kay turned to her. 'It's a marriage proposal!'

'Oh.' Caro looked first to her left, and then to her right. Five people she counted, filming this event. And beyond that, lined up all along the bridge, people were whooping and cheering. Strangers, childishly excited by the sight of more strangers making what was, what should be, a private decision in a private moment. She pulled her shoulders together, straightened up and turned away, her mouth making a hard line. She was exhausted and irritated. She'd barely had five minutes to herself to consider her own private decision. Shook's question. A question that required the kind of space and silence sorely lacking in Vegas. 'Why does everything have to be so bloody public!' she sighed, looking at Kay.

But Kay was another world away, caught up in the moment, smiling a very goofy and un-Kay-like smile. 'I think it's lovely,' she murmured.

'Really?' Helen said.

Kay sighed. 'Martin slapped the Argos catalogue on my desk. Told me to take my pick... From the pages he'd folded over.'

Chuckling, Helen turned away to watch the newly betrothed couple on the gondolier.

Caro too turned to watch. 'How long had you known him?' she said suddenly.

'Martin?'

'Yes.'

'Mmm.' Kay frowned. 'I can't remember. A few months I suppose.'

'Just a few months?'

'That's long enough isn't it?

'Is it?'

A slow smile turned the corner of Kay's mouth upward, she put her head to one side and looked at Caro as if she was looking at a painting. 'I don't know, Caro,' she said finally. 'I could say when you know, you know, but I'm divorced, so maybe I didn't know.'

'And maybe you did?' Caro said quietly.

'Or maybe I just took a chance,' Kay said and the look she gave Caro was so loaded, it could have carried lead.

12

Back in the cool of the air-conditioned foyer, Helen made a beeline for the elevator. The damage wrought upon her feet by her choice of footwear was incalculable. Three blisters that she'd counted so far and a bunion the size of a doorknob. So focused was she on the cushioned plasters in the first aid kit she'd sensibly packed (old habits die hard) that she snapped as she felt Kay's hand on her arm, pulling her back. '*What?*'

'It's Marianne!' Kay said.

And standing behind Kay, Caro now nodded across the roped-in rows of queueing arrivals, towards the front desk.

Helen looked up. She recognised Marianne immediately. The military-style severity of her haircut, and the bulky shoulders squeezed into a sleeveless dress so tightly, red marks where the straps cut into her flesh were clearly visible. She was wearing white sneakers, carried a white hat and had a huge straw handbag slung over her arm. All in all, it was the kind of holiday-in-the-sun-outfit that belonged in the pages of a woman's magazine, circa 1983. She felt a pang of sympathy. Kay had said that one of the reasons she'd asked Marianne was because she hadn't had a holiday in years. Next to her stood a tall, grey-haired man who looked familiar. Very familiar, like a relative she hadn't seen in twenty years. 'Who's that?' Helen whispered, leaning in to Kay.

Kay shook her head. 'No idea.'

'He looks an awful lot like Blake Carrington,' Caro said.

'John Forsythe's been dead for years now,' Helen muttered.

'I think he looks like the cowboy guy from *Dallas*,' Kay said.

'JR?'

'No.' She turned to Helen. 'He was the baddie, not the cowboy. The cowboy was a nice-guy.'

Helen shook her head. 'Well whoever he is, I've definitely seen him before.'

They stood, ducks in a row, the same incredulous expression on their faces as, across the foyer, Marianne and her companion chattered amicably with the receptionist.

'Is she writing you another note?' Caro said drily, as the receptionist slid a piece of paper across.

Helen squinted. 'What on earth is Blake Carrington wearing?'

And again, they leaned in, like skittles.

'Whatever it is, it's a little tight,' Caro murmured.

'The actor!' Kay gasped. 'It's the actor!'

'What actor?' Both Helen and Caro spoke together.

And as they did, Marianne turned from the desk, looked across the foyer, dropped her pen and cried, 'Kay!' In another instant she was across the room, embracing Kay, once, twice and then a third time. She turned to Helen. 'And Helen Winters! The one with the husband!'

'Not for long.' Helen said lightly.

Marianne kissed both Helen's cheeks. 'It hasn't been as exciting at the Hotel Adagio since you all stayed.' She looked at Helen and winked.

'No, I suppose not.' Helen attempted a smile. Not many guests, she supposed, created the kind of drama that had surrounded their trip to Cyprus and the hotel where Marianne worked. Lawrence turning up the way he did after hearing about her holiday romance. The awful bout of food poisoning that had resulted in her discarding the contents of a plant pot, and filling it with her regurgitated seafood lunch. Blushing, she said, 'How is your orchid now?'

'Flourishing!' Marianne beamed.

'I'm glad.'

'And how is your marriage? If I may ask.'

'Over.'

'I am sorry.' Marianne stopped smiling. She dropped her head to one side. 'I'm not surprised, but I'm sorry.'

'Don't be,' Helen said.

'Ok.' Smile returning, she patted Helen's arm. 'And Kaveh sends his love.'

Helen's blush deepened. Kaveh had been a brief and beautiful moment in her life, and had she been a young woman she might have persuaded herself that she was in love with him. Might even have done something stupid like move her world to be with him. But she wasn't a young woman, and thank goodness for that. 'Send my love back to him,' she answered, aiming for detached coolness, aware that the heat of remembered passion in her cheeks wasn't completely on her side.

'I will.' Marianne gave her a knowing smile and turned to Caro. 'Caro!' Without warning she took a step forward and threw her arms around Caro, and because she was so small and Caro was so tall, her head came to rest against

Caro's chest. 'I was so sorry to hear,' she whispered. 'About your baby. So very sorry.'

Caro's face went very pale, but she didn't move. She stood, waiting awkwardly for Marianne to disengage herself.

Which she did, eventually. 'Well, who knows?' Marianne shook her head. 'Maybe it is for the best? I've been cooking for days, just so I can leave my son for a week. And he's twenty-seven!'

Standing a little to one side now, Helen glared at the back of Marianne's head. Caro's miscarriage wasn't something they had discussed. Wasn't something, Helen was beginning to think, that would ever be discussed. Not now, not with the way things were. And it was fine. Everything was so horribly complicated between her and Caro anyway, she wasn't prepared for any kind of conversation that dipped below the surface. Which made it all the stranger to understand the level of irritation she now felt towards Marianne, waltzing in with clumsy comments. That habit of concern towards Caro, a habit she'd first developed when they were students, living together, was obviously still there. She glanced first at Kay, who looked to Helen to be equally uncomfortable, and then at Caro. But to her surprise, Caro was smiling. If Marianne's comment had re-opened the wound, she was hiding it well. And before she could give it any more thought, Marianne turned and said, 'I must introduce you to my friend. *Come!*' she mouthed, waving her arm to call the grey-haired man over.

He waved back as he walked across, loose hipped, considering his age, hair a bright blue-grey and skin so smooth it reminded Helen of Lawrence's Lycra cycling outfits.

As he reached them, Marianne grabbed hold of his arm

with both hands. 'This,' she said, 'is my old friend, Tony Larson!'

'Otherwise known as Anthony Larson,' Tony said with a broad smile.

Anthony Larson. Helen blinked. The name rang bells more distant than those at her wedding.

'From *Dallas*?' Kay said.

Helen stared at him. It wasn't *Dallas*. Definitely not *Dallas*.

Again Tony smiled. '*Knots Landing,* a little *Cagney and Lacey.*' He shrugged. '*Days of Your Lives*, *General Hospital* and of course, *Odysseus Returns.*' He turned to gaze down at Marianne. 'Which is where I met this exquisite creature.'

At which, Marianne contracted with pleasure, like a crunched sweet wrapper.

And Helen actually felt herself tip forward onto the balls of her feet with sheer surprise. Marianne was all sorts of things, but *exquisite* hadn't been on her list. She wanted to turn to Kay, or Caro, to gauge their reactions, but she couldn't, and she sensed they couldn't either. In fact the only person capable of movement was Marianne, who'd leaned into Tony, her blush spreading from the top of her head, down her neck and across her crêpey décolletage. '*Knots Landing*?' Helen managed. 'Now I remember!' And she did, vague memories of lying on her tummy watching the TV, a keyhole-shaped road with enormous houses and people living in perpetual sunshine. No wonder he reminded her of a distant relative. 'So.' Astonishment had scraped all the filling from her voice. 'How umm... how did you two meet?'

'I know!' Kay laughed. 'In Athens? When you were working there?' She looked from Tony to Marianne. 'Is this the actor you told me about?'

'Yes,' Marianne said, laughing as she nudged Kay's arm.

Helen watched. It was clear they had a rapport, Kay and Marianne. She sneaked a glance at Caro, whom she felt sure had also noticed. How could she not? In Marianne, it was obvious Kay had found the kind of easy companionship the three of them had once shared. An ease in each other's company she couldn't help but feel was gone forever. The evidence of it, there in front of her, shrank her a little.

Marianne raised the sunhat she was holding and held it against her stomach, as if to hide herself. 'It was a long time ago,' she said. 'I was very young then. I—'

And with a manly sweep of his arm around her back, Tony cut Marianne off. 'Marianne,' he gushed, 'was working the front desk at the hotel the production company had put us in.'

'The Four Seasons,' Marianne interjected. 'Such a beautiful hotel.'

'She was the most exotic creature I'd ever seen in my life.'

'Oh!' Marianne put her palm against his chest. 'This was in my prime.'

'*This*,' Tony smiled, 'is your prime.'

His teeth, Helen noted, were extraordinarily white. She pressed her own lips together. Under Tony's honey words, Marianne was melting faster than candle wax.

'Is this the time your...' Kay hesitated.

'My wife turned up?' Tony finished.

'What?' Helen snapped her head from Tony, to Kay, to Marianne. '*What?*'

'It's true. I'm not proud of it, but...' And here, Tony paused (a little dramatically Helen thought) to gaze down at Marianne. 'No one was more suitably named. She made me forget everything.'

'Including the fact you were married,' Caro said, lightly.

Helen snatched a glance at her. She'd been about to say the exact same thing.

Tony dropped his chin. 'Like I said, I'm not proud of it.' He nodded. 'My wife arrived a day earlier than expected and we... we were a little engaged, weren't we?'

Marianne blushed. 'I had to pretend to be room service. Do you remember?'

'Everything,' Tony purred. 'I remember everything.'

'And I was wearing your Nirvana t-shirt. I had to throw my uniform on over the top.'

Helen's eyes went to the paunch of Tony's stomach, swelling out Kurt Cobain's face.

He leaned in and kissed the top of Marianne's head. 'So kind of you to return it, my dear.'

And no one spoke. And even though they were standing in a busy foyer, of a busy hotel, in a busy city, seas of incredulity seemed to have parted to leave them stranded. Helen nodded. She was trying desperately to think of something to say, but her mind was blank with astonishment.

And then Caro smiled, and in a smoothly pleasant voice, said, 'Goodness, how amazing.'

'Isn't it?' Marianne beamed.

Helen pressed her lips together. She had a tremendous urge to laugh and she knew, she just knew, from the tone of Caro's voice that she was experiencing the same temptation. Marianne and Tony were preposterous, but also quite wonderful. Almost fantastical, and so much of her wanted to turn and wink at Caro, to share a moment of appreciation at the burst of colour and fun this moment had brought, like so many other colourful, fun moments they had shared. But she couldn't find a way of doing it, because she couldn't get past the spinning wheel of those words. It. Was. A. Mistake.

And then Kay said, 'So... how did you get back in touch?'

'I sent him a message on Twitter,' Marianne said. 'Asking if he remembered me.'

'The internet,' Tony nodded, 'is a marvellous thing.'

'Yes... yes, it is.' Helen nodded back, joining in with the general consent. Now the initial amazement had worn off, her feet were making themselves felt again. A regular throb, like jungle drums. She really, really needed to...

'I'm afraid I need to sit down,' Caro winced.

Helen turned, looked down at the shoes Caro wore, as foolish as her own, and then looked up and smiled. And Caro smiled back and in moments like this, she thought, it was very easy to believe that nothing had happened, that they were as they had always been, a bit bumpy, a bit tetchy, but friends, always friends.

'Shall we take some coffee?' Marianne asked.

And together the three of them let out a collective groan.

'No?'

'We had the most enormous breakfast,' Kay said. 'I don't think we could manage anything else.'

'And the queues,' Caro added.

Marianne turned as she looked around the foyer. 'There doesn't seem to be anywhere to just sit.'

'Ladies.' Tony beamed. 'This is Vegas. Would you let me escort you to the best seats in town?'

'Please do,' Helen said, her smile a little tight now. He was as slick as an eel. Slippery too; still, if he knew somewhere they could sit down, without queueing, without eating, without drinking, she'd follow him all day

13

W eaving in between bored young women twirling fingers through hair, slow pensioners, babies in prams, loud men and kamikaze toddlers, they followed Tony along the colonnade, the click of hundreds of shoes loud against an Italian-marble floor. Either side rose the colossal columns that gave this passageway its name, and, arched above, richly coloured fresco after fresco depicted blue skies, outstretched arms, flowing robes. Helen turned to look back. At the far end of the colonnade the golden sphere radiated like a meteorite, hand-placed by some celestial entity.

'It is quite extraordinary,' she started and didn't get to finish because Caro said, 'My God!'

'Slot machines?' Helen turned.

The colonnade had opened up, the hand-cut tiles of the floor rearranging themselves into a wide and perfect circle, so that now they stood underneath a fountain of a chandelier contemplating what could only be described as an army of slot machines. Thousands of them, blinking and shrieking warnings, ringing bells, blowing whistles. Above each machine, an LCD screen flashed blindingly bright images, superheroes jumping rooftops, grizzly warriors fighting games of thrones, cartoon pigs building houses of straw. On repeat. Over and over.

'You're in Vegas.' Tony laughed. 'There is no better way to spend your time.'

Helen frowned. The ocean ahead of shrieking, whistling, honking machines looked to her to offer no more sanctuary than a seat on the last train home from King's Cross on a Friday night. 'What do you think?' she said turning to Kay.

Kay shrugged. 'I don't know. I've never played slots.'

Tony beamed. 'It doesn't matter if you win or lose,' he said. 'That's not the point.'

'It isn't?' Caro asked.

'Not at all.' He smiled. 'Why do you think there's a scarcity of chairs about the place?' Nodding to the machines, he added, 'Those chairs are the most comfortable in town, for good reason. The air is cool and the drinks are free. Slots in Vegas are like shopping any place else. They're just a way to pass the time.'

'Sounds like the plane,' Helen murmured. She was thinking of the free drinks and the cool air and most of all, her reclining seat. If the slots were anywhere near as comfortable, she might never leave.

'If you play the penny slots,' Tony shrugged, 'you're just cheating time anyway.'

Kay smiled. 'I'm all up for cheating time.'

And for the second time that morning, Helen and Caro's eyes met in a glance as complicated and unique as a snowflake. Helen looked away. They had discussed Kay's illness with any real depth only twice. The day Caro had turned up at her house, to break the news, and leaving the hospital on the day of her operation. Since then, with treat-

ment underway, it had become harder to think about it. Life
did what it was prone to do, it carried on relentlessly. Libby
had been in the thick of re-taking her finals, so there had
been an awful lot of grandmothering duties to undertake.
Caro had been away much of the time. On those occasions
that she had seen Kay, she'd looked well enough, reporting
back that her scans were good. And so as the distance
between the initial shock of hearing the news had
expanded, so Kay's cancer itself had receded. Kay was still
Kay. Relentlessly wise, and alive. A few times, Helen had sat
herself down and forced herself to concentrate upon what
she had learned from her mother's illness. Survival rates,
secondary sites... But still it remained abstract. How do you
understand an illness, until its trajectory is spelled out in
the physical reality? She lifted her chin as she looked across
at the strange and noisy landscape. She had, she realised
now, been expecting to talk all this through with Caro. It felt
like another blow, and tears of angry frustration welled.
How could Caro have behaved the way she did? Friends this
long-standing weren't hanging from every tree. How could
she have thrown away such a precious resource? And for
what? A man?

'Ladies?'

Startled, Helen turned.

Tony had lifted his arm, was funnelling them now, easy
as water, past the front line of slot machines, and then the
second and the third, until looking around it was clear to
Helen that the landscape had transformed. The ceiling felt
lower, the lights dimmer, all exits vanished. They had
stepped through the wardrobe, slipped through the looking
glass. She strained to look back at the way they had come,
but all she could see now were people and machines,
machines and people, through three hundred and sixty

degrees... machines, people. She rose up onto her toes. All the pain in her feet and the heat from the sidewalk vanishing. The room was unspeakably noisy, but the air was so cool! And maybe it was the nostalgia of long-remembered childhood memories that set her excitement levels racing. She'd always loved seaside arcades, the delicious and slightly naughty refuge they offered on a wet seaside afternoon. Her mother mildly disapproving, but always ready to press a fifty pence piece into her hand. She'd continued the tradition with her own children, despite Lawrence, who'd never bothered to hide his contempt and who'd always tried to sabotage things with a fossil-hunt suggestion. But Jack and Libby always chose the arcade, and yes, the glow of a small victory had been nurtured as they'd left him to his wet and sandy hour. Once again, just as it had on the strip, the thrill of Vegas touched her. 'Sure beats the arcade on Newquay seafront!' she said.

'Chairs!' Caro gasped.

Helen turned. Caro was right. Finally there were chairs... Everywhere! Great, huge, comfortable-looking chairs! With ashtrays, if she smoked, which she didn't. Still she thought she might start. Just to kick off her sweaty sandals, lean back and light up!

Caro had already hobbled over and was just about to collapse into the nearest one when an elderly man in apricot shorts called out, 'You might want to give that one a miss!' He was pushing an equally elderly woman in a wheelchair, complete with oxygen bottle, as casually as if they were strolling down St Albans High Street.

Caro looked down at the chair.

'It's a little damp.' The man nodded. 'They'll be along soon enough to sort it.' And he tipped his baseball cap at Tony. 'How you doing?'

Tony raised a hand in greeting.

'Does he know you?' Kay asked.

He shrugged. 'I still get recognised. It comes with the terrain.'

Beside him, Marianne flushed with pleasure.

'Did someone spill a drink?' Caro had moved around to the side of the chair and was now leaning over it, a hand stretched out ready to test the seat.

'I wouldn't do that if I were you,' Tony said. 'Sometimes folk don't wanna leave a machine, if you know what I mean.'

'I don't,' Caro said archly. 'My feet are somewhat—'

'They don't always make it in time.'

'Don't make it...' Halfway through her sentence, Caro's words dried up. She stared first at Tony, then at the damp patch, and then slowly straightened up. 'Ah. I see. I'll umm... I'll stand for now.'

So she did, and beside her Helen and Kay stood too. A curiously still island in the midst of this electronic jungle. Like children on the first day of school, Helen couldn't help thinking.

'So ladies,' Tony said, with a huge indulgent smile. 'What's your bankroll?'

'Bankroll?' Helen asked.

'How much are you playing with?' And before anyone could answer, Tony stuck his hands in the pockets of his jeans so the thumbs stuck out like two fat worms, rocked back on his heels, swelling out Kurt Cobain's head, and took a huge breath, as if he were playing Hamlet at the Hollywood Bowl, warming up for his 'to be, or not to be' moment. 'Well,' he started, 'the rule of gambling is never to play with more than you can afford to lose.' Pausing for effect, he nodded seriously. 'So you have to ask yourselves a question.'

'We do?' Helen said flatly; she couldn't even feel her feet now.

'And what might that be?' Caro said, an unmistakable edge of irritation in her voice.

Tony turned his palms to the ceiling. '*How much can I afford to lose today?* That's it. That's the question.'

Afford to lose? Helen turned to the others. She couldn't afford to lose anything, which seemed utterly ridiculous, standing as she was in the midst of a thousand gambling machines.

Kay looked back at her, equally baffled and then Caro said, 'You mentioned penny slots?'

Helen nodded. Penny slots, yes. Penny slots sounded good. Penny slots sounded very much like Newquay seafront. And if there was one thing Caro could be trusted with, it was fiscal responsibility.

Tony let his head fall to one side as he raised his palms in an expansive and ever so slightly condescending manner. 'Absolutely!'

'Perfect,' Caro said crisply. 'Can you show us the way?'

'I can.' Tony smiled. 'Yes I can, but you have to be careful. You can lose pretty big, pretty quick, if you start on the wrong slot. A couple of rolls and you're done, which won't give you any time at all to get to know if you've struck a loose one.'

'A couple of rolls? That's only two pence... I mean two cents,' Caro said.

'Oh no.' Tony shook his head. 'No, no, no.'

One no, Helen thought, would have sufficed. Just one.

'All the pennies are different,' he continued. 'You got your quarter dime penny slot, and your five-dollar penny and your ten-dollar penny...'

'And you said a loose one?' Caro frowned.

'Means more chance of winning. Some slots,' Tony winked, 'give up easier than others.'

'Really?' Caro's features remained perfectly still as she said, 'I read that they were completely random. That they're all computer programmed.'

Tony laughed. 'That's a nice theory, Caro. A nice enough theory.'

With the smallest sense of unease, Helen glanced at Marianne. She was glowing, as vibrantly alive under Tony's spell as the last nurtured embers of a much needed fire. And as she watched, what she felt was worry. How vulnerable she seemed. How deeply embedded the need to still be desired was. Then again, hadn't she perhaps felt and looked the same under Kaveh's spell, in Cyprus? When, she wondered, would it ever leave? And would she miss it when it did?

'Say your bankroll is fifty dollars.' Tony interrupted her thoughts. 'And you're looking for a hundred bets. That's gonna be fifty cents a bet. So in that case I'd be looking for a two credit, quarter dime slot. Like that one over there.'

They all turned to look where he pointed. Helen blinked. What on earth was he talking about? She had no idea what she was supposed to be looking at, and no idea what a two credit quarter dime equation was.

'I *think* we should start with the penny slots?' Caro said, her eyebrows making tight little arches.

'Good choice. Penny slot will give you a hundred rolls, might be just enough to get a feel.'

'A hundred rolls?' Helen sighed. 'I thought they were penny slots! How can you get a hundred rolls from a penny... I mean a dime?' She looked at Kay in desperation. She felt like a third former in a maths class.

'Penny slots, I'm guessing,' Kay said, looking at Tony, 'that take a dollar minimum bet?'

'Exactly.' Tony smiled. 'Clever lady.'

'And where might they be?' Caro snipped.

Helen looked at her feet. 'As long as they have a bloody chair, I don't care.'

'They're scattered in betweens,' Tony looked up. 'Keep an eye out for the one cent sign hanging above.'

On cue they all looked up and sure enough across the aisle, like stars on a moonless night, 1c signs began to materialise, floating above the honking, flashing signs and screens of Ghostbusters, Lord of the Rings, Game of Thrones, Star Trek, Indiana Jones, Jurassic Park, Family Guy, Friends, House of Cards, Scooby Doo, Wonder Woman.

'Whatever happened to the bunch of cherries?' Kay sighed.

'I DON'T UNDERSTAND,' Helen groaned for the umpteenth time, swinging her chair in circles, like a bored child in their parent's office. She didn't. Caro had been playing Titanic for a good ten minutes... she guessed. She had no idea. She was in a place where intervals of space were measured not by clocks – there were no clocks – but by a thousand electronic ring-tones, or bleeps, or bells. They could be in here for a week without knowing it. And Caro, with all her fiscal responsibility and talk of random odds, didn't look as if she was ready to give up anytime soon. Leaning forward on her elbows, she stared up at the slot screen as golden keys whizzed past, compasses, miniature Kate Winslets, stop-watches and... 'What's that?' she said.

'Rose's hair comb,' Caro answered without looking away.

'How many violins do you need?' asked Kay. She was sitting the other side of Caro.

'It's a cello,' Caro muttered.

'Looks like a violin to me.'

'It's a cello!' Caro snapped. 'The orchestra played 'Nearer my God to Thee', Kay. It's a cello.' She banged her hand down on the play button.

'When's the iceberg coming?' Helen said, and winking leaned back to look at Kay.

Kay laughed, shook her head and mouthed, *Don't.*

'I just need...I just...' Caro's lips continued to move as she frowned. 'I just need one more comb...' Again, she banged down on the start button.

'How about we leave you on this and we find another one?' Kay said, standing up.

Caro didn't answer.

'Send a text when you're done and we'll come back?'

'I'm not sure we'll find it,' Helen muttered. She too stood up.

'I'll find you,' Caro answered, wholly distracted by a new roll of cellos and combs.

'Right then.' Kay looked to Helen. 'Shall we?'

'We shall,' Helen sighed and linking arms, they began a slow meander away.

'I never thought I'd see the day Caro got sucked into a slot machine,' Kay said, laughing softly.

Helen nodded. It was funny. Caro, so organised and sensible, fixated on what was nothing more than the random roll of a dice. A penny gamble.

'Where on earth did we leave Marianne and Tony?'

'Oh.' Helen stopped. 'I don't know,' she said. And she didn't. There wasn't a single identifying landmark with which to guide themselves. 'Shall we just walk?'

So they did. Past rows and rows of slots, the wash of fluorescent light, ghastly blue on players' faces, as if a hundred fridges had been opened and a hundred faces sat, staring in. Past people weaving scooters and wheelchairs, people clutching oxygen machines, holding canes, folded over walkers. For Helen, Newquay arcade had been as navigable as a duck pond compared to this, the fifty pence piece in her hand more than capable of satisfying her childish dreams. But this? She felt uprooted, as if she walked in chaos. All the talk of max credits and bonus spins left her cold. Caro had grasped it. And Kay. They'd worked out Titanic in a few minutes, while she'd watched, as lost as any third-class passenger in the bowels of that doomed ship. It was beyond her. As far away conceptually from the seaside arcade of her childhood as it was geographically.

Trundling on they turned another corner, walked straight into a pot plant and were – or Helen was – wholly amazed to see Tony and Marianne almost exactly where they had left them. Had they walked a full circle? She had zero idea. *Zero.*

'Having fun?' Tony asked. He had bent to collect a handful of winnings from the slot he was playing.

'Caro is,' Kay said. 'She's found a Titanic slot.'

'Titanic!' Marianne's eyes lit up. 'I loved this film! Apart from the ending. The ending was bad. She should have let him get on that door with her. There was plenty of room.'

Tony laughed. 'Artistic licence, my love. Although, I would always have made room for you.'

'You're just in a good mood because you won!' Nudging his shoulder, Marianne beamed. 'One hundred and twenty dollars.'

Helen's eyes widened. 'You just won that?'

'Told you,' Tony said, looking right at her. 'Some of them give out a lot more than others.'

'Mmm.' Helen smiled. She wasn't warming to this man at all. Neither the way he was winking at her, nor the way his pot belly distorted Kurt's head. 'It's all a bit much for me,' she said lightly. 'Max bets and all that. I never was very good at maths.'

'Me neither,' Marianne said as she slipped down from the chair. She was, Helen noticed, so short, it was a drop to the ground.

'Oh, it's simple enough,' Tony started. 'You want to be playing maximum credits to get the highest odds of winning and—'

Helen raised her hand. *Please stop,* she wanted to say. *Please. Just. Stop.* First of all, it really was hopeless. Like all those awful Sally had five apples and Billy had three, problems she thought she'd left decades ago... Secondly, she really was having trouble liking him.

'Maybe...' Tony shrugged. 'You should try one of those newer machines. They're proving pretty popular and they seem darn simple to me. There's one over there. No bets. It's just a claw, to grab a prize.'

'A claw?'

'Like the pub machines back home,' Kay said. 'You can do that, Helen.'

She could. How many times had she taken control from a furious Libby, or a miserable Jack, as they'd tried repeatedly and failed to win some hideous, highly flammable bright green ball of fluff. And her win ratio was surprisingly high. The best in the family. Which wasn't saying so much considering that Lawrence never tried and the kids had been useless.

'Where is it?' she asked now. Claws she could do.

Tony pointed it out.

'Shall we try?' Marianne said. 'I'm fed up with this machine. It's always whistling at me.' She turned to Tony.

'Ah.' Tony turned his winning chips over in his hand. 'If you don't mind.' He turned to Marianne. 'I was thinking of playing a couple of hands of cards? I'm a little clumsy with that thing.'

'Do you play?' Kay asked, her face suddenly animated.

'A little. You?'

'Oh, not really. Not at the level I suppose they do here.'

Tony nodded. 'Understand. You need your wits about you to play it here.'

'Ha!' Helen snorted. 'Kay's got wits coming out of her ears. She's a maths teacher.' The line was delivered with more punch than she'd intended, but something in Tony's manner really irritated her. A superciliousness. As if he were the only one in possession of wit.

Tony put his head to one side, his eyes narrowing as he studied Kay. 'Want to join me?'

'Oh... I don't...' Kay hesitated. She looked first at Marianne, who said, 'Go. I think I'm going to find this Titanic.' And then at Helen, who said, 'Go!' And for the first time Helen felt thankful that Tony had turned up. It was as clear as day that Kay was tempted. 'Go,' she urged. 'I'll stick with the claw. That's about my level.'

14

'And then reality TV became the big new thing. They came knocking of course. *Dancing with the Stars?* I said to them, I'm an actor. I've worked with the greats. Mel Gibson once watched me deliver a death sentence to an empty chair and slapped me on the back after for a job well done! I'm supposed to waltz for my supper now?' One confident stride ahead, Tony stopped walking and turned back to Kay. 'The boozy who should have been in the chair by the way, was flat out drunk in his trailer. But the show must go on, huh, Kay? Anyway, here we are!'

Snapping to attention, Kay rewound the last words she'd heard. 'Reality TV,' she managed. 'Yes, it's very big now.' It was the best she could do. She'd stopped listening. At some point, in the few minutes it had taken them to navigate their way from the slots, through the electronic gaming machines, all the way to the back of the casino floor where the games room was situated, she had switched off. She'd had to. Tony talked non-stop. Working his way through four seasons of *General Hospital* then, without taking a breath, moving onto *Days of Your Lives*. She'd stopped listening around 1998. She looked up and a soft *'Oh'* escaped. There was nothing about the room in front of them that she understood, or had anticipated.

The carpet was a geometrically patterned blaze of red and gold, the chairs were striped and the felt-covered tables shaped as randomly as if a five-year-old had been let loose with a pastry cutter. Dark wood panels lined the walls. The carpet under her feet was thicker than it had been in the slots room, the lighting more subdued, the ambient noise muffled by the thick green baize of the tables. The stakes, it was clear, were higher here. And, as she looked across at all the players, she began to feel an intense embarrassment creeping up from her toes to her knees, her stomach and her face. She was an overweight, fifty-plus maths teacher from suburbia. Back home, on that afternoon in the coffee shop, Helen had asked her where in the world, and she hadn't hesitated. She'd found her answer easily, and hadn't given it any thought, not even after Caro had put the ticket in her hand. This daydream of a land that her mother had sung along to as she'd washed dishes on a Sunday afternoon. Abba's 'Money, Money, Money' on the transistor in the corner of the kitchen, her father and her playing cards at the kitchen table. Gambling away whole packets of matchsticks!

Shall we go, Kay? he would tease. *Win our fortune? Buy your mum a hostess trolley.*

We'll go, Martin had promised. *We'll definitely go,* after she went out and blew a week's wage on that jacket.

And now she was here, she'd finally made it and it was a revelation to realise how unexamined this long-held, quietly stored dream had been. She hadn't even needed to leave home to find it in the first place. The lyrics of a song on the radio? The gentle teasing from her father? Was that all it had taken? She'd put it together, and put it away and, if she was honest, never really tried to follow through. It was this last thought that hit the target. That had her smiling weakly at Tony as she followed him in, like a lamb, or a child, certainly a someone who had never even tried to follow dreams. It was Caro who had asked why she hadn't gone. Caro whose whole life had been a process of one foot in front of the other, to get where she wanted to be, regardless of the hurdles, the setbacks. So, what had stopped her? A family event she hadn't wanted to miss? A lack of funds? A leave-it-to-tomorrow attitude? Twenty-five years later and she had no idea of a single one of those over-riding, terribly important, couldn't be avoided reasons for *not* coming. What had been so difficult about fulfilling a dream? She wished she knew. She really wished someone had come along twenty years ago and given her a huge shove. Had told her how fast the years before Alex would fly by, warned her what was waiting, when the years of Alex were over. Kay! She adjusted the strap on her handbag, fingers nervously playing with the catch. *You* should have given yourself the shove, she thought. You should have shoved yourself.

Heart thumping, she followed behind Tony as he nodded at the croupiers in their smart two-tone waistcoats, and momentarily placed a hand on the shoulder of an old man sitting at a poker table they passed. Sometimes they stopped to watch the play. The pace was fast. Cards flipped and folded, chips stacked and swept. Strange words snatched up and thrown across the baize, *colour up, yo eleven, he's a wonger.* Even so, she recognised the games. Poker, Baccarat, Blackjack. She almost recognised the players, because, to her astonishment, the room was stuffed full of the most normal-looking, thick-waisted people she'd ever seen. *People like her.* Dressed in baseball caps and hoodies and jeans. People that she might find herself queueing behind at Tesco's meat counter. Or people like Sammy from her chemo group. Sammy who was, probably at this very minute, on her way to Blackpool to fulfil that dream of seeing a fake George Michael, Sammy whom she'd laughed at the afternoon of the workshop when she'd turned and said, *Why, Kay? Why didn't I ever go and see the real thing?* Surrounded by the strange juxtaposition of the familiar and the extraordinary, Kay remembered how Sammy had answered her own question. *I'll tell you why. It was easier not to and I always assumed there would be another time.*

Well. Her lungs filled, her chest swelled, her eyes went glassy, her mouth dry. Now that nowhere was easy, now that *another time* had taken on the scarcity of summer snow, here she finally was, in the games room of a Vegas casino. She was as mixed up inside as a tin of Quality Street, soft with excitement, crunched up with fear. This was no daydream of a far land. These people were as normal as her. She was an overweight, fifty-plus maths teacher from suburbia and she fitted in perfectly. *Dad!* She wanted to laugh it out loud, throw her head back and call across the ocean that divided them. *DAD! I'm here.* But as swiftly as it had arisen, the urge to laugh died. She stared across the room. If this was so easy, what else might she have done, if she'd ever taken the time to follow dreams?

'What's your game, Kay?' Tony turned to her.

'Game? Oh...' Kay took a deep breath. She looked over at the roulette table, the huge fast-moving wheel. Then she turned to the table where all the yelling was coming from. 'What's that?' she said.

'Craps,' Tony answered.

Kay watched. The craps table looked fun. It was by far the noisiest, and surrounded by a group of people who looked as if they were playing a team game as they cheered and groaned in unison. But the table itself was the most confusing thing she'd ever seen. The green baize covered in piles of red chips with white dots, or blue chips with white dots, marked with yellow lines and black circles and indecipherable script: *Insurance Pays, Pass, Don't Pass*. A casino worker stood at one end, another in the middle, translating the constant flow of chips and dice in a game that everyone around the table obviously understood. It was fascinating and intimidating, like walking into a secret club and not having a clue about the password.

'It's a game of chance,' Tony said. 'Not my bag.'

'Isn't everything?' Kay smiled. But inwardly she agreed. There had been a strategy to the games she'd played with her father. 'Blackjack,' she said, 'is what I mostly played when I was younger.'

Tony's face broke out into a wide grin. 'Good choice.'

'Is it?'

'Oh yes. Best chance of winning of any game.'

'Really?'

He nodded. 'If you're going to spend an hour in here, Kay, Blackjack is what you should be playing. And...' raising his hand, he pointed across the room. 'There's a couple of openings at that table over there.'

He might as well have pointed to a crocodile, or an approaching grizzly bear. Kay pulled back in fear. The table Tony pointed to had a sign floating above it. Only this one didn't say, *1c*. This one said *$10, minimum bet*.

Tony looked at her. 'Is that what you were thinking?'

Matchsticks. She swallowed. If she'd been thinking anything, it was matchsticks. The leap to ten dollars a hand was a leap to another world.

Tony smiled, a kind smile that reached his eyes. 'Why

don't you just watch me for a hand or two?' he said. 'Join in when you're ready... or not at all.'

'Is that allowed?' She was so unsure of the protocol, the rules, the etiquette of a casino that she felt like a child, like one of the kids she taught.

'Sure it is,' he grinned. 'We're in Vegas! Everything's allowed!'

Oddly disappointed, Kay followed him across. A part of her, she was beginning to understand, would have responded to some persuasion on his behalf to get her to play, wanted in fact to be persuaded, but he hadn't even tried. Risk, she supposed, just wasn't in her DNA, and he probably sensed this. She was, after all, an overweight, fifty-plus maths teacher from suburbia.

BUT A MERE THIRTY MINUTES LATER, and any feelings of disappointment were as lost to Kay as size eight jeans. She was deep in the game, the lost song of all those childhood Sunday evenings, playing with her dad, coming back to her. Because the game, it turned out, was the same wherever it was played. And because she knew the rhythm of it in her bones, she'd only had to be reminded. Tony, she could see, knew it too. Despite his self-absorbed ramblings of earlier, his mind as far as Blackjack was concerned was sharp as a scalpel. He was now – she did a swift tally of his chips – up three hundred dollars. Whereas the player opposite had, in the time she'd been watching, lost just short of five hundred. And although the numbers made her palms sweaty, the game didn't. Swap out those ten-dollar chips for match-sticks, and she'd play. She knew she would. She knew she could. Already she'd begun to second guess the bets Tony would make. A rusty old calculator rising up from her pool of memory and cranking into life, running odds in her head, tossing up probabilities and coming, she could see, to the same conclusions as Tony. And he was three hundred dollars up in... Twisting in her chair, Kay looked for a clock. There was, of course, no clock to be found. It didn't matter. Three hundred dollars! Three hundred dollars... That was half a week's wages, and clock or no clock, if there was one thing Kay was sure of, it was that she hadn't been sat here on this stool for half a week. Again, autonomously, that calculator started up. How much over the course of a day? If she played the same strategy...

Two things happened at once that, together, jerked her out of her reverie.

Abruptly, Tony stood up, handed the dealer a pile of his chips and took fewer different-coloured ones in return. At the same time, she felt, through the fabric of her handbag, the vibration of her phone.

'Are you done?' she asked, disappointment rising again.

Tony shifted his tokens into one pocket, slipped his hand in and stretching the fabric jiggled them around. 'May I give you a tip?' he said, but he didn't wait for her to answer. 'Quit when you're winning, Kay. *Always* quit when you're winning.'

Kay smiled. 'Of course.' She looked down at her phone. It was a text. From Helen. Two words.

I'm lost!

PHONE PRESSED TO HER CHIN, both arms waving in the air, Helen rose onto her tiptoes and yelled. 'Here! I'm here!' She'd caught sight of a head of silver hair and had followed it, waiting, hoping, praying that it belonged to Tony, who should be with Kay. It was essential they saw her. They might walk past, they might not notice her at all, and she didn't think she could face another minute in this whistling, jangling, horn-blowing, electronic hell. She'd given up with the claw long ago, and for what felt like an age now had walked around in circles trying to find someone, anyone that she recognised. Every time, every single time, she'd ended up back where she'd started.

'Here!' she yelled again.

And to her immense relief, Kay waved back.

'Thank God!' Helen sighed. 'Did you play?' she asked as they approached.

'Tony did. He won three hundred.'

Helen's jaw went slack. 'Three hundred! You've had a great afternoon!'

'Yep,' Tony said, nodding amiably, as if winning hundreds of dollars was something he did every day.

'Where's Caro?' Kay asked. 'And Marianne?'

Helen shook her head. 'When I told her that Caro was playing Titanic, she left to try and find her. For all I know she's still looking, this place is a maze. I've been walking in circles for ages.'

Tony laughed. 'They do it on purpose, to keep you from leaving.'

'Well it works,' Helen muttered.

'Oh boy.' Kay sighed as she surveyed the plain of slot machines stretching away on all sides. 'How on earth will we find them?'

'That's easy, ladies,' Tony grinned. 'I suggest you follow me.' And he turned and set off the way he and Kay had come.

· · ·

ASTONISHINGLY, for Helen, within a short minute they had found both Marianne and Caro. They were still playing Titanic, Caro banging on the play button with a jaw as rigid as a steel box and Marianne standing to one side, shifting her weight from hip to hip, impatiently waiting her turn. Both of them so engaged, a flying elephant could have passed by and they wouldn't have noticed.

'It's so stupid!' Marianne cried, as they came closer. 'There was plenty of room.'

'What's stupid?' Tony called.

But Marianne hadn't heard.

'I'd have to disagree,' Caro hissed. She didn't take her eyes off the slot as she hit another roll. 'She'd have tipped herself over.'

'What are they arguing about?' Helen said.

Kay shrugged.

'But she didn't even try!' Marianne threw her arm up. 'What kind of a love story is that, when she didn't even try to save him?'

'She would have frozen!' Caro banged down on the play button.

'Hey!' A heavy-set man in a floral shirt playing the slot next door turned and glared. 'Lady!' he growled.

'Tell her,' Tony turned to Kay and Helen, 'not to bang. Other players don't like it.'

Helen nodded. Caro, she could see, was unlikely to hear anything she might be told.

'Don't bang the machine,' Kay said gently.

'What?' Caro looked at Kay blankly, then turned back to the slot. 'I just need one more Heart of the Ocean.'

'And then it's my turn,' Marianne muttered.

The counters rolled. One heart, two and then none.

Caro rolled again.

One heart, two and then none.

Moving in, indefatigable as the iceberg itself, Marianne nudged Caro aside, and pressed to roll.

Helen's heart sank, as surely, she thought, as the bloody heart of the ocean thing. Her blisters had started up again, circles of sharp pain rubbing at the back of her heels. Dully, she watched the slot spin.

One heart, two and then none.

And again.

One heart, two and then none.

'My turn—'

'Caro!' Helen said loudly, a little more loudly than she'd intended.

And suddenly, Caro broke free from her spell. She pulled back and looked around. 'Goodness! There you all are.'

And now Marianne turned.

Tony laughed. 'You see? This is how time passes in Vegas.'

'Gosh.' Caro gave a small embarrassed laugh. 'These things are addictive.'

'Vegas,' Tony smiled, 'is addictive.'

'How long have we been here?' Marianne said, looking back at the machine, her hand itching towards it.

'I have no idea,' Helen sighed. 'But I do know, I could really do with a coffee now.'

'Me too. And something else...' Marianne snorted as she picked up her handbag. 'Whatever anyone says, the ending was ridiculous. She had plenty of room on that door. What do you think, Kay?'

But Kay didn't answer.

Helen looked at her. The whole time they had been waiting, Kay, she'd noticed, had watched almost mesmerised as the slot had rolled around and around. 'You ok?' she said now.

Kay startled. 'Yes,' she said. 'Fine.'

'They are addictive,' Helen said. 'Even just watching them. I'm glad I'm not a gambler.'

And once again, Kay didn't answer.

15

Two days of hectic sightseeing passed, Tony as an occasional guide. They'd ridden the Deuce bus up and down the strip, seen the Sphinx, had their photo taken with Big Elvis. They'd watched the Bellagio fountains pop and jerk to Billie Jean, gazed at flamingos cruising a cement-lined pool, tasted Coke flavours from around the world and tried as many different colours of M&Ms, from the M&M shop, as were made. Helen still couldn't get over this. A shop that sold nothing else *but* M&Ms? Having decided they should all choose at least one thing, she had opted for the CSI experience. She was even wearing her t-shirt today: *People lie, evidence doesn't.* She'd bought one in extra-large as well. For Lawrence. A little reminder of the secret second mortgage he'd taken out to fund his Everest trip.

They'd taken another walk along the strip, this time in sneakers, and this time at night. But it had been just as hot, and every few minutes they'd had to loiter in the doorways of various restaurants, where misting fans blew preciously cool air. It was always older women, Helen had noticed, taking refuge alongside them, yanking open t-shirts as they turned their faces to the welcome mist. They'd passed men bearing sandwich boards: *Ride Over the Grand Canyon*, and guys sporting fraternity letters. Micky and Mini Mouse, who were clearly going through some marital strife, and Darth Vader, rasping like a man in need of a pair of resuscitation paddles. Water grottoes and waterfalls, indoor rainstorms and colour changing fog. A grove of olive trees, a gangplank of pirates, a lone leprechaun. Donny Osmond's face, twenty storeys high, and too-many-to-count, three-feet-long plastic tubes filled with brightly coloured liquids... greens, oranges, pinks.

What is that? Helen had called at a man slurping from a green tube. *A three-foot daiquiri,* he'd laughed. Of course it was! And of course she'd bought one, the words of that thong-wearing angel ringing in her ear: *You haven't lived, girl!* Marianne had chosen orange, Kay pink. Only Caro had declined, and as they'd walked along, slurping and staring at the extraordinary sights, Helen had had to concede, the angel was right. She really hadn't lived. What was she doing, putting dinner-parties on a list of things she really, really wanted to do, when all this world was out here waiting to be experienced? For the first time since Cyprus, she felt alive! One hundred and a thousand percent alive! Anything felt possible. She was after all, younger today than she ever would be again. Which meant she was at her youngest! She did not feel like a grandmother. She was not thinking of the house and how to proceed with a divorce and, for the first time since she'd heard them, she'd even forgotten those words *It was a mistake*. Vegas was a city for starting over and starting again. A city where anything went. And its free-wheeling, can-do, live and let live spirit (along with the rum from the daiquiri) rushed her veins like a drug.

Caro's choice of tourist activity had been the Bellagio Conservatory and Botanical Gardens, which, despite the fake orange trees and pumped-in floral fragrance that had Caro sneezing the entire time, had turned out to be an oasis of calm, the yin to the yang that made Vegas, as far as Helen was concerned, such an extraordinary experience.

That was yesterday; today it was Marianne's turn to decide and she had chosen Madame Tussauds. After which, Tony had pulled an ace from his pocket and invited them all to an afternoon at his ranch, followed by a barbecue under the stars. It sounded wonderful and Helen was as excited as any kid in any sweet shop. Kay too was glowing. She was, Helen could see, thoroughly enjoying herself and it was a joy to witness.

But first came breakfast. Again. Which didn't seem possible. It felt to Helen like she'd only finished eating five minutes ago.

'I'm not even hungry,' Kay sighed, as they stood clutching plates to their stomachs like a row of orphans.

Helen looked behind her. The queue for breakfast seemed even longer today than it had been the day before. Behind them stood an elderly couple, and behind them a group of men trailing suitcases, their crumpled clothing and exhausted faces testament to the journey that had brought them here. Beyond them, two young women, still dressed from the night before, heels and handbags and slinky dresses and glitter eyeshadow.

'Have they been out all night?' Caro whispered.

Helen turned. 'I hope they had a better time than I did.'

'How do you feel now?' Kay asked.

'I'm still full from dinner,' Helen groaned. Dinner had been another enormous buffet. Foot-long steamed crab legs, Cajun dirty rice, gumbo and sushi, all piled onto one plate.

More in one meal than she usually consumed in a week. All prepped, cooked and served. How on earth were you meant to refuse? Perhaps, she considered now, by remembering the after effects. She'd been in and out of the bathroom at least three times during the night.

'You know,' Kay said, 'the waiter yesterday told me that the amount of seafood consumed in Vegas is more than the rest of the United States combined.'

'Well, no one can say I didn't do my part,' Helen muttered. 'I consumed enough for California. Why do I always overeat?' She put a hand on her belly and grabbed a fistful of flesh. 'Ugh.'

'We could always skip breakfast,' Caro said.

'I need to sit down,' Kay sighed. 'I need a coffee before I can face another Elvis.'

'THAT'S IT,' Helen gasped, half an hour later. She pushed her plate away. 'Now I really am stuffed.' Leaning back in her chair, she undid the button and then the zipper on her shorts. 'Why did I eat all that? Hash browns? Bacon and sausage? I don't even know what breakfast ham is, but it doesn't stop me eating it!'

Kay laughed.

And beside Kay, Caro smiled. Having spent a considerable amount of time in luxury hotels serving luxury breakfasts, she had built up a resistance to laden buffet tables. She was practised in restraint. 'Does anyone know what time we're leaving for the ranch?' she said.

Opposite, and barely meeting her eye, Helen gave a quick shake of the head before picking up her phone.

'Not sure,' Kay said lightly.

Caro nodded.

Helen's reluctance to engage with her remained painfully obvious, and short of confronting her, Caro didn't know what to do. It was true they hadn't seen much of each other since Kay's operation. But the few times they had met, Caro had gone away feeling reassured that their friendship had been sufficiently repaired. Last August had been receding, a kink that the perpetual pull of time, she'd thought, would eventually straighten out and maybe flatten altogether. It was this feeling that had propelled her into booking the trip, into *doing something spontaneous*. And Helen, she'd presumed, had felt the same. Otherwise, why would she have thrown that Christmas dinner party? It wasn't just for Kay, Caro was sure of that. And it had been such fun. Almost like old times, only better for Caro actually, because the happiness she'd felt with Shook had been such a different sort of happiness than she'd ever experienced in her younger years. She'd been excited to introduce him properly to Helen, keen to gauge her reaction and... Coffee cup at her lips, Caro's face froze, her eyes wide as she stared across the restaurant. She'd also been keen to let Lawrence see, once and for all, that there would be no more room for his sly flirting... But he'd slobbered in her ear and stuck his hand up her skirt. The heat of memory struck, her cheeks warmed and all around a thousand pieces of crockery fell silent. The restaurant blurred, as something new came into an uncomfortably sharp focus... The fleeting, barely there, reflection that had moved across the window of Helen's living room and then vanished. A movement that hadn't lasted more than a second, that Caro had, with the nerves of presenting the tickets, forgotten about almost immediately. Shook had come back into the room and stood close to her and any fear she might have harboured that the shadow had been him had melted away with his reassuring smile, dissipated in the deep waters of unconsciousness, as she'd turned the light of her mind to the moment and concentrated on Kay. Yes, Kay's delight, her genuine surprise and the sure knowledge that she had gotten it right. She had, perhaps for the first time in her life, pulled off something spontaneous and gotten it right. She hadn't, not even for a moment, given any further thought to the shadow. So now, as the realisation arrived for the very first time, it was so cold and so bright it made her wince, and sent a ripple of goosebumps along her arm. Helen had seen. Helen had seen Lawrence's hand up her skirt, his face so close to her own. It was the last brick removed in the dam of misunderstanding between them. It had to be, because everything flowed now. Everything made sense.

'I think we should get it sorted,' Kay was saying.

'Sorry?' Caro turned to her.

'The Grand Canyon.' Kay laughed. 'Where were you? I was saying we should book it today. I'd hate to miss it.'

'The helicopter?' Caro said blankly.

'Yes.' And again Kay laughed. 'Helen's got it on her phone now. Where were you, Caro?'

But before Caro could answer, Kay's phone pinged.

'Marianne,' she said, slipping her reading glasses on to squint at the text. 'She says Tony has some business downtown and she'll be over by ten.'

'Did she stay with him last night?' Helen asked.

Kay nodded. 'Last two nights. Apparently he's got some fancy suite over at another hotel.' She took off her glasses. 'She's smitten, that's for sure.'

'Mmm,' Caro started. 'He seems...' but she didn't finish. She put her cup down and smiled too tightly. Too many thoughts were now racing around her head. She wasn't even sure what she had been about to say.

'Nice?' Kay offered.

'Not very trustworthy,' Helen said bluntly, and looked at Caro.

'I didn't say that,' Caro flushed.

'Nooo,' Helen stretched the word. 'But I did. Anyway, I'll get this booked.' And she looked back down at her phone.

Caro nodded. She tucked the same strand of hair behind her ears twice, blinking hard. Her eyes stung, and in the midst of this chaotic and bustling restaurant, sitting opposite one lifelong friend and beside another, she was engulfed by a sudden and profound loneliness. The message that had just been passed from Helen was unambiguous. *Not very trustworthy.* Helen wasn't just talking about Tony. Within that description, she included Caro and Caro knew this as sure as she knew it was day. With Kay still texting Marianne, Caro swiped the screen to unlock her own phone, looking for a message from Shook, looking for company, support, a little love. But there was nothing. He'd said he wouldn't contact her, and if there was one thing she was sure of, it was that he was a man of his word.

'Ah!' Kay had her glasses back on, reading through another text that had just arrived. 'Marianne says we're leaving for the ranch at three. It's about an hour away.'

'That sounds great,' Helen said, the note of determination in her voice unmistakeable.

'It does,' Caro managed, but she was empty as a drum. This trip, this dream trip she had so carefully constructed, had been built upon sands she didn't even know had shifted. A knot formed, deep in her belly. A knot of worry. One way or the other, no matter how difficult, no matter how awful the confrontation would be, she had to talk to Helen. Explain what Helen had seen, explain that although, yes, there had been times – distant and incredible as it seemed to Caro now – when, Helen having left the room, she had let Lawrence rest his hand on her leg. But not now. That wasn't something that was even possible now. The coffee she was drinking too quickly scalded her mouth, and as the burn travelled down her windpipe, Caro felt she deserved it. She wouldn't have done anything. All those distant and incredible times... nothing would have progressed. She knew this now, but it was no comfort because the knowledge had come too late. Like being handed a compass, after she'd found her way home. It was the friendship that mattered most, far more than the value she'd mistakenly placed in Lawrence's attention. The friendship with Helen that had sustained her through three decades of life, and that had proved more constant than any other source of emotional support in this lonely world. What was clear, what was blindingly obvious, now that she was out of the storm, safely anchored with Shook, was that her loneliness had been a house with no walls, leaving her vulnerable to every passing change of weather. It wasn't much of an excuse to explain why she'd always allowed Lawrence to overstep the boundary, but it was the only one she had. No, she would never have hurt Helen and yes, she would have staked her life on this. What she didn't know, what she had no idea of, was how she was going to get Helen to see that.

16

The knot was still there, only now it had unravelled, to coil, parasite like, around Caro's intestines, as she stood staring blankly at Hugh Hefner and the bunny girl in bed next to him.

Madame Tussauds? In Vegas? She didn't get it. Didn't see the point or the enjoyment to be gained as she watched yet another middle-aged man, with stiff joints and sweaty hands that he wiped on his trousers, clamber up onto the bed, ready for his middle-aged wife to take the photo.

She'd tried. She'd shaken Elvis's hand and managed a smile as the waxwork responded with a static *You've sure gotta lot of nerve, baby.* She'd stood alongside an enormous basketball player while Kay took her photo. She'd slapped her hand over the hand of Eric Clapton, displayed alongside Paul Simon's and Janet Jackson's, on a Wall of Hands. She had stood and watched, as obese teenagers grated behind Beyoncé and not once had she been tempted to join in. To get *interactive* with the waxworks, as they had been encouraged to do upon entering. A stance, she was acutely aware, that set her apart from the others. Because up ahead, Kay, Marianne and Helen were having a great time.

It's ok to touch, the screens in every room repeated on loop. And so they had. Helen especially, immediately jumping right in to pick up a prop sword and decapitate Jack Sparrow. As if, Caro couldn't help thinking, she was on a mission to keep herself distracted, to put distance between them and keep it that way.

And because everyone else was so intent upon having fun, she had continued to try, always feeling deeply uncomfortable and always keeping her mind focused on the bottle of hand sanitiser at the exit. She was counting down, waxwork by waxwork. But each new room was a form of mild torture, with the one she found herself in now perhaps worst of all. No, she was as far from seeing the point of all this as she'd ever been.

The middle-aged man shuffled himself off the bed, stuffing his shirt in to cover a huge protruding belly. *Did ya get it?* he called to his wife and his voice woke Caro from her thoughts. When she looked up, she saw that apart from this man and his wife, she was alone in the playboy room. The others had moved on. She eased past the couple, who were now checking the photograph, and entered a passageway that was dark and narrow. Up ahead, she could hear Kay laughing and she smiled, momentarily forgetting her discomfiture with Helen, with Hugh Hefner and Bunny Girls and Vegas in general. Something was obviously funny, and this was Kay's trip. No matter how silly, how tacky, how difficult she was personally finding it, Kay was enjoying Vegas immensely, and to hear her laugh like this was a balm. The passageway opened up into a room backdropped by a gauzy silver curtain. In front of the curtain stood a waxwork of a tuxedo-wearing George Clooney. Did he ever wear anything else, Caro wondered as she edged to the side. George's hand was stretched out, for whomever wished to take it, distinguished streaks of grey in his sideburns. And there, hobbling and wobbling on one leg was Marianne, stuffing... Caro blinked, yes... stuffing herself into a wedding dress.

'What's going on,' she said, her voice as light as she could manage.

Kay had the back of her hand pressed to her mouth, tears running down her cheeks. 'Marianne is going to marry George Clooney.'

Even Helen, standing behind Marianne to help her into the dress, had visibly relaxed. She was laughing too, and it was easy to see how genuine the laughter was, how unforced.

'You need these.' Kay stooped to pick up a large plastic bouquet of white roses.

'I need to get this on first,' Marianne gasped.

From behind Helen bent and gave a great upward tug on the dress.

'Ouch!' Marianne yelped. She dropped forward and stuffed her arms through the sleeves, then stood, resplendent in cheap white satin that had bunched and strained across her belly. 'How do I look?'

'Awful,' Kay said, pushing the roses into her hand.

And before Marianne could respond, Helen plonked a veil on her head. 'Ta dah!' she laughed, her head tipping back.

Caro smiled. The dress was hideous, the roses were hideous, even George himself was hideous. Alongside the cheap curtain was the type of large urn, adorned with plastic flowers, that wouldn't have looked out of place in a high street undertakers. The whole scene was absurdly ridiculous, and as she watched, she had the idea that she might, finally, see the point of it all. Her face broke into a wider smile. 'It's awful,' she said nodding. 'Perfectly awful!'

Thrusting her elbows back, Marianne puffed her way to George. 'Come in,' she waved to Kay and Helen. 'I need some bridesmaids. Caro?'

'Oh no.' Caro took a step back. 'I'll take the picture.'

It took less than a moment for the wedding party to accept this and arrange themselves accordingly, and as they did, Caro was filled with a regret that surprised her. Why hadn't she just said yes, and dashed in to join the group? Then again, why hadn't they insisted she join them? She lifted her phone to frame the photo and was struck by the image it captured; three middle-aged women, giggling like teenagers. Hadn't that once been Kay and Helen and herself? Wasn't there something wrong with this picture? The answer hit, winding her like a fist in the stomach. She was out now, and Marianne was in. And suddenly all her latent childish feelings of inadequacy roared into life. She was as she'd ever been, a nervous and too eager-to-please girl, in awe of all those other girls, the ones who laughed so easily, whose mothers laughed easily too, who dreamed of white weddings and got them, whose lives didn't haunt them...

'Caro!' Helen yelled. 'Take the picture! I can see a tall, beautiful human rights lawyer coming around the corner!'

Marianne and Kay tipped their heads back, roaring with laughter. Caro snapped the picture. And there it was. The three of them. Helen, Kay and Marianne.

At fifty-one, feeling as lonely and misunderstood as she ever had, her words fell like bombs upon this happy landscape. 'Shook,' she said, 'has asked me to marry him.'

The wedding party froze.

Or did Caro just imagine they had?

Because in the next moment Kay had disentangled herself from George Clooney and was bringing her hand to her mouth, a look of amazement on her face. Marianne too had lowered her flowers.

But Helen, and this Caro knew she hadn't imagined, Helen hadn't moved. She was stood staring at Caro, as if she had seen a ghost.

'IT'S COMPLICATED,' Caro said in answer to Kay's tentative *Well?* She pressed a glob of hand sanitiser into the palm of her hand. It felt cool.

They had reached the exit of the museum, where the music level was slightly more tolerable. It hadn't been inside. It simply hadn't been possible to have any kind of coherent conversation and she'd used this as an excuse to carry her through the rest of the very few exhibits left, her blurted confession ushering a sobering reality into the experience.

Concentrating on the sanitiser, she didn't add anything else, and as no one else did either, Kay's *Well?* drifted away. She hadn't meant to blurt it out, she hadn't meant to say a word, not until she'd come to a decision, which she hadn't. Firstly, because there really hadn't been many quiet moments in which she had had time to herself. And secondly, the few moments there had been, before bed, after a shower, when she'd run it through in her head and reached a point where she was ready to say yes to what she thought she was being asked, she had been overwhelmed by fear. Life, in this last year, had plunged depths Caro hadn't known existed. Had shown, with a clarity she could not have imagined, what loneliness really looked like. This side of fifty, it was ugly. The scenery had been pushed aside, the veil lifted, and she had seen, had briefly known, what it was to be old and to be alone. And it was nothing like the flimsy notions she'd carried around in her late thirties or early forties, as everyone else had partnered off and married. It was nothing like those days, because then she could still turn a head with her slim figure, then she still had the respect of her work colleagues, and the purpose of a career. Recovering from the miscarriage, the fallout with Helen, saying goodbye to her mother, coming to terms with the fact that she was going to lose Kay, was walking a tightrope across a volcano. She'd only just kept herself upright. So what if she accepted Shook's proposal and it all went wrong? If he proved to be crushingly disappointing to her, or she to him? Then she'd fall, and this side of fifty she wasn't sure she could find the strength or the energy to climb back out, to stop herself becoming engulfed in a loneliness as premature as it was profound, and from which there might be no escape. So she didn't know. And she didn't know how she would know. And turning now to see Kay's expectant face, Caro was filled with conflicting emotions. Why had she said anything at all? On the other hand, who would she have spoken to if it wasn't Kay and Helen... if Helen would only just look at her... These were her friends. Still, just about, her friends. 'It's complicated,' she repeated. 'I'm not even sure how I feel...'

And at this, Helen turned and walked away a few paces.

'Helen,' Kay called. 'Wait up!' Looking at Caro, she said, 'It's honestly not that complicated, Caro. Don't overthink it,' then, 'Helen?'

But Helen didn't respond. She'd reached a small table, with a lone empty chair. Hand resting on the chair back, she turned to face them. 'I need some air,' she said. 'I just need some air.' And without another word, she turned again and walked away.

'WHAT WAS ALL THAT ABOUT THAT?' Kay's face was pale as she watched Helen melt into the flow of people. 'What is going on?'

'Kay...' Caro paused, seemed as if she might speak. But she didn't. She shook her head and she didn't say a word.

Kay breathed in, nostrils flaring, weariness threatening. She wasn't even surprised. She had, she found, almost been expecting it. It was clear that ever since they'd left the UK, Caro and Helen had been playing an odd game. A game that involved the continual passing between them of something fragile; a something that had obviously just been dropped. She had an idea it was Caro that had done the dropping, but why on earth Helen should have a problem with Shook asking Caro to marry him, she couldn't guess. Caro knew. It was written all over her face, and surrounded by the glitz and pretence and heat of Vegas, Kay experienced an epiphany. She didn't care. She wasn't going to ask what the issue was, because she didn't care, and she wasn't sure she ever would again. Maybe it still led back to that August night, when Caro had taken Libby's baby. Maybe they simply weren't able to put it behind them, and in a small, but disappointed way, Kay thought now, she understood. Nothing in life stayed the same, let alone people. And it might have just been too much to hope that the friendship they'd shared as young women could be sustained now that they were all so much older and yes, uglier. Life had left them chewed up and storm damaged. Maybe it was inevitable that the distance forged by husbands and children and marriages would cement over, become impassable. Maybe, it was time to accept that an exchange of Christmas cards was the way they were heading. Trips together like this were perhaps better left to the 18 to 30 group, when loyalties hadn't really been tested, the girth of forgiveness not yet been measured. She stuck her hand under her waistband and hitched up her shorts, shifted the strap of her handbag. Part of her wanted to ask Caro about Shook, but not a big enough part. Tussauds had been fun. Silly, easily achievable fun that she wanted only to keep going. She turned to Marianne, but anything else she might have said was pre-empted by Marianne's huge snort of air.

'Whatever is the matter?' said Kay.

Marianne scowled. 'Tony wants to play Blackjack again.'

'Oh.' Kay nodded. Her mood lightened, like blinds had been opened, like someone had come along and slapped the day a lovely lilac. 'Is that bad?' she asked lightly.

'For me it's bad!' Marianne muttered. 'I don't want to play Blackjack! I don't even want to know how to play Blackjack! Last night there is a drunk Korean guy, trying to explain me that numbers two to six are worth one point and tens are minus one. If I do this I have an advantage over the house of this.' Exasperated, she threw her hands up in the air. 'I don't know. He plays a lot. Too much I think.'

Kay smiled. 'He's talking about counting cards. And the house advantage.'

'Counting cards?' Caro asked. 'Isn't that illegal?'

'Think so.' Kay nodded. She wasn't thinking about the legality of it, she was thinking about how astonished she was she'd remembered. Because what Marianne now described, she could recall perfectly. It was a counting system, where low cards had a plus value and higher cards a negative value. Her father had taught her. Something she'd completely forgotten about until she'd perfectly remembered. The more high cards left in the pack, the greater the odds of going bust. Of a dealer going bust and a player winning. An itch began, starting in her fingertips, moving her toes. An itch that, although she'd been trying to ignore it, had started that first day in the games room with Tony and hadn't ever really gone away. Because hadn't it kept her awake these last couple of nights? The itch to go back and play this time. The constant calculations of how much she might walk away with. It wouldn't be a fortune. But it would be a start. Maybe even the five thousand Caro had talked about, to start Alex's pension fund. Maybe spare for a holiday, a last holiday with her dad and Alex, her mother. Nowhere fancy. Devon. Norfolk.

'Whose house are we talking about,' Marianne said, frowning.

'The casino, I suppose,' Caro said.

Marianne pursed her lips. 'The only house I know about, is mine back in Cyprus, gathering dust and getting dirty, because if there's one thing I do know the odds of, it's that my lazy son won't be lifting a finger to clean it. Any other houses,' she waved her hand, 'I don't want to know about. One is enough!'

Kay turned to her. 'So, it's safe to say you're not going to play?'

'No!' Marianne exclaimed. 'I didn't come all this way to play games! If I wanted to do that I could have gone into Kyrenia and joined all the old men, sucking their teeth and wasting their lives, playing backgammon!'

'Would you mind if I played with him?' Kay said, the question popping out like a pip. Easy. Simple. But goodness she wanted to play. More than anything, armed with this new memory, she wanted to try her hand and play!

Marianne shrugged. 'I want you to do whatever you want, Kay. This is your holiday.'

Beside them, Caro shifted her weight.

'What will you do?' Kay asked. 'It's a few hours, isn't it, before we leave for the ranch.'

Marianne lifted her chin. 'I think I'll go to the spa. I haven't been to one since the last century, so yes. I think I can easily go there now.'

'Caro?' Kay turned to Caro, whose face was such a mosaic of conflicting emotion that she was almost ready to crumble, and say, *Let's go for a coffee, let's go and talk, tell me what's going on.* And maybe would have, except Caro got in before her.

'Go and play, Kay.'

'Don't you want to talk?'

'*No.*' Caro shook her head, the word vibrating with a sadness that was untouchable. 'What I want,' she managed, 'like Marianne, is to see you having a good time. This is your trip.'

'But—'

'But nothing, Kay. I'll work it out with Helen.' Caro turned and looked across at the crowds of people queueing for tickets, at the crowds of people shopping, at the crowds, just crowding. 'Or I won't,' she added. 'Besides, I think I just want to find somewhere quiet. To think a while.'

Kay followed her gaze. 'I don't know where you're going to find that.'

'The spa,' Marianne said. She put a hand on Caro's arm. 'Come with me, Caro. Have a massage and pretend to be asleep and you can think all you want about this proposal. That's what you need the quiet for? Yes?'

Swallowing hard, Caro nodded. 'That, and other things.'

'You really don't know?' Kay said.

'I don't.'

'He's such a good man.'

'They all are,' Marianne sighed, 'in the beginning.'

'True.' Kay nodded. She turned to Marianne. 'Tony seems like a lot of fun.'

'He is fun,' Marianne said and looked at Kay sideways. 'But remember how I met him the first time? He was cheating on his wife. Of course I was too young and selfish back then to understand. But leopards don't change their stripes, Kay.'

'Spots,' Caro murmured.

'Yes, spots. Don't worry. I have my eyes wide awake.'

'Open,' Caro murmured again and this time smiled. 'Sorry.'

'Come to the spa,' Marianne nudged her. 'You need to relax. It's a good idea.'

'I will,' she said. 'I think so too.' She turned to Kay. 'And you go and play.'

17

_____

Finding her way to the games room proved as hard as Kay had imagined it to be, but once there she spotted Tony straight away and waved to him.

'Marianne said you wanted to play?' He smiled.

'Well...' she started, nervous all over again. And before she could finish, a man wearing a washed-out pink t-shirt that barely covered his stomach called to her. 'Come on in third base!'

Third base?

Tony waved her in to the table. 'That's the name of the player on the right of the dealer.'

'Ah.' Kay glanced at the other players. Besides the man in the t-shirt, there were two. Another man and a woman, both wearing the same inscrutable expression of extreme concentration. The chair on the right of the dealer was indeed empty.

'Or we can move to a lower limit table?' Tony said.

'What's this one?' Kay whispered.

'Twenty-five dollars.'

Twenty-five dollars! She nodded, her hand flipping the

catch of her handbag up and down, her eyes taking in the piles of chips by each player's hand. *Twenty-five dollars?* Twenty-five dollars on one hand meant the very real possibility of being a hundred dollars down in five minutes. Three minutes even. Twenty-five dollars was several hundred matchsticks out of her comfort zone. 'A lower-limit is a good idea,' she swallowed.

Tony slipped off his chair. 'The five-dollar table is nice and empty. I'll just colour up.'

'Colour up?'

He grinned. 'Watch.'

So she did. Focusing as he exchanged a large pile of red chips for a smaller pile of green. And a heap of green chips, for a few blacks. 'They get heavy,' he smiled.

'Black is a hundred dollars?'

'And red is five, and green, twenty-five.'

'Ok.' Over eight hundred dollars then, she'd counted going into his pocket. What did she have in her purse? Fifty in cash. Fifty in cash meant, ten hands. And suddenly she was as excited as a puppy let off its leash. Suddenly, ten hands of Blackjack seemed the most sensible and productive way of spending fifty dollars imaginable. Hadn't she just spent almost that amount to kiss a plastic George Clooney? And heaven knows how much stuffing herself with food that she could neither smell, nor barely taste. 'Let's play,' she said, her toes curling with excitement.

AT THE FIVE-DOLLAR TABLE, she took the seat to the immediate right of the dealer, while Tony had slipped to the bathroom. 'Third base,' she said to the woman next to her, as she sat down.

'Emma,' the woman replied. She was eighty if she was a

day, and almost bald. Through the pitiful scrap of hair she had left, she'd scraped a diamond hair slide into place. How it stayed, Kay had no idea.

'Joanne,' the woman opposite growled.

'Oh.' Kay looked from one to the other. 'I didn't mean, I'm called third base. I...'

But she was cut off by Emma waving a hand and letting out a laugh so croaky it sounded like a frog. 'Honey, we know. We're teasing.'

Kay smiled. Emma had her diamond hair slide and Joanne wore a sparkly jumper, bright red and covered in sequins. Kay glanced down at her own t-shirt. She felt hopelessly dull. Why wasn't she wearing her jacket? Nearly five thousand miles she'd travelled to finally make it to a real gaming table and play a real game. Next time, she thought, and her eyes widened in surprise. She was already thinking there would be a next time? 'I like your jumper,' she said to Joanne. 'I feel a bit underdressed, I'm new to all this.'

Joanne nodded. 'We're here every couple of months. Beats sitting at home in Miami, comparing dead husbands.'

'Oh.' Kay glanced at Emma, and back at Joanne. 'I'm sorry.'

'What for?' Joanne rasped.

'Your husbands. They're dead.'

'Not all of them.' Emma snorted. 'I've still got one above ground.'

'Me too.' Joanne shrugged. 'And I've had five. Three passed, one vanished and one drip-feeds. And you honey? How many do you have?'

'Husbands?' she stammered. 'Just the one. Ex.'

'Very sensible,' Emma squinted. 'Yes, you look like a sensible kind of gal.'

Kay smiled. Sensible? She might as well have it tattooed

on her forehead. So sensible, strangers could decide it within seconds. She felt something heavy turn over in her chest. She was sensible and she was dying, two words that shouldn't be in the same sentence and never would have been if she too had managed to work through five husbands.

'Ladies.' Tony returned, nodding as he slipped into a seat next to Joanne.

Joanne and Emma nodded back.

'Do you know them?' Kay whispered.

'They're regulars,' Tony whispered back. 'Are you ready to jump straight in? What's your strategy going to be?'

'Strategy?'

Tony smiled. 'You don't have one?'

Kay shook her head, all sorts of ideas competing for attention. Was now, for example, the time to confess that she had never done this before? That the most she'd ever staked was a pile of matchsticks? She wasn't like Emma and Joanne, in their glitter jumpers and diamond hair slides. She was sensible Kay, with one ex-husband and a Vegas jacket that had been worn to various suburban parties, a few upmarket dinners, but not once in the place it had been bought for. A destination so extraordinary in the life of an overweight, middle-aged maths teacher, that even when Caro had presented the tickets, when the plane had touched down, when they'd walked along the strip and mingled with the Elvis lookalikes, she still hadn't quite understood her dream. Yes, Vegas was fun, yes she had thoroughly enjoyed herself but (and for the first time ever she thought she was finally beginning to understand why she had never come, why she had never even tried)... *this* was the dream. Never mind everything else that Vegas had to offer, it was the chance to pit her skills against real players, at a real table in a real game, that she had unconsciously harboured, and equally unconsciously dismissed as being for other, more adventurous types. For those prepared to take a gamble, which she wasn't. And yet, finally, here she was! And it felt exactly the place she should be. And she wondered why she'd excluded herself all these years, come to such quick and restrictive conclusions about herself.

'Never split on a twenty,' Tony was saying.

Kay Burrell. That's who she was. Kay Burrell, with a first-class degree in mathematics, and a brain still as sharp as a shard. And she was also Kay Burrell, with stage four melanoma, so what exactly – her hand balled to a fist – yes, what did she have to lose? 'That would just turn a good hand into two mediocre hands,' she said as she turned to Tony.

His eyes opened.

'And when the dealer draws a six, it's good. He has to deal to seventeen, right?'

Tony nodded.

'So the next draw can only take him to sixteen, and then the odds of him drawing five or less aren't as good as him going bust?'

Tony's smile was slow but wide. 'I can see we're going have some fun,' he said.

'Hope so,' Kay said and smiled, a sea of prickling excitement running up and down her arms. She wasn't in the land of matchsticks now and she couldn't have been happier!

'Ok.' Tony dropped his voice, his face serious. 'But a couple of things you might not know. Hand signals are obligatory. Wave your right hand above the cards when you're sticking.' He mimed the movement. 'Tap the table with your finger for a hit.' He rolled his eyes to look up at the ceiling.

A Midlife Gamble

'Eye in the sky,' Emma drawled, 'needs those hand signals.'

'Got it,' Kay whispered. My goodness, she was excited, like she was ten years old and on the threshold of being initiated into a very cool and very secret club. And although her nerves hadn't completely vanished, she looked across the table at Joanne, and then back at nearly-bald Emma. If ever, she thought, a group of women were on borrowed time, it's us. And she opened her purse and took out her money.

Mathematician or not, she was an unmistakable novice at professional Blackjack, finding herself on the receiving end of reprimands from nearly everyone at the table. Placing her bets in the wrong position, touching her cards, even at one point forgetting those all-important hand signals. But it was all good natured.

'It's the five bucks table, honey,' Emma explained. 'Nobody gives a shit.'

Which seemed remarkable to Kay, because five dollars or not, the chips were stacking up. On her first hand she went bust. Five dollars down. On her second hand the dealer turned over a natural Blackjack. Ten dollars down. The third hand she was dealt two queens.

'Double down,' Tony whispered.

Kay separated her cards, took another chip and placed it on the second queen. She tapped the table, watching as the dealer turned over first a nine, and then a ten. Then feigning confidence, she waved her hand a little dramatically across her cards. Her heart picked up; her mouth pursed. Win or lose, she was ready to laugh. She was in for twenty dollars now. Ten on each hand. The dealer drew first a ten and then a four. The odds were in her favour. She bit down on her lip, her eyes on the dealers' hands. He turned over an eight. Twenty-two! BUST! She could almost hear her father's voice, see him gathering in his matchsticks.

Twenty dollars! Turning to Tony, Kay grinned and he was grinning too. He'd won as well with a much larger bet. But twenty dollars! The thrill was such that it could have been twenty hundred.

Within another ten minutes her bankroll had grown to eighty dollars. Another ten and she was nudging a hundred. Not that she had any idea of the time. She'd forgotten what time was. She'd forgotten the way Helen had stalked off and she'd forgotten Caro's strained expression. She even forgotten Caro's news. Her mind had narrowed down, focused itself on everything that she was innately comfortable with. Probabilities and advantages and the instinct to keep a track of those high value cards. *Statistical advantage, Kay.* Now she could hear her father's voice. It was so clear and she was so sure of the memory that if she could have called him, she would have. Interrupted his early evening television to ask. *Do you remember, dad?* But she couldn't, and so she just kept playing and she just kept winning. And somewhere she knew it wasn't down to pure luck.

After a while, Tony put his hands on the table and, pushing down, flexed his fingers. He looked across at her pile of chips and then back at his. 'What do you say we change tables?' he said.

Kay looked at her chips and then his. From her side view, she thought she saw Emma and Joanne exchange a glance.

'Go a little higher?' Tony shrugged. 'We seem to be lucky. You and I.'

She looked across the room, back to the table where she'd first found him. Twenty-five dollars a hand.

'I'll tell you what,' Tony said. 'We'll play two hands there. That's all. And if we lose both then you're only back to where you started. More or less.'

'That's true,' Kay murmured. If she lost both hands, she would only be five dollars down from where she'd begun, however long ago. And for the sheer enjoyment of the time she'd spent playing, she would have paid a lot more than five dollars. How much had it cost to go on the High Roller? Or take a gondola ride? It was, she decided, money well spent. And the relief of that conclusion had her pushing her stool back and standing up. Gambling with real money was a heck of a lot more exciting than gambling with match-sticks. 'Ok,' she said, as much to herself, as to Tony. 'Colour me up!' she said to the dealer.

Emma flicked her fingers in Kay's direction. 'Look at you,' she cackled. 'Got the lingo down pat.'

And now she laughed. She was in Vegas! Asking a dealer to colour her up! Playing cards at third base and winning! For the first time in a long, long time, she was winning at something! 'It was lovely meeting you ladies,' she said as she turned to go. 'Maybe see you again?'

'Oh sure,' Emma rasped. 'We're here pretty much all the time.'

'Almost as much as Tony,' Joanne muttered.

But Kay didn't hear. She was already onto higher stakes, where the winning continued.

One bad hand and then three winning hands in a row and she was looking at just short of two hundred and fifty dollars in chips, stacked up in front of her. Tony had kept on winning too. And together they were like a couple of naughty kids. She saw him glance down at his phone a couple of times and although she guessed it was Marianne, any feelings of guilt she might have had at keeping him at the table were easy to bury, spiralling away and thinning out like a smoker's exhale. This was her trip, she reasoned, her time, and she might never be here again.

For the third time since she'd started playing, she was dealt a matching pair. Again she split her bet and in a moment the like of which Kay had never experienced before, she took four green chips and placed two above each of her cards. Now she was in for a hundred dollars! So what! It was the most unrealistic hundred dollars that had ever passed through her hands. Hard plastic discs that could just as easily have belonged to the *Connect 4* she'd spent hours and hours playing with Alex when he was a child. She hadn't had it ten minutes ago, this hundred dollars, so it hardly seemed to matter if she would have it in another ten.

But she did. The chips came back to her double-fold, because the dealer dealt her a king and a seven and then dealt himself twenty-six. So now she was four hundred and fifty dollars up, from a fifty-dollar start. She stared at the little stack in front of her. Doubling up on the next hand, pushing another hundred in, she'd be looking at six hundred and...

And then Tony stood up and put his hand on her shoulder.

Startled, she looked at him.

'We're a good team, aren't we?'

'We are,' Kay laughed. Tony had won as well. An awful lot from what she could see, but he was betting larger amounts and she couldn't quite see, because he'd pushed his stack to the dealer.

'Remember what I said when you were watching a

couple of days ago? Quit while you're ahead, Kay. *Always.*'
And he nodded at her stack of chips.

'Of course, of course.' And although she didn't want to,
she knew he was right. She stood up, bubbles of excitement
forming. Four hundred and fifty dollars! She couldn't wait to
tell Alex. And Helen and Caro. She could buy a bottle of
champagne for Caro... If Caro was going to accept Shook's
proposal, she would buy champagne... And then she
remembered... She looked down at her chips, and juggled
them from one hand to the other. Helen would need to
come back from wherever it was she'd gone. And even then,
if she bought the champagne, what would they all do?
Drink it in silence?

'FIVE HUNDRED DOLLARS!' Kay said again, her face animated.

Helen smiled as she turned to look out of the window.
There wasn't much about the way they were travelling to
Tony's ranch that felt cowboy-like to her, but she didn't
mind. The windows of the SUV were tinted, the seats a
polished leather and the air, thank goodness, deliciously
cool. She was far enough away from Caro, who sat the other
side of Kay, for the rope of tension between them to have
taken slack. Much of which had to do with Kay's win. Five
hundred dollars was a lovely amount. Helen's heart swelled.
Kay was delighted, and in return, Helen was delighted for
her. And the timing couldn't have been better. Like a table-
cloth shaken in the air, Kay's good fortune had swept away
the crumbs of tension from earlier, her buoyancy infectious.
It was, in fact, keeping the day afloat. So much so that Helen
had been able to pass off her earlier behaviour with the
excuse of a headache, the sudden need to get some fresh air
and stretch her legs after the stuffy close-up experience of

Tussauds. It hadn't even mattered that no one except Tony had believed her. The excuse was sufficient in itself. Like a ladder thrown across a crevasse, it was the only way to keep going on a path none of them could turn back from. Everyone had grabbed it. Turning back, she patted Kay's knee. 'Don't get addicted now.'

'Oh,' Kay laughed. 'I don't think so.'

'Good. Dinner's on you then!'

Through the rear-view mirror, Tony looked back at them. 'Not tonight. Tonight Lula is cooking up steak and baked potato, BBQ beans and homemade coleslaw.'

And despite everything, Helen's stomach gave a low growl. When was she going to stop eating?

'Lula?' Marianne asked.

'The housekeeper,' Tony answered.

'He must be absolutely loaded,' Helen whispered.

Kay nodded. 'And he just won a lot more than I did.'

Helen nodded, lifting her chin as she looked at the back of Tony's head. Her eyes slid across to Marianne, sitting up front beside him. She wasn't sure if she was amused by this unlikely relationship, or envious of it. Unable to decide and unwilling to give it a moment's more thought, she leaned her head against the window and closed her eyes. A respite from the overload of Vegas was exactly what she needed. Rushing out like that, into the heat of the sidewalk, the sounds and the smells and the constant movement of people, she'd felt disorientated, her senses muffled, as if the city itself were underwater and the real world out of reach. She was looking forward to getting to the ranch. *It's complicated,* Caro had said. At which point, Helen had felt as if she had two stark choices. Stay and confront Caro. Or leave. But, weakened as she had been by the threat of confrontation with Caro, Vegas had engulfed her. Other people's elbows nudging, other people's hair touching, their smell, their voices. And there had been nowhere to retreat to.

She'd crossed the boulevard to find herself in the entrance of an indoor shopping centre, a tall area, flooded with natural light and brimming with greenery, where vines climbed twenty feet upward and lavish hibiscus flowers grew in abundance. An unexpected oasis that had allowed her the respite to sit, and breathe, to study closely the tiny browned edge of the hibiscus flower close to her hand.

Except a cleaning lady had arrived, taken out a can of industrial cleaner and set about polishing the flowers one by one. And when, confused, Helen had stretched her hand out to the soil, the surface she had met with had been cold and hard. Cement. Coloured brown to look like soil. As fake as everything else.

Tony's chatter weaved in between her thoughts like a tap left dripping. Her eyes were heavy, but she dragged them open and looked at the back of his head again. He talked without pause, and it was clear to Helen that no one was expected to join what was obviously a soliloquy. On he went, something about the tedium of location work, a snippet of *Knots Landing,* which had her vaguely interested. Across the scrubby wasteland that was the outskirts of Vegas, she saw a man exercising a dog and the sight was odd to Helen; until she realised that in the time they had been in Vegas, she hadn't seen a real person doing a real thing. No one taking the trash out, no one walking dogs, no one sitting on public benches passing the time of day. There were no public benches. Vegas, with its perfect artificial flowers and its cleanly swept pavements, was a mirage. And real life, by contrast, felt to Helen hopelessly messy and imperfect. That was the last thought she had. Unable to resist the weariness of her mind, her eyes slipped closed and by the time the SUV had left the city perimeters, she was asleep.

SHE WAS WOKEN by a dragging sensation. The feeling of rising very slowly to the surface of dark water. Opening her eyes, she realised they had slowed to turn off the highway. The road ahead was unpaved and sure enough, the SUV began to bump and jolt. Helen sat up, tugging her t-shirt smooth over her belly. This at least was a little more cowboy like. She pressed her forehead to the window. Outside, plains of orange stretched away to the Spring Mountain range, but the glass she was looking through was tinted and it wasn't until the SUV had turned through an arched gateway into the ranch proper... It wasn't until she opened the door and stepped out, that the true measure of the landscape they were now in became clear.

Everywhere was desert. A lunar-scape of pink and orange and deep rusty reds, pitted all over with boulders and rocks. Some the size of houses, others small enough to hold. Above, a great dome of blue sky arched on and on, parallel wisps of cirrus clouds stretching like a celestial highway thousands of feet above the snow-capped peak of Mount Charleston.

She felt the brush of air on her arms, temperate and warm, and the infinite variety of movement of fresh air. In Vegas, she realised now, even the air was regulated. Outside, it was hemmed in by buildings and left to simmer. Inside, it was artificially cold. But here it was free, carrying with it the dust of the land it had crossed. She could feel it, settling already amongst the fine hairs of her arms, could see it, in the way the Joshua and sagebrush moved. She did a full turn, three hundred and sixty degrees: mountains, sky, desert. Sky, desert, mountains. Behind, the low rustic spread of the ranch and a dog... Another real dog, raising his head to watch them. Wind and space. She breathed in. The ringing in her ears from the thousands of slots had ceased. She could hear the silence. And it was wonderful!

'Oh the light!' Kay too had stepped out of the SUV and now Caro, and Marianne, and for a moment they stood, hands raised to foreheads squinting behind sunglasses. Because yes, the light was extraordinary. Like God had determined this part of the world be forever rose-tinted. It was fresh and soft and it felt to Helen as if she'd been dipped in sunrise.

'And all this is yours?' Marianne said as she turned to look at the ranch.

Tony beamed. 'Welcome, ladies,' he said, 'to Hidden Valley Ranch. 'Mi casa ar su casa.'

18

A somewhat hurried ten-minute tour of the ranch later, Caro, Marianne and Kay stood with chins leaned against the rough-hewn fence of a large corralled area, the same expression of stunned disbelief on their faces. On the other side, tied to a long hitching rail, several horses waited, tails twitching, feet shuffling. Alongside the horses, Helen also waited, listening to the instructions of Gabe, the ranch-hand Tony had just introduced them to.

Glancing sideways first at Marianne, and then at Kay, Caro guessed they were thinking exactly what she was thinking. *When*, and *by whom*, were horses mentioned?

'We have them for all abilities,' Tony had said just a moment ago, obviously sensing the reluctance emanating from this side of the fence.

To which Marianne had replied archly, 'But do you have them for all sizes?'

Remembering this brief exchange, Caro smiled. She slid her hands between her chin and the warm wood. There had been an unmistakable hint of annoyance in Marianne's voice. That of a woman shown a carnation and told it was a rose. She understood why. *No one* had said *anything* about horses. Not when the ranch was first mentioned, nor on the journey down. Tony had sold them a lazy afternoon walking around the ranch, followed by a campfire barbecue. But horses? It was clear from the expression on Marianne's face, they weren't her thing. They weren't Caro's either, or Kay's. In fact, the only one who had been anywhere near enthusiastic was Helen. Just like Tussauds, she'd jumped in, had already been assigned her horse and was now leaning close into its neck, her hand on its flank. Looking, Caro thought, as if she'd spent half her life in a corral full of these giant creatures. She watched now as Helen put her foot in the stirrup and, with help from Gabe, was eased over the horse's back. She didn't know what was surprising her most, Helen's physical courage or the fact that Tony, whom she'd come to such unflattering conclusions about, owned this magnificent place.

'Well done, Helen,' Kay called.

Caro nodded. 'Yes, well done.' At this rate Helen would be halfway to the Pacific, before anyone else was in the saddle. She was, it was very clear, intent upon maintaining a distance and, right now, Caro didn't want to think about that. There was something else that she needed to think about first. That needed solving, and if only she could get a little space and time, she would. The spa had meant to offer her that, but her masseuse had talked non-stop, asking question after question about London, without pausing to listen to a single answer. People like that amazed Caro, the kind who went through life blithely unaware of what a conversation was supposed to consist of. There hadn't been a moment's peace and she was thinking now about the swing chair on the porch of the ranch. She'd seen it when they had first arrived, and immediately considered that it would be the perfect place, the perfect opportunity, for her to sit and think this proposal from Shook through logically. All the pros... all the cons... Plus, she could feel the heat of the desert sun on her head. Her hair was thinning, another hour exposed like this and her scalp would burn. She needed shade and she needed space. Easing back from the fence, she got ready to excuse herself.

'Marianne!' Tony cried, all teeth and arms as he walked towards them. 'You'll be fine. You're a doll. You should see the size of some of the folks these guys take.'

'A doll,' Marianne said archly, 'who has just had a very expensive manicure.' She stretched her hand forward to show five polished nails, deep maroon, with a white sequin glued on each.

'That looks divine.' Tony winked. His dusty Stetson shadowed his face as he took Marianne's hand and kissed it.

Moving aside, Caro pulled her sunglasses down. Ranch or not, Tony's enthusiasm was too oily for her. Still, he wasn't her problem. She opened her mouth to speak.

'I don't want to get dirty,' Marianne said bluntly. 'You know how much this cost?' She waved her hand. 'What if I fall off? What if they break? Seventy dollars of nail, lost in horse-shit. No thank you!'

At this, Kay laughed, and Caro too smiled as she pretended to look away. The more time she spent with Marianne, the more she liked her.

'Marianne?' Tony pleaded.

'No.' Marianne stood her ground.

He turned to Kay, but she too was shaking her head. 'I think I've pushed my luck far enough today. Quit when you're winning, you said?'

Tony put his hands on his hips. 'I did indeed. Well

ladies, make yourself at home while we're gone.' He turned to Caro... who made to scuttle. But there was nowhere to scuttle to. This desert had no corners. One moment, she'd been in the process of a subtly planned retreat, and now... Now she wasn't.

'So Miss Caro, come and choose your horse.'

And because she didn't know what else to do, because she was stalling for time, she eased her sunglasses off her head and rubbed them on a corner of her shirt. When, finally, she looked up, Kay was looking right at her.

'You don't have to stay with me. I'll be fine.'

'Oh I wasn't... That's not what...'

'Marianne's here. We'll just take a seat on the porch and wait there.'

Wistfully Caro glanced across at the swing chair, the quiet spot she'd intended to claim, the space in which she needed to make perhaps the most important decision of her life. Half of her wanted to explain this, point by point, make her case. The other half was already resigning herself to the inevitable. She folded the arms of her sunglasses together. And then there was another consideration, which there could be no denying, Kay, she was sure, would rather have Marianne's company. This place was so peaceful. Why would Kay want it tainted with the fall out of tensions from earlier?

'Don't you want to try?' Kay asked now.

'It's not that.' Caro turned to look back at the horses. It was entirely that. She didn't want to try. She was scared.

Gabe was still talking to Helen. 'Keep the ball of your foot on the stirrup,' she heard him say. 'That's important. Without a heel you got nothing to stop your foot getting caught.' And to emphasise his point, he jiggled the stirrup.

'If your horse decides it's gonna run, and your foot is caught, you're in trouble.'

Caro stretched her foot forward. 'I don't really have the right shoes,' she said, as she looked at her sneaker.

'Neither does Helen,' Kay answered.

'Noo...' She turned her sunglasses over in her hand. 'But Helen's done this before, Kay. She had riding lessons as a child.'

Kay tipped her head back and laughed. 'Forty years ago, Caro.'

Pressing her lips tightly together, Caro didn't answer.

'Are you scared?'

'Yes,' she said, then, 'you know Helen, she's always been braver.'

'I wouldn't say that.'

'About things like this, I mean. Sailing and...'

'Bravery,' Kay smiled, 'comes in different forms.'

Unintentionally Caro glanced down at Kay's puckered scar, the tail end of which was visible from the neck of her t-shirt. A feeling of shame arose. Courage? What kind of courage did it take to live under the threat of death? Turning back to watch Helen, a thought struck her. The years of her life in which not much happened were gone. Those times when ten or twenty years might pass, with nothing more dramatic than a change of address. When her parents still lived and the shape of her own future was still malleable. She put her sunglasses back on and turned to watch the horses, shuffling dust, flicking their tails. In the space of twelve months, she'd been pregnant and had a miscarriage that had ended any chance of her becoming a mother. She'd become an orphan, quit her job, and miraculously stumbled upon a new relationship, unlike any other she'd ever been in. She'd been proposed to. For the first time in her life, she had been proposed to! And her best friend was dying, and her other best friend was retreating, irreversibly as a glacier. What on earth would it matter if she got on a horse or not? And if she didn't do it now, when would she ever get the chance again? Probably never, and this she knew because if there was one thing this last year had taught her, it was that chances are finite and the last one rarely bothers to make itself known.

'I think it would be good for you,' Kay said softly.

Caro nodded. From the beginning, the very beginning when they were gauche eighteen-year-olds, Kay had always seemed to know what was going on in her head. Blinking back a tear, she nodded again. What on earth was she going to do without her?

BUT JUST GETTING in the saddle was such a finely choreographed dance, fraught with so much danger and so many rules, that if she could have pressed abort, she would have. Last chance be damned.

Gabe called instructions. *Approach from the left side. Come in at the shoulder. Hold the reins in the left, keep them loose. Check your girth.*

What did that mean? She had no idea.

Don't kick the horse as you swing your leg over.

Why would she do that? Panicked, her mind shifted a gear, throwing up image after image of the horse bolting, her foot catching, her body dragging. To calm herself, she concentrated on its quivering warm flank and tried to ignore the wild white of its eye, all the time acutely aware that on the other side of the corral, Helen was already astride her horse.

'Foot in the stirrup, Caro!' Tony grinned.

But when she lifted her foot, her supporting leg went to jelly. Knees shaking, she clutched at the reins.

'Atta girl,' Tony said. 'Now press down.'

'Press down? What do you m—'

But Tony's hands were on her bottom, hefting her up like a sack of potatoes, so now she was rising... up... up... and it was all too late.

'Swing your leg! Keep a hold of the reins!'

And what could she do? She was well past the point of no return. Setting her jaw in grim determination, she swung her leg over the bridge of the horse's spine and landed with all the finesse of a wet towel, plumb in the saddle. She had a moment to cherish the relief of finding herself on the horse, rather than in a heap on its other side, before the animal snorted and began a jolting shuffle sideways. Caro froze. It was one thing to know in theory that this was a live animal, quite another to experience how powerless she felt now, sitting atop. The ground was suddenly a long way down, and the realisation that she had ceded control to such a huge and powerful creature filled her veins with ice. She was terrified. If she could have slipped off, she would have done so. But this wasn't a fairground carousel. What if she got it wrong? Got her foot stuck in the stirrup, angered the horse and... Panicked, she looked around for help. Someone needed to tell her what to do, and how to do it. *Now.* Things had to be learned, spelt out, planned, but Tony had moved away and up ahead Helen's horse was walking slowly out of the paddock, tail flicking, Helen astride, looking as comfortable as if she'd been born on it.

Where the hell had Tony disappeared to? Caro twisted in the saddle and as she did, she jerked the reins. Her horse let out a shrill whinny, tossing its head in an alarmingly violent manner. 'Woah!' she called, jerking the reins again, at which her horse stumbled back, lifting its feet, head rearing. Her eyes filled with hot terrified tears. She had no idea what to do. This was chaos. She'd ceded control and the result was as alarming and chaotic as she'd feared. *Help me,* she whispered. *Help me.*

'Ok... ok.' From nowhere, a man's hand appeared at her left side, pulling the reins slack. It was Gabe. 'Gentle,' he said. 'Go gentle.' As he slackened the reins, her horse settled.

'I don't think I can do this,' Caro blurted. 'Really... I don't think this is for me, it's...'

'Do you want to dismount?'

Caro opened her mouth, but nothing came out. Yes she wanted to dismount, more than anything she wanted to dismount, but even more than that she did not want to fail.

Gabe moved in close to her horse, resting his palm on its neck. 'His name is Jangles,' he said. 'And he's a career trail horse. A little taller than average, but he knows what to do.'

'I'm glad one of us does.' Caro laughed, trying and failing to hide the abject terror she felt.

Gabe looked at her. 'You have to trust your horse,' he said. 'Once you're in the position you're in now, you don't really have a choice.'

Trust? *You can trust me,* Shook had said. Those had been his exact words. She wiped her palm on her jeans, where it left a dark mark.

'I'll walk you around a little,' Gabe said, 'until you're comfortable with each other.' His voice was low and calm as he talked, not to Caro but to Jangles, leading the horse back a few steps and then beginning a wide lazy circle of the corral. Jangles snorted but offered no resistance.

Gabe looked up at Caro. 'Best thing you can do is relax.

Don't fight your horse. He's your partner and you gotta learn to let him lead.'

Caro's smile was tight as she nodded. Jangles was a horse, not a partner. And she'd never allowed anyone to lead, ever.

'Horses,' Gabe continued, 'respond to pressure and release. Pressure from the side, here...' and he patted Jangle's flank, 'will tell him to go forward. Pressure on the bit, will tell him to slow down. He's smart. He'll listen. And when you release that pressure you're telling him he did the right thing.'

Again she nodded.

'So relax.'

'I am.'

Gabe looked at her. 'If you say so,' he smiled and turned to lead Jangles on.

In the saddle, Caro swayed. *Relax*, she chanted, *relax, relax, relax.* It was exactly as Gabe had said. She didn't have a choice. *Relax*, she murmured again, giving her shoulders a little shake, *go with it, go with it.* And without being wholly aware that it was happening, every step that Jangles made had the knots of terror and resistance Caro had tied herself in unravelling. The rhythm was hypnotic. And when Jangles came to a halt and the swaying stopped, Caro looked up, surprised to see that they had left the corral and were now on the trail path.

'How you doing up there?' Gabe said, still walking alongside.

'Fine.'

'Want to try a little stop and go commands?'

'Ok. So... pressure here?' She squeezed her knees and Jangles began a slow trot.

'And let's stop,' Gabe called.

Gently Caro pulled back on the bit. Jangles came to a stop.

'See, it's all about trust, Caro. You're doing great.' Gabe put his hands on his hips. 'For the duration of this ride, remember, Jangles is your partner and partners look out for each other. So pay attention to how he's feeling. If he's tense, or side-stepping, or jumpy. He may have a trigger nearby. Keep an eye out for safety risks, that's your job. Low hanging branches and stuff. Jangles knows what he's doing, but he's tall and he's heavy and he's shit scared of plastic bags skittling outta nowhere.'

'Oh.' Caro blinked. She looked down at her horse and the thought of this massive and powerful animal being terrified of a piece of plastic filled her with compassion. She leaned forward and stroked Jangle's flank. 'Don't worry,' she whispered. 'I'm taller than average and I'm a career kind of person as well. I'll trust you if you trust me. And I promise I'll keep you safe from those plastic bags.'

19

s the last swirls of red-grey dust thinned, and the shuffling sound of the horses' hooves fell quiet, Marianne turned to Kay.

'I hope they don't kill each other.'

'Caro and Helen?' Kay tried to laugh it off, but it wasn't convincing. 'Oh, they'll be alright.'

'Will they?' Marianne said, tapping her fingertips against the rough wood of the corral. As she did, the sequin from her middle finger dropped off, falling into the dirt. 'Hassiktir!' she muttered, and squatted to pick it up. 'Now what do I do?' she wailed. 'Seventy dollars!'

'If you lick it, it might stick again,' Kay suggested.

'With what? My tongue?'

Kay shrugged.

Marianne shuddered. Closing her eyes, she stuck her tongue out and gave the absconding sequin the briefest, cat-like lick, before pressing it into place. 'I knew they were impractical! I told the girl this would happen, but she insisted.'

Kay shook her head, trying not to laugh.

'So!' Marianne said, one fingertip still pressing down. 'What is going on with them? I thought they were supposed to be friends.'

'They are... Or they were. I told you what happened last year.'

'You told me, yes.'

'It was an awful evening, Marianne.' Kay sighed. 'Helen had every right to be angry.' She turned to look away at the small rise over which the riders had disappeared. 'But I really thought we... I thought *they* had managed to put it behind them.'

Marianne nodded. She released the sequin, satisfied herself that it was safe and then stood, watching the same space that Kay watched.

'Shall we sit?' Kay said. She felt weary. Helen and Caro's absence was proving heavier than their presence, allowing as it did time for her to make an inventory of the tensions between them. From the stiff politeness of their exchanges, to the way Helen always positioned herself as far away as possible from Caro, to the avoidance of eye contact. The events of last year had left the terrain between them as treacherous as a minefield. Their friendship was now a place where all of them, herself included, were on guard, acutely aware of how damaging one false step could be. Experience whispered to her that, in time, it would be ok. That eventually everything softened, everything melded. It's just that if there was one thing she had precious little reserve of, it was time. The situation saddened and deflated her. She had no answers and expected no resolutions.

'Sitting is a good idea,' Marianne said quietly. 'The porch?'

'The porch, yes.'

They walked across the yard, the warm earthy smell of

horse lingering in the air. Kay breathed it in greedily. It felt real, exactly what she needed. She climbed the rough-hewn steps to the porch and sat down on a swing seat covered in a fabric that was worn and sun-faded, but still intact. Marianne sat beside her, and in silent harmony, they pushed back on their heels. The seat swung forward and then back, forward and back, forward and back.

A wagon wheel hanging from the far end of the roof caught the sun, splintering it into golden segments that had Kay squinting as she shielded her eyes. Rusty nails held rusty horseshoes to an upright post, and a butterfly, wings tipped the yellow of Inca gold, settled itself on the porch rail. Kay watched as it stretched out paper-thin wings, its clubbed antennae so fragile and so alert. She lifted her chin to the sun. Miles away on the horizon a lone cloud sailed across the sky, a breeze as warm as blood passed across her face and an irresistible surrender overwhelmed her soul. Her body responded accordingly; tears spilling down her cheeks. 'What am I going to do,' she whispered and felt the warmth of Marianne's hand cover her own. 'What am I going to do?'

'You're going to sit,' Marianne answered.

'They're both godmothers to Alex,' Kay whispered. 'How can I rely on them when... when the time comes.'

Staring out at the desert, Marianne was silent.

'Alex's father, Martin, he's around but...' Kay sighed. 'He has this new partner, and a new family. He's not good at multi-tasking. Let alone multi-relationship-ing.'

'Of course.'

'And I always thought... I thought, if anything happened to me, at least Alex would have his godmothers. I didn't have sisters. Or brothers. But if they're not even talking to each other, how is that going to work?'

Marianne's silent nodding of the head turned into a silent shaking.

'I know,' Kay continued, 'they're only doing it because of me. This trip. The whole trying to get along.' She glanced sideways at Marianne, and then fell back, her head tipped to the sky.

'You know what I'm going to do?' Marianne said after a long silence.

Kay looked at her.

'I'm going to get us some coffee. Tony said to ask the housekeeper if there was anything we needed, and I think we need a cup of coffee.' She stood up and as she did, she gave Kay's hand a firm pat. 'Also, I've never had a housekeeper to ask before. Do you want coffee?'

'I do,' Kay smiled. 'Yes. I do.' She turned her head to the desert, then just as Marianne had opened the ranch door, said, 'He's very nice, isn't he? Tony?'

Marianne smiled. 'He is.'

'Do you...' Kay paused. 'Do you ever wonder what might have happened if—'

'If?'

'You know. If he hadn't been married all those years ago?'

'No.'

'No?' Marianne's response had been so swift, it had Kay turning to her in surprise.

'No,' Marianne said again and shook her head. 'The fortunate thing about me, Kay, is that I was raised in religion.' She shrugged. 'We have fatalism running through our veins, like you have blood. So... what happened then, is, I have always thought, what was meant to happen. I'm too old to start thinking another way now, and anyway sometimes it makes life easier.'

'Do you think so?'

'For me. I'm only talking about me.'

And for a long moment they looked at each other.

'Coffee then?' Marianne said.

'Yes please.'

A FEW MINUTES later Marianne was back, holding out an enamel mug filled with steaming milky coffee.

'Just like real cowboys,' Kay said, as she took the mug. 'Aren't you having one?'

'I am. But I'm also having an interesting talk with Lula. Very interesting actually.' Marianne paused, looked at Kay as if she was about to say something and then with a slight shake of the head and a smile that Kay saw took some effort said, 'Do you mind if I go back and finish it? I thought you might want to sit for a while.'

'Take your time,' Kay said. 'I'm fine. It's so peaceful here, I'm really fine.'

As Marianne went back inside, Kay shifted her weight, easing off her sneakers and stretching her legs along the cushions of the swing chair, so she faced the desert. Her hands, cupped around her mug, rested on her stomach, her head leaning back against the frame. Yes, this was fine. To sit and swing, to gaze out at the mountains and the desert, to watch for John Wayne kicking clouds of dust on the horizon, was all she wanted to do. She brought her hand to her eyes. Way up against the perfect blue of the sky, the dark shape of a bird made long fluid loops, and across the yard, a shirt, hanging from a makeshift washing line, moved in the breeze. Silence, sacred as a church, brushed against her elbow and lapped at her toes and Kay felt as if she were looking at a painting, an immortal landscape, that, if only for this moment, she was a part of. Relief touched her. She felt it as a hand on her shoulders, a cool palm against her brow, a whisper of permission so persuasive that, hand trembling, she only just managed to get her coffee onto the porch before the tsunami struck. The violence of a grief she had managed to hold back since the first minute, of the first hour, of that very first day when her doctor had asked her to sit, with such a gravity of tone it had turned her legs to water. Because not once had she given it house room. Not like this. Not through all the months and weeks that had followed, in the company of her family, in the company of fellow patients, with professionals or strangers, not even at home, had she found a space safe enough to let it out, a space large enough to accommodate. But this place... Fist at her heart and mucus stuffing her airways, making every breath a struggle, Kay lifted her chin, her eyes taking in the expanse of the horizon from north to south, over every ridge and peak of the distant mountains. This place she knew could bear the weight of her damaged heart. This desert would swallow her tears. Here she was safe and she could cry forever and for everyone. For herself, and all the things she wouldn't now do. For Alex, and all the children of the world left motherless too soon. For parents who outlived their babies, for last times that she hadn't understood were last times, for the easy joy of youthful friendship... All of this, plus an infinity of human woes and still, it wouldn't make the slightest difference. Her tears wouldn't leave a mark. Here, it was easy and comforting to begin to under-stand the pitiful insignificance of a human life. Against those mountains formed millennia ago, in amongst this dry red soil which was once blue sea, she was tiny and she was nothing and even if she lived to be a hundred, she would still have been tiny, and she would still have been nothing.

The absolute truth of this covered Kay like cool mist. It opened her pores and expanded her lungs so all at once, within the armour of worry and sadness that had locked her in from the beginning, there was suddenly more room to breathe than there had ever been. She tipped her head back, spread her hand wide on her chest and breathed in, really breathed in, Marianne's words ringing in her ears. *What happened, is what was meant to happen.*

Something that could only be described as a consolation had her sitting up and blotting her eyes. Every last living thing, she was thinking, as if the idea were entirely new, is temporal. Set against the sublime and ancient lines of the earth before her, every living thing was nothing but a blip, and as she thought this, she also thought it was wrong. Very wrong.

She reached down for the coffee, lifted the mug to her lips and sipped. And this time she really did think she could smell it. A smoky, nutty smell that she filled her lungs with, and held, as the kernel at the heart of her thoughts revealed itself. Love was not a blip. Love, and only love, continues, handed down, generation after generation. How else to explain the fact that although her mother's presence on this earth was more fragile by the day, the love Kay had for her was as vibrantly alive as that golden-winged butterfly. It informed the way she lived her own life, showing itself in inherited mannerisms and nuances of voice. For as long as she lived, her mother would. As she thought this, she sat very still and the world hushed and time, accommodating her, stood still, opening up a vista wide enough for her finally to understand that she wasn't leaving Alex. She never would leave Alex. Because just like her mother before her, she'd planted her love inside him, deep enough, nourished and cared for it long enough that it wouldn't die with her, and she knew this now like she knew the sun in the sky above. As long as Alex lived, she would remain with him. 'Thank you,' she whispered, to the desert and the mountains and the red red soil, and forever after would remain convinced that she had been answered, that the sagebrush had lifted its leaves and kissed a whispered response across the earth.

20

'It started out quite flat, so that was fine,' Caro said, excitement rushing her words. 'And I remember crossing this river bed and actually thinking how calm I was. I mean there were boulders, but they weren't worrying me, which was amazing given the state I was in before we left. I don't know if you saw...' She turned to Kay. 'I was terrified to be honest, but by the time we had gotten to this part, I knew Jangles would manage, and then... Then we stopped at this outcrop to take in the view, and it was just breath taking. Absolutely breath taking!' Smiling with the memory, Caro leaned forward and poked at the fire with a long stick, two spots of happy-pink glowing on each cheek, a million stars glowing in the sky above. 'Didn't you think, Helen?'

Glancing up, Helen gave a short non-committal move-ment of the head that might have been a nod of agreement. She was sitting on a fold-out chair, on the other side of the campfire from Kay and Caro, thinking about the stars above and what it would be like to fulfil that long-held dream of sleeping under them. The attempt at a nod was the best she could do. She wasn't even sure what Caro had just said, because she was trying not to listen. The fresh air out on the trail had swept her mind clean and the rhythmic sway of her horse had been a soothing balm. So much so that it was hard for her to remember a time when she had experienced such profound peace of mind. In her garden on a sunny afternoon dead-heading roses, or trimming back clematis? That was peaceful. Pushing Ben in his pram, just as it had been when Libby and Jack were tiny, was peaceful, but wasn't there so much more to experience? Other trails to meander along? All this had absorbed her, keeping the rumble of overheard conversation at bay, allowing her to concentrate on what life might look like if she ever got beyond a divorce that at times seemed as unreachable as the stars above. If she ever left a job that required nothing more than treading water. Because if this trip had shown her anything, it was just how closed down and walled in her life still was.

'What struck me, was the silence!' Caro's enthusiastic voice dropped into her thoughts like a stone in water. She was still standing, holding the stick upright in one hand, her glass of wine in the other. 'Sooo peaceful,' she said. 'I wish you had come, Kay.'

'I'm glad I didn't.'

'Really?'

Kay smiled. 'I needed a little space, Caro.' Turning to wave her arm at the expanse of black desert that encircled them, she added. 'It's quite easy to find that here.'

And this time, Helen's nod of agreement was real. Looking up, she watched as Kay pulled the blanket that covered her knees higher up her lap. In the melée of emotion she'd been operating under, she had, on occasion, forgotten about Kay. And that was unforgivable. 'Are you ok?' she asked. 'Are you warm enough?'

'I'm fine,' Kay said. 'How could I not be? This place is magnificent.'

'It is, isn't it!' Caro said. She threw her arms out and tipped her head back and turned to the desert. 'And the stars! Just look at them!' Above, in a clear black sky, infinite galaxies encompassed the night. Silver pin after silver pin, clustered together in milky wisps, or scattered singly like a string of broken pearls. 'It's just astonishing,' she said, 'how it takes so long for the light to reach us. Some of these stars are already dead, but there they are! Shining away like that. Isn't that sad?' And shaking her head, she turned back to the campfire and sat down, her eyes bright, her face glowing. 'Anyway, by the time we were on the way back, I think I knew.'

'Knew what?' Kay let her head drop to one side as she smiled. 'What are we talking about?'

Helen didn't say anything.

Caro sat back on her stool. Her back was upright, the stick and the wine glass clasped between both hands. 'Sometimes,' she said, 'it's just so obvious that things happen for a reason. You needed to stay, Kay. And I needed to go. I was meant to go on that ride. I did it, you see!'

'Did what?' Kay laughed. 'Honestly, Caro, you look like the cat who got the cream.'

'I let go,' Caro answered.

'Let go of what?'

'*Control!* Gabe didn't know it, but when he called Jangles a career trail-horse, he put my mind at rest. It just made sense to me. I mean there I was, a career woman, on a career horse. He's terrified of plastic bags; I was terrified of him! And who could honestly say which one of us was being irrational?' She lifted the stick and pointed it at Kay. 'Don't answer that.' She laughed. 'It doesn't matter. What matters is that it started me thinking. I mean, the first time Jangles left the trail and headed towards a tree, I panicked. I was an absolute bag of nerves, but thankfully, Gabe was behind me and he said Jangles was doing that—'

'Because the ground is less stony there,' Helen said, her voice flat. She kept her chin lowered as she looked across the flames toward Caro. 'It's less painful on their feet.'

'Exactly! Anyway...' Caro leaned forward, picked up the half-empty bottle by her feet and topped her glass up.

And something in the flourish of the wave from the stick she held sent a warning signal to Helen. She rubbed her foot back and forth in the dust, concentrated on burying a few glowing embers with her sneaker. Caro, she sensed, was building up to saying something of importance. Something significant. She could tell from the increasingly excited tone of her voice, the fluttery movements of her arms, the confidence she obviously needed from the wine. Well, whatever it was that Caro was getting excited about, Helen did not want to hear.

'And then when we reached the plain, on the way back, Gabe said, I should go faster, let Jangles stretch his legs. I won't deny it, that *really* scared me, but I think it was then that I decided. I remember quite clearly making the decision in my head. *I'm going to release the reins and let go!* It was quite an epiphany.'

'An epiphany?'

Caro turned, stick upright. 'Yes, Kay. For me, an epiphany. I don't think that's too strong a word. And, I honestly think, in that moment, I've never trusted anyone quite like I trusted Jangles. I put my life in his hands... well hooves. I really did.'

'Trust?' Helen said, her tongue thick with the weight of the word.

'Yes!' Caro put her hand on her chest, the stick angled now across her face. 'I know it might sound silly. And I think it's ironic that it's taken me coming all the way out here to experience what it's like to relinquish the reins.' She laughed. 'I know why they say that now! Fifty-one and I've finally let go of the reins! But you both know me. I hate not to be in control, not knowing what's going to happen next. Trusting a horse? Well, trusting anyone hasn't been easy.'

Helen looked down at her glass. The way Caro held the stick, it cut her face in two. Divided it into the two faces of Caro. On one side a friend of thirty years, on the other a person who would deceive anyone and everyone to get what she wanted. She stared at her wine and tried desperately to take herself out of the moment. To remember the warmth of her own horse's neck as she'd leaned in during the ride. The skin soft as it was tough, tiny wiry hairs that moved under her palm like ocean waves. The warm and earthy smell that was a childhood smell, producing memories of Saturday mornings, when her mother was alive. Before she grew up and did grown-up things, got married, had children of her own, forged grown-up friendships that were so much more complicated than childhood friendships. Before anything got complicated. *Trust?* If she said any of what she was actually thinking on the subject of trust, it could never be unsaid. It would mean, quite simply, the destruction of everything.

'So anyway,' Caro continued, blithely unaware. 'As you both know, Shook has asked me to marry him.'

Kay nodded.

'And, I've been thinking about it a lot. The trail ride

really gave me time. And...' Caro paused. Lowering her glass to the ground, she rolled the stick along her jeans. 'Helen?'

Helen looked up. A strange vibration starting in her ears. Was Caro going to bring it all up?

'Do you remember what I said that day at Stonehenge?'

Her eyes flicked across to Kay. 'No,' she answered carefully. She was thinking about Kay, and about how all that was going to be said should not be said here, should not be said now. Could probably only be said when Kay was gone... as in never coming back gone... as in dead. Stonehenge? She frowned. The day, just weeks after Caro's miscarriage when Kay and she had driven down to find Caro, worried sick. And Caro had been fine. Or she'd said she was fine, and then she'd driven back and taken Libby's baby and stayed out so long the police had been involved. So she hadn't been fine.

'No,' Caro murmured. 'Of course you don't remember. With everything that happened... after.'

Helen stared into the fire. The flames, fluid as water, melted and separated her thoughts. Everything that had led up to the night Caro took Libby's baby, had been a runaway-train wreck, fuelled by heartbreak and loneliness. Caro's heartbreak and loneliness. And as much as it had hurt, it had, Helen knew, been a hurt she should learn to navigate. That all the good people of the world would learn to navigate. So she had begun to. But she wasn't perfect. Libby had walked through fire that night. They all had, and they were all still a little scorched and every time she saw again her daughter's stricken face in the hours Ben and Caro were missing, she found another layer of resentment that she'd worked hard to keep buried. But those feelings were diluting. Caro and she were, tentatively, back on the same track... Until, that is, she'd come to the dead-end of that overheard conversation. *It was a mistake.* His hand on Caro's knee and Caro just sitting there, allowing it. How could she find a way to water all that down? She hadn't even tried. The fact that her marriage was over, she accepted, and had in fact instigated. The fact that it had been a sham all along was harder to swallow. But even worse (because having had time to think it through, Helen understood that she had expected more from Caro than she ever had from Lawrence) was the fact that Caro had played the role of friend on the one hand, and been so ready to betray her on the other. The dual nature of her best friend distorted the view of her own life. Turned it upside down, placed her on the outside, like a spectator.

'I made a promise that day,' Caro was saying. 'And it was to be more like you, Helen... But... It's complicated.' She shrugged. 'It's just so complicated.'

'Like me?' Helen whispered. The vibration in her ears was constant now, a relentless thrum. Was this the moment Caro was going to tell her that she was in love with Lawrence? And that Lawrence was in love with her? And that all those years ago, they'd both made the biggest mistake of their lives? Half of her wanted to laugh. A physical response to the unbearable constraint of social conformity. The way some people laugh at funerals, the way naughty kids laugh in front of the teacher. She got that now. The more she knew it would bring everything crashing down, the stronger the urge to tip her head back and laugh out loud at the absurdity of it all. Which would be the last time any of them laughed. Ever. Because if... *if* Caro opened this can of worms... which would have to be opened, would surely one day need to be shown the light of day... how would they ever get them back in? Tramp them down, silence and squash them? Panic scored her, and again the urge to giggle was ridiculous. They couldn't close the lid on this. They would *never* be able to do that. And it didn't matter. Here underneath galaxies of stars, in the great scheme of life, amid all the blood and heartbeats of this world, it really didn't matter. Except it did. And how would they get through the next two minutes, let alone the next two days? She didn't speak. She stretched her legs out and stared at the fire. She was thinking of Kay, whose outline she could see next to Caro, whose holiday it was and who was dying. 'Why would you want to be more like me?' she said, her words dripping out loud and resonant, like water in an empty space. 'So you could take my place?'

The shape in the darkness that moved was Kay. Not much. A sway backwards, and definitely a movement.

'You're brave Helen!' Caro laughed. She swirled her stick in a merry wide arc. 'You always have been! And on that day, I made a promise to myself to be more like you. To be braver. But it's so hard when—'

'I am not brave!' Helen's hiss was laser sharp. It decapitated Caro's sentence, which was fine by Helen. Just fine. Because whatever Caro was going to say next, she wouldn't hear it. For a long time now, there had been a part of herself that she'd hated, that she'd been trying to starve into submission. It was the part that had been aware of Caro's jealousy and had, in an awful *awful* way, fed off it. All those years when she had had the house, and the husband, the right kind of tableware and the right kind of newspaper. When she had thrown the best kind of parties and had the best kind of fun (*she was fun!* Didn't all those fun Facebook photos prove that?), this part of Helen had grown comfortable. And the fat lazy lie she had told herself, the version that had proved more palatable, because it didn't involve addressing that very deep, but very constant seam of dissatisfaction, was that if someone else wanted everything she had, was jealous of it, and, more, was someone she actually admired, then those things – the house, the husband, the plates, the parties – must have had value, mustn't they? For so long she'd held onto this like a talisman, clutching it long after it was obvious that what she was clutching was an empty pod, the seed of life within it long since dispersed on wind after bitter wind of disappointment. Well, enough! She didn't want Caro to be jealous, because there was, and never had been, anything to be jealous of. And she certainly didn't want to stand and hear Caro say how she wanted to be more like her. Who the hell was she to be emulated? What the hell had she ever done? Married a man whom, it turned out, had never loved her? Nurtured a long and close friendship with a woman who was quite capable of deceiving her? It was all... It was all so fucked up! 'I am not brave,' she said again, the words slow with finality. And she saw how Kay had put her glass down and leaned forward to cover her face with her hands.

'You are!' Caro smiled.

'When,' Helen seethed, 'have I ever been brave?'

'You went sailing!' Caro exclaimed. 'I couldn't have done that. And today, you climbed right onto your horse without even a second thought. You've always been braver than me, Helen.' And suddenly Caro stopped talking, the stick lowering. 'What did you say?' she said slowly. 'Take your place?'

'I heard you,' Helen whispered.

'Heard me?'

'At that stupid dinner party I had. I heard you and Lawrence. I heard what was said, Caro.' She turned to Kay. 'I'm so sorry, Kay. I really am. I *never* wanted this to come out, not now, not ever really, but I can't sit here anymore and listen—'

'What did you hear, Helen?' Caro interrupted.

Helen stared at her. 'Are you going to make me repeat it? You're really going to do this?'

'Whatever you heard—'

'Lawrence had his hand on your knee!'

Swallowing hard, Caro nodded. 'Yes,' she said. 'Yes he did.'

'And I heard him say, that you were both the same. You and him. That it wasn't too late. That you should have told him how you felt. That he thought it was just a shag, but you should have told him... and that twenty-five years ago he made a mistake! It is... it was... Jesus, Caro! It's one thing to find a marriage isn't working anymore, but it's something else to find it was a sham all the bloody time! And you... You slept with him! You were supposed to be my friend...You... I... You...' As her voice finally failed, Helen shook her head. She was empty. As lifeless as any of the rocks scattered out there in the sea of desert beyond. What she had said to Kay was true, she hadn't wanted to speak of this, she really hadn't. Across the flames, she could see Caro's face, the wide-open astonishment, and now the dark narrowing down that a reckoning brings. She didn't, as she watched Caro, notice the black outline that was Kay stand and move away, and by the time she might have noticed, it was too late. The outline had gone, swallowed by the night.

Caro too was oblivious.

So they sat and the only light came from the flames between them, and the stars above; the stars that were dead, as luminous as those that lived. The night stirred a breeze, a lapping at their ankles, on the back of their necks.

And then Caro tipped her head to the sky and whispered, 'I knew I should have told you. From the very beginning, I knew.'

Helen didn't speak.

Dropping her chin, she pinched the bridge of her nose. 'I'm sorry, Helen, and I always have been. I never intended to hurt you. It's like I said... if I'd had an ounce of your courage, I would have told you a long time ago.'

'*Stop it!*' Helen shouted. '*Please*, just stop it! Stop going on and on about my courage.' Tears streamed down her face. 'You've hurt me, Caro,' she cried. 'Can't you see that? Lawrence? Well, the more I learn about my husband, the more I can't believe I ever loved him in the first place. But *you!* You were my friend. I expected more from you. I *needed* more from you because... because I need my friends! You...' She bent forward, great wracking sobs folding her over. 'I trusted you! I thought we'd always be friends. It hurts, and I'm sorry, Kay. I don't know what I'm going to do without you. I thought... I thought I'd still have Caro.' Hopelessly Helen looked up, her face stilled by confusion, her eyes straining to make sense of the empty space where Kay had been sitting.

21

Each step up the porch felt to Kay like a mountain climbed. She was drained. Wrung out. And the only thing she was sure of was that she couldn't listen to another word of the argument about to explode between Helen and Caro. Years and years ago, when milk still got delivered in bottles, Caro had slept with the man that Helen had gone on to marry.

Kay had known about it at the time and, for maybe a week, had given it headspace, because within that brief window, it had seemed worthy of headspace. Lawrence and Helen had seemed serious, and when in the following months it had become evident that they were serious, Caro had come to her, and Kay had advised her to try and forget it ever happened. It had been easy and natural advice for Kay to dish out, because by some great fortune, she'd been born immune to the Lawrences of this world, the way they crossed her path with their bonhomie and magnetic charm and minuscule depth. She'd been happy enough to go along with their *what a great girl she was* act because they were nothing to her. Not that they ever suspected this.

Their very worth depended upon making sure that even the plainest girl in the room knew just how unlucky she was not to be in serious contention, and yes, even Lawrence had tried. She'd shut his advances down faster than a Venus flytrap. But Caro hadn't been able to, and although it had always been obvious to Kay that Helen was going to win, she'd never understood why Caro couldn't also see this. From the little she knew about Caro's family, Kay had put it down to appetite. Caro hungered for attention. At the time it had been mystifying, now it was obvious. Caro had been chronically undernourished, and who could blame a hungry child for lapping up crumbs? All this was a hundred years ago. Summer had come, as it always does. The lease on their student flat had ended. Parents had arrived in cars to pack boxes and suitcases. Caro took a job in the city and within two weeks had flown to New York to start a training course. Martin turned up in Kay's life. They had all begun their grown-up lives and she hadn't, if she was honest, really thought about the episode since.

She paused, turning now on the top step of the ranch to look out at all those far away stars, which, as Caro had said, might be dead, but whose light she could still see, whose beauty she could still appreciate. So, Lawrence was still manufacturing bullshit. Whispering sweet nothings into Caro's ear. For a long time, Helen's marriage had been a happy one and Kay didn't believe in his talk of 'mistakes' any more than she believed her cancer was curable. She was almost sure that Caro didn't either, but it was too late. She just didn't have the energy to stick around and find out. Or the time. No, definitely not the time. Stones in her heart, she pushed open the door to the ranch-house and went inside.

Marianne and Tony were sitting at either end of a long

couch. Tony leaned forward, elbows on knees, head in hands. Marianne ram-rod straight, lips tight as a bud.

'Howdy partner,' Tony said as he dropped his hands and smiled a lop-sided smile that was about as believable as Lawrence's bullshit.

'What's the matter?' Marianne shuffled to the edge of the couch.

Kay could have laughed. The difference between men and women. 'Nothing,' she said.

And of course Marianne wasn't fooled. 'Are they arguing again?'

Kay nodded. 'A little.'

'What about?'

Flopping into an armchair, she leaned her chin in her hand. 'Helen's husband. Apparently he said something to Caro that Helen overheard. I wouldn't trust that man with a ten-foot barge pole, and I'd be very surprised if, after all this time, Caro did. But...' She shrugged.

Standing up, Marianne shoved her feet into her sandals.

'Really Marianne, don't worry,' Kay said watching as Marianne's toes squeezed through the jewelled leather thong. 'It's probably best to let them talk it through.'

'You know what, Kay?' Marianne said archly. 'I think I need some fresh air anyway,' And as she passed, she looked older, more weary, heavier of body than Kay thought she'd ever seen her.

As the rush of cool night air swept in and the ranch door swung shut, Kay turned back to the room. It was soothing and comfortable and designed to reflect the desert terrain outside. The effect was that of an oasis. Every piece of soft furnishing bore the colours of the earth, cushions scattered on the chairs were robust blues and burnt orange. Tufted rugs, woven in bulky yarn, lay on the floor and every surface was a coarse wood; the stair-rail alone was a slender and whole trunk. Subtle lamps gave off pools of dreamy yellow light and pottery in fiery reds and yellows splashed colour. From the ceiling above the kitchen sink hung a feathered dream catcher. Loose-limbed in her armchair, Kay looked up at it. Alex had a dream catcher above his bed. She'd hung it there for him as a small boy and he still believed in it. She knew because when the bedroom had been re-painted a couple of years ago, he'd put it back up. Narrowing her eyes, she concentrated on the colourful beads, tied together with fine leather. What she wouldn't give for someone to tell her that they worked. That trapped within those feathers and beads was every last nightmare and fear her son had ever had, with infinite room for all those still to come.

'How you doing, Kay?' Tony's voice carried across the room slow as a winter shadow.

Kay turned. Tony looked as weary on the outside as she felt on the inside. Coupled with the look that Marianne had given him on the way out, it was clear they'd just had an argument. Love's middle-aged dream. She wouldn't ask. She didn't actually want to know. 'Well,' she sighed. 'I have to admit, I've been better.'

From under deeply hooded eyes, he almost smiled. 'Ditto, my friend. Ditto.'

'It's such a beautiful place you have,' she said. 'Thank you for inviting us.'

Nodding, he looked down at his hands. He didn't speak.

Kay leaned back in her chair. The silence in the room was profound, rich as an ocean, as multicoloured and various, filled with shoals of thoughts never destined to surface, currents of emotion that always threatened. She looked across at Tony's bent head and his sloped shoulders. A minute passed, maybe longer. And then Tony looked up and said, 'Shall we play?'

But she didn't understand what he meant.

'Shall we go back and play?'

'Blackjack?'

'We were lucky before. You and me.' He shrugged.

'Well...' Instinctively she turned to the window. Far across the yard she could see the flames of the campfire where Helen and Caro still sat. Against the backdrop of black, it looked tiny and she had no way of knowing if they were in fact still there. 'What about the others?' she said, understanding that Tony's *we* hadn't included them.

Again, Tony shrugged. 'I need to get outta here,' he said.

Kay looked at him. Whatever had just happened between him and Marianne had obviously tipped him over into this rudderless swell she felt that she was also caught in. Torn between a certainty that she couldn't leave Helen and Caro, and equally determined to steer away from them.

'I'll ask Gabe to drive them in, when they're ready. He paused. 'If there's trouble, perhaps it's best to let them talk it out.'

'What about Marianne?'

Tony smiled. 'Marianne will be glad of the space,' he said. 'Trust me.'

And here was the weathervane she'd been hoping for. Practical aspects answered, a compromise seized that would enable her to say yes to Tony's suggestion. She didn't want to go out and sit by the fireside with Caro and Helen. She didn't want to get dragged into the discussion. Not at all. The silence and peace of this place had worked its magic, massaged a poisonous dose of grief out of her and now she was ready to go back. And yes, to play. To gamble. Why not?

For the first time in her short life, why shouldn't she take a chance?

'KAY?' Helen called again. She was standing now, her voice higher with every repetition of Kay's name.

'Kay isn't here.' Marianne answered and her voice was shrill with impatience, rising like a flare in the desert night as she approached the campfire.

'Where is she?' Caro said. She too was on her feet. 'She was here a moment ago... where is she?'

'Don't panic.' Sighing, Marianne collapsed into the fold-up chair Kay had so recently vacated. 'She went inside to get away from you two. Which is good for me, because Tony is very annoying.' She crossed one leg over the other and bouncing her foot, shook her head vigorously. 'So!' she declared, and looked first at Caro and then at Helen. 'Now you have me instead!'

'Inside?' Over the flames Helen's eyes met Caro's.

'Is that what she said?' Caro turned to Marianne. 'To get away from us?'

Marianne nodded. 'This is what she said. Just now, and all afternoon actually.'

'All afternoon?' Helen echoed.

'Yes. While you were riding, we sat for a while.' With a wave of her hand, Marianne indicated that they should both sit down, that she was here to talk.

'And she really said that?' Caro's eyes had widened with disbelief.

Helen looked at her. She was at a loss as to why Caro should find what Marianne was saying hard to believe, because she wasn't remotely surprised. In fact, the only thing that surprised her now was that Kay had agreed to come on this trip in the first place. She closed her eyes, momentarily subdued by the understanding of the leap of faith Kay must have taken. After the way the Cyprus trip had been derailed and the troubles of last year... Yet again, they had failed her. Swallowing down the lump in her throat, she looked at Caro whose desolate expression must, she thought, mirror her own. They had let Kay down. Oh, how they had let her down. Turning to Marianne, her voice was quiet and slow. 'She's been talking to you for a while now, hasn't she?'

Marianne nodded. 'Since the diagnosis.'

'And... I suppose she explained what... the problems we've had?'

Again, Marianne nodded.

'What else did she say,' Caro whispered. The stick in her hands snapped in half. Dropping the pieces to the ground, she sat staring into the fire.

Marianne wiped the palms of her hands together. 'It's almost as dusty here as it is in Cyprus.'

'Marianne?' Helen pleaded. 'Can you tell us?'

'I can.' Marianne nodded. 'Although it's hard for me to do so, because I might lose my temper and I am not a pretty sight when that happens.'

No one spoke.

'My mother was half Serbian.'

Still no one spoke.

Marianne snorted air and again, wiped imaginary dust from her hands. 'What does it matter!' she suddenly cried. 'I haven't been a pretty sight for many years...' Pausing, her nostrils flared with irritation. 'You are both godmother to Alex, yes?'

Caro and Helen nodded.

'This is one of the things that troubles her. She thinks

that when she dies, you won't be there for him.' Marianne pressed her chin to her chest and, looking down, slapped a palm across her collarbone. 'I already told her,' she said, lifting her hand to inspect the object she'd just crushed. 'Not again,' she muttered, as she licked whatever it was and pressed it onto her fingernail. 'I said that Alex can come to Cyprus and live with me. We have hundreds and hundreds of orchids to keep him happy.'

Helen's mouth fell open. 'Alex doesn't need to go to Cyprus! We... we'll always be there for him!'

'Will you?' Marianne answered, her eyes very small.

'Of course,' Caro said. 'That's a given. Of course we would.'

'And tell me how are you going to make that work? How can you make a decision between you? You can't agree on anything. How can he take advice from two women who can't agree? Do you think it will help him to be hearing different things? I have never met him, but from what Kay has told me, I don't think it will be good for him. Not at all.'

Helen looked at Caro, who was looking right back at her.

'This afternoon,' Marianne continued, waving her arm. 'When Caro says something very important, about Shook – which is no name for a husband, but there you go – you storm off Helen! And Caro doesn't know why, and then we get here, and you're in the saddle faster than the Lone Ranger.'

'There was a reason—'

'Psshht!' The burst of air that was Marianne's hiss blew Caro's words away. 'And I watched you both!' she steamed on. 'All through dinner. Caro is here.' Marianne pointed to one side of the fire. 'And Helen is over there, so interested in her plate of food and *only* her plate of food. I know I like to eat, but I've never seen someone pay so much attention to beans!'

'It was that obvious?' Helen whispered.

'It was more obvious than Tony's bullshit!'

'Tony seems...' Caro hesitated, stilled by the death-stare Marianne now gave her.

'I haven't finished,' Marianne said, as if it were necessary. 'She is even having nightmares about you arguing at her funeral.'

'No.' Helen sat up.

'No...' Caro echoed. 'That would never happen. That ...'

'If there is one thing in life I have learned Helen...' Marianne said, one finger pointed toward heaven. 'It is *never,* to say *never*! Hassiktir!' she hissed and turned her finger, so she could see the nail. 'I will never listen to a twenty-year-old again,' she hissed, inspecting the other nails. 'Three left! Three out of ten!'

'Helen... there was a lot more that you didn't hear—' Caro started.

'Again, I haven't finished!'

Caro's mouth opened and closed.

'Thank you.' Marianne stretched out her leg and deep in thought, looked at the toenails of her raised foot, her mouth pulling down at the edges. 'I had a friend once,' she said. 'Louise. She was British too. We met in London, when we worked together in the eighties at The Strand Hotel.' As she spoke Marianne's mouth softened, and her eyes became jewels, wet with tears that would never be released. 'We also argued.'

The fire crackled. Helen watched as deep within its depths a tiny explosion of sparks fired up and vanished. A birth and an extinction of energy. There was, she felt, more life in that single moment of combustion than she feared she might ever possess again. Neither Caro, nor she herself, had seen Kay leave. Kay whose peace of mind they had managed to fracture. What did that say about them? She felt dull. Flattened by the understanding.

'I always liked British people,' Marianne said. 'They have a good sense of humour. No dress sense, but a good sense of humour.'

Helen looked up. 'What happened?' she said. 'You said *had*. You *had* a friend.'

'Louise got herself an American boyfriend, and then a visa. She was going out to live with him.'

'You lost touch?'

'No.' Smiling, Marianne shook her head. 'Her plane never arrived. This was December 1988.'

'Oh my God.' Caro covered her mouth with her hand. 'Lockerbie?'

Marianne nodded. 'It can happen so fast,' she said and her left eye twitched, like a speck of dust had blown in. One twitch and nothing more. 'It's been over thirty years and I still think about her. I didn't have another close friend after that. When you're young, and so many people are in your life, you don't understand. You don't know what makes a friend, so you think everybody you meet is your friend. But they're not. They're just passing through. Louise though?' Marianne smiled. 'I like to think that the troubles we had, we would have got over them. We would still be friends. We had already been through so much together.' She looked up. 'History. You call it history? Who else was I going to get that from?'

Helen took a long and deep breath. Once upon a time history had been her subject. And Marianne was right. It was non-transferable, it couldn't be peeled off and stuck onto the next likely candidate that came along. She stared at the flames. She had no idea what to think, or what Caro might say next. What part of their shared history she was going to re-write. In the end it didn't matter, because whatever it was, she was going to have to face it.

'When you all stayed at the hotel in Cyprus,' Marianne continued, 'I was envious. You seemed such good friends. I watched you and then I went home to my little house and I thought about Louise. I wondered what our friendship would have been like, if she had lived. I was jealous of her. That's all it was. We were not on good terms when she died and that was my fault. She was on her way to America. Maybe a whole new life, and I felt like she was leaving me behind.' Marianne sighed. 'I hope that she would have come to forgive me. I hope that I would have been mature enough to apologise, that we would, in time, have laughed about it.'

Caro looked up. 'About what?'

'My jealousy,' Marianne said simply. 'The fact that I was jealous, when there was nothing to be jealous of. Life isn't a race. I know that now. There was no prize between us and nothing to win. She would have had her life, and I would have had mine, and just to have had such a good friend through it all, would have been prize enough. Anyway...' She lifted a hand, waved an open palm to the sky and then let it fall again. 'When Kay emailed me, after your holiday, it was a little miracle. Yes.' Nodding, Marianne looked from Caro to Helen. 'She doesn't have so much time left. Is it really so unforgivable, Helen? What happened with the baby?'

'No,' Helen whispered. 'But it's not as simple as you think Marianne. There's—'

'Your husband said something to Caro?'

Helen looked at her.

'Kay told me.'

She nodded.

'What did he say?'

But Helen shook her head. She didn't want to repeat it. Not ever.

And across the other side of the fire, Caro stood up. 'You only heard half the conversation, Helen. Yes, he had his hand on my knee, but did you see me take it off?'

Helen didn't answer.

'Because if you didn't see that, then you didn't hear what I said after. And I need you to know. I need you to know what I said.'

Still Helen didn't respond.

'I said, I pitied him, Helen!' Wringing her hands together, Caro took a step forward. 'That's what I want you to hear. It's not a pleasant thing and I'm sorry. But that's what I said.'

'Pity?'

'Yes.'

Confusion clouded Helen's face. Her body hadn't caught up with her mind. She could feel her head shaking, refusing the rest of the conversation, whilst knowing that everything depended upon hearing it. 'Why?' Her mouth made the shape anyway.

'Because he was losing you, Helen, and I wasn't!' Caro's voice was a plea, a cry to be heard. 'I told him that the only mistake I ever made, was in risking our friendship by sleeping with him in the first place. Risking the friendship of a loyal and funny woman. A brave woman, who always told me the truth. And not because she wanted to hurt me. I knew that, Helen! I never wanted to hear it, but I knew it was because you wanted the best for me. You're loyal. You've always been loyal to me.'

'But you slept with him?'

'Yes.' Caro nodded. She thrust her hands into her pockets and as if the admission were too awful to face, twisted away to look at the sky. 'That bit is true,' she whispered in a voice whittled bare. 'I'm so bloody sorry it ever happened. If I could rewind thirty years and take it back, I would. And I'm even more sorry it's taken me so long to work this all out.'

In between them, Marianne drew in a long and silent breath.

'When,' Helen managed. 'When did you sleep with him?'

'Three weeks before graduation,' Caro said flatly. 'I don't have an excuse. I was twenty-one and still a virgin and I was jealous of you. It was so easy for you.'

The corner of Helen's lips twitched. A storm of emotions pushed through. 'To lose my virginity!'

'No! I mean, life! I mean, everything! But I don't think that now. I understand now. Nothing has been easy. I'm talking about my twenty-one-year-old self here, Helen. What she was thinking!' Looking at the ground, Caro sighed. When she spoke again, her voice was heavy with regret. 'Please try to forgive her. She envied you so much.'

Helen leaned forward and dropped her head into her hands. She was trying to find a response, but it was like trying to scratch fire from wet wood. The only thing Caro's admission had sparked was a dull nothingness. No white-hot anger, no throbbing wound... nothing. In an ironically detached way, it occurred to her that another lifetime ago, there might have been some moral high ground available, to which she might cling. And do what? Sit in righteous and cold solitude? Because it would be cold. Any heat of emotion that belonged with this episode had long since died away, like ripples on a lake, melting back into the darkened surface from which they had arisen. The only thing that remained now were Caro's last words, *she envied you so much.* Raising her head, as if to memorise those words before they disappeared forever, Helen stared into the fire. Envy, envy, envy. How much of her life had she wasted at her own kitchen sink, indulging in that same four-lettered utterly useless pastime? And what would it have taken for her to stop envying the choices Caro had made with her lie? Losing Caro completely, like Marianne had lost her friend? Her voice was quiet, but nonetheless perfectly clear. 'I'll forgive her,' she said, 'if you will do something for me?'

Caro turned to her.

'Tell her,' Helen continued in a croak, 'tell her, that she will have nothing to envy? That Helen will get married to a selfish and shallow man, who she will stay with long after she should have left...'

'Helen—'

Helen raised a hand. She wouldn't be stopped. What was going to be said, had to be said. 'Tell her, that the Helen that Caro admires so much, will grow into a coward. That life will swing her such a blow...'

'Daniel?'

Tears streaming down her face, Helen nodded. 'Such a blow,' she whispered, remembering the stillbirth of her first child. 'She'll lose herself. She'll spend years and years, terrified of her own shadow. I've been hiding for years,' she said hoarsely. 'Whereas you? You went out and got what you wanted, Caro. You put the effort in. So tell her, *please* tell her that she's got it all wrong. That it's Helen who should admire Caro. That it's Helen who will be envious of Caro. It's Helen who'll spend weekends at the kitchen sink, wondering about you. Where you are, or what you were doing. You always seemed so free. You were always true to your course, when sometimes it has felt as if I have let everything and everyone, blow out everything I thought I was, and anything I ever wanted.'

Beside her, Marianne nodded, put a hand to her eye and wiped away what might have been a tear.

'I'm sorry, Helen. I was so jealous.'

'I know,' Helen whispered.

'Of the life you had.'

Rubbing at her forehead, Helen stood up. 'I want to stop this,' she said. 'I don't care about what happened thirty years ago, and I want to be able to put last year behind us. Completely behind us. But I don't know how... I don't know what to do.'

'Start again,' Marianne said.

Both Helen and Caro looked at her.

'I have had so many dreams,' Marianne said, and her voice cracked. 'So many nights when I have woken up with a wet pillow, because every time the dream has always ended the same way.'

'With what happened?' Caro whispered.

Marianne shook her head. 'No. I never dream about that. In my dreams, Louise and I are always starting again. It is always at the beginning. We are young and we are in London and we have always just met.'

Caro looked at Helen. 'Modern philosophy,' she whispered. 'Remember?'

Helen smiled. 'You looked like the kind of girl who was determined to do well. That's why I sat next to you.'

'I'm so glad you did, Helen,' Caro cried. She took a wobbly step forward and so did Helen and they met in front of the fire and held each other, and behind them Marianne nodded as she used her thumbs to blot her eyes.

22

The radio was playing country music, one mournful vibrato after another. In another time and place, Kay would have turned it off. The last thing she needed right now being lament after lament about the sadness of life. But here, cocooned in the air-conditioned comfort of the SUV, the Mohave desert flashing past on either side, the music felt perfect, made it easier to forget she'd left the others behind and easier to pretend she was a twenty-first-century cowgirl, a pioneer, a someone other than herself. Because the unease lingered. She'd left, with no warning. And she'd left to come back and gamble. Tony, who seemed subdued but none the less more at ease than herself, had tried to reassure her several times now. Lula would let the others know and Gabe would drive them. Kay hadn't felt wholly comfortable with the idea, but who was she to intervene? Hidden Valley Ranch wasn't her ranch and Lula and Gabe weren't her staff. She leaned her elbow against the rim of the window, and stared out into the black of the desert. There wasn't much to see – the occasional outline of a tall spiky yucca against the mauve sky, sometimes the elongated glow of approaching, but still distant, headlights. To distract herself from the discomfiture that lingered, she turned to Tony. 'Why don't you carry on?' she said, forcing a lightness into her voice at odds with the darkness they were surrounded by.

'Carry on?'

'Yes, from where you left off the other day.' Kay tried to laugh. She was nervous and the more she allowed herself to think what they were heading back to, the more intense that worry became. The chips she had won earlier were still in her purse. She hadn't cashed them up, because... She'd told the others that there hadn't been time. There had been plenty of time. She hadn't cashed the chips, because she wanted to do it again. An itch, which didn't sit comfortably. It was obviously much easier to walk away from a pile of matchsticks than a pile of genuine Vegas chips. 'You were telling me about your work. We got up to when you were cast in *Days of Your Lives*.'

'Oh, you don't want to know about that.' And in Tony's voice, perhaps for the first time, Kay recognised a deep and rather sad note of authenticity. It surprised her. It had her turning to study his profile, but his expression was... expressionless.

'I hope I'm not speaking out of turn...' she began.

'Speak away,' Tony said as he turned briefly and smiled, a frankness softening his eyes.

'Is everything ok? I mean, I know it's not.' She waited. Tony didn't speak. 'Is Marianne ok?' she added. The look Marianne had given her on the way out of the ranch house rose up now, clear as it had been then. Loosening her seatbelt, she turned to face Tony.

'Marianne,' Tony said, 'is disappointed.'

Kay didn't speak.

'In me.'

'Oh.'

'She thought...' Tony began. He lifted a hand from the steering wheel, held it aimlessly for a moment and then dropped it back down. 'Truth be told, Kay, I'm disappointed in myself, but what can you do? The older I get, the more I tend to think it's a natural part of ageing.'

'To be disappointed?'

He shrugged.

Kay turned away. He meant what he said, that was clear, and although she didn't know why, she felt a tremendous sympathy for him. Here he was, a successful man, living the life he pleased and still, under the surface, he was as full of worries and sad regrets, it seemed, as everyone else. As herself. 'You've had such a successful career though,' she said.

'Acting?' Tony glanced at her. 'Pretending to be someone else all my life?'

'I couldn't do it.'

'You could,' Tony said. 'It's easy.' He shook his head. 'Maybe too easy.'

'Why do you say that?'

Tony smiled. 'If you're uncomfortable doing something, pretending to be someone else makes it more comfortable. Which isn't good in real life. Gets you into all sorts of trouble in real life. Anyway!' He tapped the steering wheel with the heel of his hand. 'I don't know why we're talking about this. You'd never need to pretend. I've never seen someone so comfortable in their skin.'

'I don't know about that,' Kay said quietly.

Tony cleared his throat, but he didn't speak.

'Maybe Marianne has told you,' she started, and when he didn't say anything, she took a deep breath and continued. 'I have melanoma. It's spread and so they've told me it's incurable. I'm on a huge cocktail of drugs and no one knows how long or how well they'll work. Borrowed time I suppose.'

The stillness in Tony's face as he turned to look at her did not surprise Kay. In this new world she inhabited, she had become accustomed to the reaction that followed, whenever she told people, which she rarely did. 'I'm sorry,' he said. 'I'm really sorry to hear that.'

Kay looked down at her hands. 'So, as you can see,' she finished. 'I wouldn't mind pretending to be someone else, for a while.'

Tony nodded.

'And thank you!' Kay said suddenly. She was thinking about earlier, when she'd sat on the porch and lost herself in the expanse of scenery, and later around the campfire the millions of stars above. She would always remember that. Always.

Tony frowned.

'For bringing us out here, Tony. I didn't even realise all this was so close.'

'You didn't? Where did you think Vegas was?'

And now Kay laughed. 'If I tell you why we came, you'll laugh.'

Tony was smiling now. 'Well,' he said, 'I think you should tell me. I think we both need to laugh, don't you?'

'Yes, definitely.' She shook her head as if she was looking at something distant, but fondly remembered. 'I have this jacket.'

'A jacket?'

'Yes. It's always been called my Vegas jacket. I bought it years and years ago.'

'To wear here?'

'Yes.' She nodded. 'But I never made it out here.'

'That happens.'

'It does, doesn't it? Anyway, Caro booked this trip, mostly because of the jacket, and my doctors said I should go, if I felt well enough. They almost ordered me. My son did order me.' She smiled, remembering how Alex had been angry with her when she'd dithered and started to find excuses. 'How could I not come?' she finished quietly. 'It was decided for me.' And as she turned to stare out the window, a dull feeling arose. Looking at things clearly, the way she just described it, was exactly the way it had happened. Caro had booked the trip and everyone had ordered her to go. And if they hadn't, she probably wouldn't have, and then she wouldn't have spent the last few hours in this extraordinary place that had given her so much. So very much. Gratitude swelled, washing her light again. 'Yes, thank you. I mean it.'

'Kay.' Tony's voice was strong and clear. An actor's voice. 'I want to tell you something and I want you to listen.'

'Ok.'

'There are two types of player in this world. You gotta trust me here, I've been around a lot of players, thousands of them, hundreds of thousands and there are only ever two types.' He looked at her. 'Ok?'

'Ok.'

'Most of them fall into the first type. Those that want the dealer to make all the decisions for them.' Tony shook his head. 'I've seen it so many times, I can't tell you. You get a player that can't decide whether to double down on a sure thing, or even to play a soft ace hand.'

'You always play an ace hand,' Kay whispered.

Tony turned to her, the accomplice in his eyes welcoming her in. 'The second type of player are those that think for themselves. They make their own choices. Just like life. *And* I know what kind of a player you are, Kay! Remember, I've seen you. Here you are, in Vegas despite everything life has thrown at you. You think for yourself. You make your own choices. You've got guts, Kay. Real guts.'

23

G*one.*

The word echoed around the room, passed from Marianne to Helen and back again like an unwanted relay baton.

'Gone,' Lula repeated. She turned her palms to the ceiling, as if to show that, yes it was true, she wasn't hiding them and neither Kay, nor Tony, was in the room. 'Mr Tony has gone ahead with the other lady.'

Helen scratched her head. Her hair was full of dirt and dust, and the ranch consisted of one room so it must be true. In the far corner, stairs led up to a sleeping area (she supposed) and there was a small bathroom off to the back, which is where Caro was now. Tony and Kay, *gone.* It just didn't make sense.

'He has asked Gabe to take you all back. But Gabe is asleep I think.' Lula shrugged. 'I will have to wake him.'

'Why?' Helen frowned. She was having trouble keeping up.

'We have to get back to the hotel somehow,' Marianne said flatly.

'No, not just this.' Lula shook her head. 'The boss is coming tomorrow and if the SUV isn't here at the ranch, where he expects it to be, there will be big trouble. Gabe needs to bring it back.'

'The boss?' Helen turned to Marianne. 'I thought Tony owned this place?'

'Tony?' Marianne snorted. 'I will find it hard to believe he owns the shirt on his back!'

At this, Lula crossed her arms. 'Amen,' she nodded. 'Amen.'

'So, are we ready to head back?' Caro came in.

Immediately Helen turned to her. 'Kay's gone.'

'Where?'

'*Gone,* gone.'

Eyes opening in surprise, Caro looked from face to face.

'I'm guessing...' Helen started, although actually she had no idea what she was guessing. 'They've gone back to Vegas?'

Marianne's features had set like poured cement. 'I would guess that too,' she said bleakly.

'Why?' Caro asked.

Helen shook her head, her shoulders rising as she breathed in and walked across to the kitchen sink. It had been positioned under a window, and just like her own kitchen at night, the image reflected back was that of herself and the domestic scene behind that she was a part of. 'To get away from us,' she said flatly, and thank goodness, the reflected face that looked back at her was so obscured in shadow, she couldn't quite make out the expression. 'To get away from us,' she repeated.

'This is my fault,' Marianne muttered. 'I should never have contacted him!' She dropped onto the nearest sofa like a stone into water, and the soft whoosh of air escaping from the cushions had Helen turning back to the room.

'What is going on?' Caro repeated.

Staring straight ahead, Marianne said, 'Tony doesn't own this ranch.'

'He doesn't? Who does?'

'A friend from Hollywood. A *rich* friend from Hollywood.'

Caro looked from Marianne, to Lula, who shrugged, shoulders rising to her ears.

'Lula told me,' Marianne continued. 'When you were both out riding. I came in for coffee and we had a chat. Stupid me! Going on and on about what a lovely place Tony had, and so she told me.'

'Told you what, exactly?' Caro said.

Marianne's head shook, side to side like it vibrated, like what she had to say was so shameful, her body refused to allow it.

Across the room, Lula picked up an empty wine glass from the table and, holding it in both hands, said, 'Mr Tony is a friend of the boss. I think they have known each other a long time. He lets Mr Tony come and stay when he wants. I don't know why. He is too good. When Mr Tony comes, he is supposed to do some jobs, but he never does. He rides and he eats and he drinks and then he leaves. And sometimes he brings friends, and they eat and drink and also leave.'

No one spoke. Eventually, still at the sink, Helen said, 'I'm so sorry. We had no idea. Obviously we'll pay for what we've eaten.'

'Of course,' Caro finished.

Marianne nodded

Lula shook her head. 'I not taking any money from you ladies.'

Turning to Marianne, Caro said, 'He lied to you?'

'He never *actually* said he owned it,' Marianne answered.

'But he let us all believe he did,' Helen finished.

'Amen,' Lula nodded.

'We believe what we want to believe,' Marianne said quietly. 'Tony,' she continued, 'Has four ex-wives. Two children who won't speak to him, no money and no career. I suppose his Hollywood friend feels sorry for him.'

'I think this is true,' Lula nodded.

'He is a compulsive gambler. And his friend is fully of sympathy, because Tony tells everyone that this is an illness.'

Lula was still nodding. 'All true.'

Helen snorted.

Marianne leaned her head back against the cushion of the sofa. 'He tried to tell me the same. *I'm sick, Marianne,* he said. If you're sick, I said, I'm a fish! *Sick?*' The heat of anger, or contempt, energised her now, and as she shuffled forward to the edge of the sofa, Marianne's face became animated. 'My mother,' she declared, 'who was half Serbian, was born with a hole in her heart. Her brother, my uncle, was crippled with polio and my grandmother lost an eye. No one knows where, but it was never found! I never heard any of them ever say they were sick! *Sick?* In my family, we don't have time to be sick.' She stuck her hands deep into the cushions, ready to heft herself upright, looked around and then as if she'd been shot, fell back again. 'I'm so ashamed,' she wailed, one hand shielding her eyes. 'What an old fool I've been.' Holding her hand up she turned it around to study her painted nails, and then around again, as if to show the room. The lone sequin left on her little fingernail caught the light and glinted. 'What a vain old fool! And now Kay! Kay is driving off with him to who knows where!'

Lula frowned, her expression inscrutable.

Still at the sink, Helen glanced to Caro. It was impossible not to feel sympathy for Marianne; on the other hand mirrored in Caro's face was a look she knew she wore herself. The resignation of being caught in a squall that had been forecast days ago. Marianne's relationship with the suave Tony was as unlikely as tulips in winter. But what could they have done? In the glow of Tony's attention, Marianne had been untouchable, walking on air, experiencing the kind of lightness-of-being that rolls around only once, or twice, in a lifetime. The kind Helen had so recently enjoyed and remembered fondly from her time with Kaveh in Cyprus. Why shouldn't they have left her to enjoy the moment? As long as there was a safety net in place. Which is what they must now be. The two of them. She nodded as Caro's eyes met hers. And then quietly she walked over, and sat down on the arm of the sofa, next to Marianne. 'The only fool I can see,' she said gently, 'Is Tony.'

'This,' Lula said, 'is also true.'

Hands at her face, Marianne looked up. 'What do we do?'

'There's nothing we can do. Gabe will take us back?' Helen said, looking at Lula.

'When I wake him.'

'So we wait,' Helen said.

Now Caro came and sat the other side of Marianne. 'We wait. We'll send Kay a text.' She was looking at Helen. 'Explaining that we've sorted things out. Between us?'

'Yes.' Helen nodded. 'I'll bet they've gone back to play cards. She was buzzing this afternoon.' And thinking this, her face drained. 'What if she loses all that money she won?'

Caro had leaned froward to rest her chin in her hands. 'We can't do anything about that. We can only be there, if she does.' Leaning back against the cushion she sighed. 'You know, I'm glad she's gone actually. This is her trip and if she wants to play, great. She'd have a lot more fun that sitting here listening to us argue!'

And at this Helen laughed. It was true and now she too was glad that Kay had taken herself off. In fact she was delighted. Good for Kay! Tony might be all sorts of things, but he wasn't an axe-murderer. Kay would be fine. In fact, once Caro and she were able to reassure Kay that it was over, all the misunderstandings and the tension, she would be more than fine. Close by, she heard a stifled sob. Marianne was weeping quietly. Helen stretched her arm out, letting her hand come to rest on Marianne's shoulders. She felt both lighter and larger than she had in a long time, newly equipped somehow to carry the weight of Marianne's disappointment, buoyed up with relief. Turning to Caro she smiled. And in return, Caro stretched her hand along Marianne's shoulders to clasp Helen's and they sat, fingers entwined, waiting for Lula to wake Gabe.

24

Standing in a hotel room which could swallow the entire ground floor of her house, Kay stood exposed as the last soldier on a battlefield.

Everything about what she was doing in the instruction manual of life that had been handed down to her, felt wrong. But how quickly it had been done. How easy to close that book, and turn to another one. *Don't get addicted,* Helen had joked on the way to Tony's ranch. Yet here she was, with an urge stronger than any chocolate craving, ready to risk the money she'd won earlier. Five hundred dollars. The most she'd ever won, and that included every raffle she'd ever entered her entire adult life. So what else could explain the ease with which she had agreed to Tony's suggestion, other than the beginning of an addiction?

She turned, walked across to the bed and picked up her handbag, opened it and looked at the pile of coloured chips nestled inside. There they were, and the urge to double, triple them was so powerful, it scared her. She hadn't known she could be so greedy. The kind of addiction that disrupted lives wasn't for the likes of her. She was too sensible, too busy, too happy with her lot. Even Alex, and all the difficulties that had come with him, had never tempted her to want more, to chase things she didn't already have. She'd never had the ambition of Caro. In fact, in the smallest of ways, it had always amused Kay to see the perpetual chase Caro's life had been. All the upgrades and improvements she'd undergone, both to herself and her material surroundings and still, she'd never seemed entirely satisfied. Which was all the more astonishing to Kay now that she too had flown business class, she too had used an executive airport lounge, stayed in – she turned to look around the room – such magnificent surroundings.

But five hundred dollars? In less than an hour?

Double that, and it could be a holiday.

Triple, or even quadruple, and she could make a real start on Alex's fund. The kind of start that, by the time it was needed, might at least be a bulwark against the harsh realities of life on a state pension.

Behind her, hanging from a hook on the wall, exactly where she'd placed it on the first day, the sequins on her Vegas jacket caught the overhead light and winked. Kay turned to face it and the jacket winked again.

You've got guts, Kay. Those were Tony's exact words.

Did she? It had been easy and, she had to admit, very pleasant, to nod and smile and go along with him, but alone now in her room, staring at her jacket, she understood it wasn't true. Not really. Her mother had been a teacher, so she too had become a teacher. Her mother had moved up to head, and that had been Kay's intention as well... before Alex. This wasn't making choices, or taking chances, this was following an example set. A good example, but nevertheless an example already set. Turning away, she caught sight of herself in the full-length mirror on the opposite wall. If they knew... If her parents could see how she was considering placing hundreds of dollars on the turn of a card, they would be horrified.

Minutes passed. Minutes that felt like hours, as she stood staring at her reflection. Minutes in which she fully expected the door to burst open and Caro and Helen to fly through. For someone to come and rescue her from a choice she was equal parts terrified of and excited by. A choice she really was making herself. A chance she really was going to take. *Who are you?* she whispered. Who was she? What would they say about her... afterwards?

She was a nice person. A good mother. A competent mathematician.

'I'm Kay Burrell,' she said to the mirror. 'The kind of woman who buys a glittery jacket and never wears it.'

Six is the worst card, Kay.

Keep a count of those high cards.

'Why shouldn't I, dad?' she said, answering the echo of memory, and in the empty room, her voice was loud. But why shouldn't she use the natural advantage she had? That innate memory for numbers and ratios and proportions? She'd spent her life trying to pass some of her ability onto hundreds, thousands of kids. Those that never stood a hope of getting past a few basic equations and the few that she'd pushed and cajoled all the way over the finishing line. Why shouldn't she be selfish now? Swap out those matchsticks for hundred-dollar chips?

Like a signal, a beam of light flashed off her jacket again. Slowly, Kay walked across and slipped it on and turned once more to face the mirror. And despite everything, despite her cancer, despite the decades that had passed, despite her weight and her weariness, despite the slog of the years, her mother's dementia, her father's frailty, despite Alex... wearing it, she felt very, very different. She felt as she had the very first time she'd tried it on in the cramped changing room of BHS, a different century and another lifetime ago – as if the world was hers for the taking. And just as they had then, the thousand sequins whispered their possibilities, reflected their light, opened up vista after unseen vista for her and made it so very easy to believe that she was, and could be, someone else. A child playing dress-up! An actor! A woman ready to mix it up with the high rollers! Ridiculous. She was an overweight, fifty-plus, maths teacher from suburbia, who'd had a lucky streak... She dropped her head to one side and frowned. Tony had said something, on the way back. Well, he'd said a lot. He did a lot of talking. But one thing particularly had struck true and she was trying to remember... Something about pretending, about...

If you're uncomfortable doing something, pretending to be someone else makes it more comfortable.

She turned on her heel, and went straight to the tall bureau, where she'd unpacked her clothes. From the top drawer, she pulled out the Roxette wig Craig had given her at Helen's house just the other week. She didn't use the mirror as she tugged it on. She was careful, making sure it was fully in place, had covered all the tufts of her own close crop, as if instead of an empty room behind her, an audience awaited. And eventually, when she did turn, jacket on, wig on, the image that presented itself in the mirror had Kay gasping in disbelief. Had her pressing her hand to her mouth. *Be blonde,* Sammy had written, and together they'd laughed at the foolishness of that old adage, *blondes have more fun.* A hair colour, was a hair colour, was a hair colour. But how different she looked! How much more indeed like Roxette and less like Kay the schoolteacher. She grabbed her handbag and swung it over her shoulder, looking back at herself one last time. If only she'd known! Thirty odd years she'd had the same hairstyle... thirty odd years.

TONY WAS WAITING downstairs in the foyer as arranged, by the golden sphere. She saw him as soon as the elevator doors opened, but he didn't see her. Or if he did, he didn't recognise her. So she did look that different! The realisation excited her. 'Over here,' she called.

As he turned, his face broke into an enormous smile. 'And you said you couldn't pretend!'

Fighting a wave of uncertainty, Kay smiled. Her hand went to the back of her ear. The wig was itchy, but apart from that no one was giving it, or her, a second glance. Was it really this easy to slip your skin?

'So is my lucky mascot ready to up the odds a little?'

'I think so.'

'Just remember, keep an eye on those high cards.'

'And never split on an even twenty,' she finished.

ENTERING the games room was *déja vu.* Everything looked exactly as it had when they'd left. With no natural light, there were no clues as to how the day had progressed. Or even if it was still day. No deepening shadows, or newly exposed sunlit corners. No clocks. The carpet retained its thick cushion, the TV screens played the same advertisements. Waitresses walked past in low-cut bejewelled corsets, and white-shirted managers stood expressionless and interchangeable. In fact, as Kay paused at the entrance, she could have sworn that over by the craps table, even the players remained the same. A middle-aged man in a washed-out green hoodie and raptor's cap, his companion, a slim Chinese man in a suit.

'Weren't they here earlier?' she whispered as she leaned in to Tony.

Tony squinted. 'Possibly.'

Possibly? He didn't even sound surprised. He led her further back into the room, further than they'd been before. Here, the tables were more spaced out and the players fewer. Here, she noticed, there seemed to be more staff.

Tony turned to her.

'Here?' she whispered. Her heart started pounding. She looked from one end of the table to the other. This was a hundred-dollar minimum bet game.

'You've gotta be in it, to win it,' Tony said, his smile easy.

'But I only have five hundred,' she whispered.

'We'll play two hands,' he whispered back. 'If you lose, we're outta here.'

'Promise?'

'Promise.'

'Ok... ok.' Her heart was racing now and the back of her neck felt cold. When she looked down at her hand, resting over the clasp of her handbag, she could see how it trembled. Tony, she knew, had won a considerable amount earlier and the nonchalance with which he'd pocketed his winnings and hadn't even mentioned it had Kay thinking how ordinary this was for him. His wealth had him breathing different air. Whatever he won, or lost, was inconsequential. The thought made her feel slightly nauseous. She drew a deep breath in, using the pause to attempt to measure just how out of depth she was. Kay the maths teacher did not belong here, no matter how quick her mind. Kay the mother… what on earth was *she* doing here? Over-weight Kay. Exhausted Kay. Conscientious Kay. Law abiding, responsible, Kay. There wasn't, in any of her lived experiences, a single scrap that she could call upon now to help. Except… she looked across the room, aware that something was missing. Wasn't there another Kay, who might be able to shore her up? The Kay who had sat and watched the desert and finally understood the scope and shape of a human life, how tiny and small its allotted place, within the great jigsaw of existence? The Kay, who might not even be here, this time next year. Whose every time from now on in, could well be the last time. What did it matter? Her heart rate slowed, leaving her abnormally calm; she pulled out a chair, and noticed that the man at the seat alongside had odd socks on. Odd socks? She could have laughed! She hadn't placed a bet or lost a dollar, she was still five hundred dollars richer than she had been this morning and she was a fifty-year-old woman with terminal cancer, so what in the world was she scared of? Reaching into her handbag, she pulled out every chip she had. 'I'm ready,' she said.

THE FIRST HAND produced a safe eighteen high, with the dealer busting out at twenty-three. Now she was six hundred dollars richer. The second hand she lost, the third and fourth she won. On the next hand she was dealt two tens. She split the play and won. Now she was nine hundred dollars richer. Within another fifteen minutes, she was fifteen hundred richer. Fifteen hundred dollars!

On the next hand she was once again dealt a lucky pair.

Tony laughed. 'Lady Luck! We have Lady Luck here!' He turned and called to anyone within earshot.

Lady Luck. Who would ever have called her that? The dealer dealt himself a six. Kay stared at it. She knew the odds. She'd been at the table a while now and seen very few high cards come out, which meant they were still in the pack, which meant the odds were in her favour that the dealer would deal himself high and go bust. Blood pounding in her ears, she split her hand and pushed one one-hundred-dollar chip onto one of her nines. And then she did the same with the other. Along with her opening bet, she was now in for four hundred dollars. It felt unreal. The money, the game, the room. Glancing up, she saw in the long wall mirror across the room a small woman with shiny blonde hair and a sequinned jacket and although at one level, Kay understood that, strip the jacket away, pull the wig off and she would be who she had always been, at many other levels, all the closer-to-the-surface levels, it was very easy to pretend that she was indeed someone else altogether. Look at her! This glamorous bright being, so at ease at the high-roller table, so alive!

The dealer went bust at twenty-eight.

Kay froze.

Tony twisted on his heels and punched the air, his eyes breathing adrenaline.

Four hundred dollars! She had just won four hundred dollars! Added to the chips she had on the table, she was now very nearly two thousand dollars richer!

'A drink, to celebrate!' Tony waved at a waitress. 'Champagne?' But he didn't wait for an answer, ordering enough champagne for everyone at the table. Including the man with the odd socks.

Three hands later, and playing more cautiously, she had only lost two hundred back. And as if she were a magnet, the table was now surrounded by spectators.

'Winners attract, Kay,' Tony winked.

A winner? Kay looked down at her cards. When had she ever been a winner? In looks, in life, in love? When had she ever won?

And perhaps it was the champagne, or Tony growing louder and more ebullient, perhaps it was the knot of people pressing in from all sides, swaying her this way and swaying her that way. Or perhaps it was simply that word: winner. What did it matter where the feeling came from, when the result was the same. She felt like a winner so she began to behave like a winner. Doubling her starting wager, playing two hands at once, doubling down on her opening bet, handling two hundred dollars as carelessly as if it were two pence. She was on a roll and there was nothing wrong with that because she had a strategy. She had been watching the high value cards and the less she saw, the more she bet. It was ratios and probabilities and she was good at it. She was a winner.

Several hands later, champagne glasses emptied and refilled more than once, the table surrounded, the dealer nodded at Kay's chips. 'Want to colour up, honey?'

Kay nodded. She slid three piles of ten across to him and he slid three yellow- coloured chips back. She looked at them. Somehow, she was now in possession of four thousand two hundred dollars. The number stood tall as the ceiling, towered above her, shone a torch in her eyes. Four thousand dollars! In disbelief, she looked up and for the first time saw clearly the faces of the people who had come to watch. The grey sallowness of skin that comes from spending too much time indoors, the unconcealed envy in their eyes as they looked at her chips. She saw the dealer, the way his waistcoat had frayed along one edge, and as the waitress passed with her empty tray, she saw the deep lines at her mouth, pulling it downward like a sad marionette. The mask, her mask, everyone's mask was slipping before her very eyes. 'Perhaps,' she said as she leaned in to Tony. 'We should quit?'

But Tony's cheeks had flushed magenta, and a delta of veins had spread across his cheeks. Drinkers' veins, yielding to the flood of alcohol. 'You're winning!' he slurred. 'Play on. Play on!'

'Bets please,' the dealer called.

Kay glanced across at the cards in the dealer's hand. They had already played twelve hands from this shoe. The most hands she'd counted all evening, before the shoe was emptied and re-filled with six new decks, was sixteen. And the number of high cards left un-dealt were more than those dealt. She didn't know how she knew this; she just did. It wasn't so much counting cards, as a brain hard-wired to take note. Once again she took two hands, two hundred dollars on each. Her first hand turned over two eights. Her second hand turned over an ace and a nine. The first card the dealer had dealt himself was a seven.

She stared at her cards. Splitting the eights and doubling the bet would see her wagering four hundred dollars again, and if she doubled down on the ace and the nine, that would be another four hundred. She was in with a statistically probable chance of winning eight hundred dollars in this one hand. Which would take her total winnings up to five thousand. It was dollars, not sterling, but it sounded the same. It sounded so very much like the amount Caro had said, *Give me five thousand and I know someone...* Her mouth went dry. If she lost she'd be back down to three thousand, but statistically she should win. And if there was one thing she knew about, it was statistics. Plus, she was a winner... Tony had said she was winner. All these people around the table were here because she was a winner. Her hand wavered. She picked up four one-hundred-dollar chips, feeling the immense weight of them in her hand. *You're a winner, Kay*, she whispered to herself. A winner!

25

Walking along the deserted grand colonnade, the slap of her dusty shoes loud against the marble, Helen saw the extravagance of her surroundings as if for the first time. And it was more opulent, more palatial, more ostentatious than she had ever thought. She couldn't work out why that should be. Why did it suddenly seem so out-of-this-world grand? And then, as she looked up at the intricate cornices of the ceiling, she understood. At this time of the night, there were no knots of women in unflatteringly tight dresses, no grey-faced parents in sloppy t-shirts and ill-fitting shorts. No electric wheelchairs, and no pink-faced boys, slurping tall drinks, all elbows and baseball caps. There were no swirled tattoos on rippling skin, no starfish gaits from the wobbling obese and... no noise. Above her head the richly painted ceiling frescoes seemed to rise up to meet her, and along each side, marble columns flowed past in seamless classical proportions. She ran her hand through her clumpy, dirty hair. Empty of people, she felt she loved Vegas even more. Felt as if she were an empress, on a victory walk into Rome.

Because if ever there was a place where you could be any and all things you ever dreamed of being, it had to be Vegas!

At the far end of the colonnade the hotel foyer opened up. She could see the elaborate queueing system, with its gold posts and heavy silk ropes, guiding nothing now but fresh air.

'Shall we see if she's in the room first?' Caro said. She was already halfway along one roped off row. 'I'll ask them to ring.'

'Right, yes.' A little unsteady, with sheer fatigue, Helen nodded. It hadn't occurred to her to do this. To ask the desk clerk to fulfil what was surely a part of his role anyway. She had been all but ready to take the elevator, traipse past a hundred closed doors, and stand knocking on Kay's door herself. And as she watched Caro now, her lips twitched. If she hadn't been so worried about Kay, she might have laughed out loud. Because for all Caro's confidence, and expectations in dealing with other people, she was now approaching the desk by walking the length of each empty row like an obedient child approaching a teacher. Up she went, turned and walked back again. Up and then back again. Why didn't she duck under? And just as Helen thought this Caro turned, raised her eyes to heaven and said,

'Why am I doing this?'

'I don't know,' Helen shook her head. 'Do something spontaneous instead!'

Caro didn't hesitate. She hoisted a rope, ducked under it and then did the same with the next one until she was face to face with the bemused clerk. 'We're looking for our friend,' she said. 'Can you ring her room?'

Smiling, Helen turned away to find something, *anything,*

to lean against or rest upon. She settled for the nearest column, where Marianne had already had the same idea.

'I need to sleep,' Marianne groaned as she leaned back against the column.

'Me too,' Helen said and stifled a yawn. She was utterly exhausted. Her hair thick, her body heavy as a sack of potatoes. She shifted her weight from one foot to the other, feeling the grit of the desert between her toes. Gabe had taken ages to answer Lula's calls. Three times she'd had to ring, and when he'd finally arrived, scowling and tucking his shirt in, it was obvious by his heated exchange with Lula, in Spanish, that he wasn't happy. And if she had to add two and two together, Helen was reasonably confident that the sum she would arrive at would include Tony. She'd heard both Lula and Gabe mention his name several times, and she had the feeling this wasn't the first time Tony had caused chaos. Still, they were back now. All they had to do was locate Kay... and then bed. Tipping her head against the marble she allowed her eyes to close, but no sooner had she done so than she heard Caro call across the foyer.

'There's no answer. She could be sleeping, I suppose?'

Helen sighed. She pulled her phone out of her back pocket and looked at it. It was quarter to three in the morning.

'What time was the last text?' Caro said.

'Just before midnight.' She'd texted Kay at eleven fifty-two.

> Are you ok? Caro and I have cleared the air. We're both so sorry, Kay, but it's all ok now and we're worried.

Kay had answered.

I'm fine. Glad you and Helen are too.

'What if she's not in the room?' Caro said as she walked back to them.

Helen sighed. Her feet ached, her mouth was dry and she could feel flakes of desert sand all down her back. A hot shower, a controlled collapse between sheets... that was what she wanted. But sleep was out of the question until they knew where Kay was. 'We'll have to start looking,' she said. 'Probably the casino.' The casino? The thought of that army of slot-machines was more than she could cope with. How would they get through it? Images of them all wandering around in circles for ever and ever squeezed behind her eyes.

'This is my fault,' Marianne said bleakly. She leaned forward to inspect her feet, the maroon sheen of her toenails completely covered now in red dust. 'All my fault.'

'No,' Helen said. She put a hand on Marianne's back. It felt warm and damp. And before Marianne could straighten up or respond, a tall blonde-haired woman clicked past on neat heels. She was dressed in the white shirt and dark waistcoat of a croupier. Her hair had been pulled back into a slick ponytail and she walked with the smooth, easy gait of the young. Almost a bounce.

'Tony Larson is back in,' she called to the desk clerk, unaware of the dusty middle-aged women, half hidden by the column, that she'd just passed.

Marianne, Caro and Helen froze.

'Does he ever leave?' the clerk asked.

The croupier laughed. 'He will soon. He's lost eleven thousand tonight. Started on the hundred-buck table, and is back on the five-buck table. He never learns. I'll take over

246

after my break, so Joel can go home. If he's still there that is. Tony's the only player left.'

'What happened to the woman he was with yesterday?'

'Which one?'

'The old one. Short and fat, has a funny accent.'

Hearing this, Marianne pulled herself up to full height, which wasn't high. All the time, Helen kept her hand pressed lightly against her back.

'Doesn't sound like his normal type?' the croupier said.

The desk clerk laughed. 'As long as she's loaded, that's his type.'

'True. Do you remember that octogenarian he picked up a couple of years ago? The one in the wheelchair?'

'The one he tried to marry? What happened there? I never did find out.'

And before either Helen or Caro could react, Marianne had stepped out from behind the column, one pudgy knee peeping from her ruched jeggings, a rash rising up like a wave across her chest. 'Yes,' she said loudly. 'What did happen? We'd *all* like to know.'

The emphasis Marianne had given to the *all*, was a call to arms. It had Helen stepping out from behind the column just in time to see surprise slap itself on the desk clerk's face, opening his eyes painfully wide, dropping his jaw.

Now Caro joined her and as the croupier turned to see who had spoken, her ponytail flipped helplessly like a puppy's tail.

'What happened?' Marianne said again. Her chin was at the angle normally supported only by a neck-brace, but, standing so close, Helen could see how her hands, balled to fists, trembled.

'Umm...' The croupier twirled her ponytail.

Helen folded her arms.

The other side of Marianne, Caro reached down, flicked an invisible speck of dust from her arm, and slowly turned her best boardroom gaze to the croupier.

No one spoke.

Marianne shrugged. 'You know what,' she said and waved her hand dismissively. 'I don't want to know.'

Half a second passed in which the croupier's face had time to begin to relax, before Marianne took a step forward and said, 'Where is he now? Playing Blackjack?'

Recoiling, the croupier nodded nervously.

'Is he with anyone?'

She didn't answer, glancing back at the desk clerk instead.

Marianne dropped her head to one side. 'This may surprise you, young lady... but even a fat old woman like me has self-respect.'

The croupier's mouth hung open. 'I didn't me—'

'*I haven't finished!*' Marianne hissed.

Helen glanced across at Caro, her lips twitching.

Caro looked back at her. *She hadn't finished,* she mouthed.

She hasn't even started, Helen mouthed back.

'So I don't care if Tony is with a twenty-two-year-old heiress. I'm asking where he is and who he's with, because I'm looking for my friend.'

'Our friend,' Caro said tightly.

'Yes. *Our* friend,' Helen finished.

The croupier bit down on her lip. 'Not now,' she managed. 'I mean, he was with a... a lady earlier. She was...'

'Old?' Helen suggested.

The croupier shook her head, but it morphed into an involuntary nod.

'Fat, but not quite as fat as me?' Marianne added.

And again the croupier's head went through a strange pattern of movement. 'She had a wig...' Horrified at what might have been another faux pas, her face froze. 'At least... well, I think it was a wig,' she whispered.

'Roxette style?' Helen said.

'Who?' The croupier frowned.

'Never mind,' Helen muttered.

'She was wearing a jacket,' the croupier said. 'A very sparkly jacket.'

As one, Helen, Caro and Marianne turned to each other.

'But she left. I mean, she's not there now. She's not playing now.'

'Did you see her?' Helen asked the desk clerk. 'She must have come this way for the elevators?'

But the clerk shook his head. 'Wait a moment,' he added, almost to himself. 'Silver jacket?'

Everyone nodded.

'I did see a woman in a jacket like that. Not so long ago actually. She went towards the square.'

'The square?' Helen said.

'St Mark's Square.'

'St Mark's Square is in Venice,' Caro said flatly.

'It's also in Vegas,' the clerk shrugged. 'I noticed because she was looking at the Armillary sphere for a long time. She even asked me what it was for.'

Helen turned to look at the large golden sphere in the middle of the foyer. 'What is it for?' she said now.

'It was used to study stars,' the clerk said. 'Before telescopes. And I remember now. She said she was going to the square to look at the stars.'

'But it's all indoors,' Helen said. 'How can she...' She stopped talking, because the clerk was smiling at her.

'Most people,' he said, 'don't care. When they come here,

they're happy to think it's real. All of it.' He drew a long breath in. 'I guess they just want to believe.'

THEY WERE HALFWAY across the foyer before the croupier had caught up with them. She was breathless, her ponytail swinging, a bead of sweat along her top lip. 'I'm sorry,' she began, addressing Marianne. 'I didn't realise—'

'Don't be sorry,' Marianne said, her voice weary. Then, with a flourish of one arm, as if she were presenting herself, head to toe, short, flabby and dusty as she was, she said, 'Be prepared.'

The girl made to smile, but it didn't quite work.

'One day,' she finished, 'this will be you.'

26

Alone in a St Mark's Square that had never seen Venice, had never been more deserted and had never been more perfect, Kay stood perfectly still. High up, rows of arched windows glowed the exact same shade of mauve-pink: a perpetual twilight, born from the painted sky. Black floor tiles gleamed, forever wet from non-existent rain, and all along the ground floor – where once upon another place and another time, goldsmiths and glaziers, cobblers and engravers, would have toiled away their time on earth – empty restaurants with empty tables and empty chairs awaited the return of tourists come only to eat the hours away. Squares of white cloth, as pristine clean now as they would be in the morning, covered the tables. No bird droppings on the smooth railings, no scratching rats scurrying into corners, no cigarette stubs, or scraps of paper, empty bottles, smears of grime on window-ledges. The clock tower, its handsome face of blue and gold, told time for no one. And although she couldn't see it, across Kay's shoulders, sequins from her jacket reflected the heavenly pink light, tiny rays like splintered sunlight, making a target of her.

In a daze she turned full circle, unable to recall quite how she'd arrived where she now stood. Between then and now lay the remnants of a few scattered images...

Tony's hand pushing her hundred-dollar chips forward, her own hand pulling them back. The dealer's last card, busting him out at twenty-four. Tony's face. The crushing groan that travelled around the table, sharp as a pin. Many pins. The sticky film of champagne coating empty glasses, the blank, almost expectant look on the dealer's face at what a disappointment she'd turned out to be, how ordinary after all. How very ordinary.

Five thousand dollars she'd had within her grasp. Five thousand dollars for those who had the guts.

Which wasn't her.

Fortune favours the brave.

And that wasn't her.

She wasn't a winner, because she hadn't even tried. She'd balked. Allowed a chink, large enough for fear and doubt, and plain old timidity to barge in and take over. Freezing the Kay who might, for once in her life, have taken the gamble.

Which she would have won.

Looking down at the wig in her hand, the ball of blonde, she tried again to remember. How had she found her way from the games room, to here?

There had been no exit signs, barely a change of light to indicate a change of room. But she remembered now. A green square, with a white arrow, that had had her shouldering a heavy door, which had led into a long corridor, lit only with ghostly emergency lights. Another door at the far end. And when she'd opened that last door, it had made a small humming noise and as she'd walked out she found herself at the edge of a large space. Empty loading trolleys lined up side by side, identification stickers fluttering in the breeze. And across the concrete barrier wall at the end of this space, a strip of highway had been visible, fuzzy with the lights of people going places, living lives. And from then it had all become real. Then she had known. She had exited the stage, gone behind the curtain of Vegas itself to find herself in a loading bay, where the props for this theatre of dreams were unloaded all day, every day.

Somehow she had found her way back to the strip, and its almost empty pavements. Just herself, a young man with no legs, asleep in his wheelchair, another man in a dusty grey tracksuit, stretched out on the steps of a topless bar, like Caesar on a couch, gazing with indifference at his empty kingdom. And along with the men, dozens and dozens of small white cards, skittling along in the breeze, every last one of them showing a photo of a young, naked girl, straddling an unmade bed: *Sandy. Call me. I never sleep.*

Yes, she remembered now. She'd taken out her phone and called Sandy because here, at last, was someone else in the world who no longer slept. But the phone had been answered by an angry-sounding man and she hadn't known what to say. *Where is Sandy? Is she awake? I need someone to talk to.*

Back at the hotel, it had become clear. *What is it for?* she'd asked, and someone had told her. The golden globe she'd admired since they day they'd arrived measured the movement of the stars, mapped the geometry of heaven. There could have been no clearer message.

This was how she had arrived at where she now stood. She was here to measure a star, how long would the light remain, how long would it last. Only there were no stars.

She had looked and looked, but there wasn't a single star. Walking backwards, hands balled to fists, Kay tried one last time. But her neck was stiff from looking up, and her heart limp. And she knew. The sky above was destined to remain forever starless; she couldn't even get this right.

Clutching the wig under her chin, like a child might hold a soft toy... like Alex had once... she stared straight ahead. Her feet burned and throbbed, the first time she had felt them in hours. As she looked down at her shoes, she became aware of all the other signs of exhaustion her body bore: a light and spinning mind on a head she could barely hold up, a dry mouth, shaky legs. A few feet away, so very close, she could see the cool blue water of the canal inviting her to sit, to lie down, to sleep. An invitation she was powerless to resist.

THEY HAD WALKED through every arch, looked behind every trash can, and had been standing on the pretend Rialto bridge, for long minutes now, Marianne, Helen and Caro. Each of them scanning and re-scanning, left to right, corner to corner. Once, Marianne had thought she'd seen a figure move behind the canopy of a restaurant, but it had turned out to be nothing. A shadow, if that were possible.

'I just don't think she's here,' Caro said for the second time.

Helen didn't answer. She hadn't answered the first time. Answering would have meant they would be moving toward a decision. A turning back, a giving in. And the idea of leaving Kay out here alone, no matter how perfect the scenery, wasn't something she felt ready to face.

'Why don't we try one last walk through,' she said, and was answered by a small but clear splash of water that sounded very close. Instantly she turned. Almost directly below the bridge, at the bottom of smooth white steps that had been closed off by black railings, sat Kay. They hadn't seen her before, because she was almost hidden, tucked up against the brickwork. She had, Helen could see, removed her shoes and rolled up her trousers to dangle her feet in the water of the pretend canal. Like a child at the seaside.

The first thing Helen felt was relief. The second thing was envy. That water looked so cool and her feet, never fully recovered from the first day walking the strip, were itching to try it. 'Kay!' she called as she leaned over the parapet.

'Where?' Caro turned.

Marianne too, the three of them toppling forward to see.

'Kay!' Helen called again.

Slowly, Kay turned her head.

'What are you doing?' Caro whispered in a loud voice. 'You're on the wrong side of the railings.'

Kay looked first at the railings, and then back at Caro. She shrugged.

'Come up!' Marianne waved.

But Kay shook her head.

'Do you need help?'

Again Kay shook her head.

Helen turned back to the empty square. There was no one in sight and if there was one thing she was sure of, it was that Kay wasn't fine. 'I'm going down,' she said, and, without hesitation, she hurried across the bridge, slipping off her sneakers as she did and hitching up her sleeves. When she reached the railings, again she didn't pause. She swung one leg as high as she could, made an odd wheezing sound and hoisted herself up.

'Helen!' Caro hissed.

Perched atop the railings, Helen looked up. 'It's just like

getting on the horse,' she giggled. Actually, it was much harder. The iron-work of the railings was a lot more unforgiving than the flank of a horse. She had a moment to wonder how Kay, who was so much shorter, had managed, and then she leaned forward, swung her back leg over and landed clumsily on the other side. Her hands stung. Standing upright, she shook them loose and called up, 'Are you coming?'

Marianne and Caro looked at each other. A moment later they were facing her, on the other side of the railings.

'You know, there are cameras everywhere,' Caro whispered.

'Why are you whispering?' Helen whispered back.

Caro giggled. 'I don't know.'

'I'll get deported,' Marianne moaned.

'We all will,' Helen said. 'And no one wants to end their professional life with a deportation notice. Do they?' As she finished, she looked at Caro. The words had slipped out before she could stop them. Parroting back to Caro, almost the exact same words Caro had used herself, all those years ago, the night she'd wanted to sleep under the stars at Stonehenge, and Caro had said, *No one wants to start their professional life with a police caution.* 'Stonehenge,' she said now, a glint of a challenge in her eye.

Caro looked at her. 'I didn't say that!'

'As good as!'

And again Caro held her eye. 'Well fuck it!' she whispered. 'I've had my professional life, it's time I started my real life!' And she bent down and pulled her sneakers off.

And as Helen watched, a feeling of immeasurable lightness lifted her. Kay was here, safe. Caro was back and Marianne...

'How am I going to get over that!' Marianne cried, waving at the railings. 'I'm not even as tall as Kay.'

'Use your hands,' Helen whispered to Caro. 'Give Marianne a lift.' She made a cradle of her own hands, to show Caro, the action reminding her of lost summers, decades ago, of fences that smelled of creosote and the tingling feeling of stepping over boundaries, every bit as real now as it had been when she was ten years old.

Marianne wiggled out of her jacket and kicked off her sandals. 'Ready?' she asked Caro, and didn't wait for an answer, placing instead the whole of her dusty and manicured foot into Caro's hands.

And watching Caro's frame stagger sideways and listening to the urgent whisperings of *Wait. Try again. You have to lift!* Helen bent at the waist, tears of laughter smarting her eyes.

'Wait,' Caro hissed again, but Marianne had already stepped forward into the thin air of a cradle that wasn't ready. Her foot came down on nothing, her balance went and she fell into a sideways hop, skip and shuffle, landing on the wet-not-wet tiles, legs splayed.

'Hassiktir!' she gasped.

Helen clutched her stomach with laughter. 'Stop it. I'm going to wet myself.'

'I already have,' Marianne muttered.

'Are you ok?' Caro managed, but she too was laughing.

Marianne wobbled to her feet. 'Catch me this time?' she said, her eyes narrowed at Caro.

'Wait, this time?' Caro responded.

And up Marianne went, Caro's cradle holding her. She landed, with a stumble, on the other side of the railing next to Helen. Within another moment Caro had joined them and they stood, looking at each other, faces flushed with the excitement of adventure.

But when they turned to Kay, the excitement evaporated. She hadn't moved. In all of the stumbling and the whispered giggles, she hadn't turned to watch, hadn't shown any interest. She was sat, still as a stone.

Helen went first, sitting herself, very quietly, beside Kay. She leaned forward, to roll up her leggings, before dipping in her feet, one by one. The water was as deliciously cool as she had anticipated. Calming and fresh. Caro joined them. Then Marianne. So now they sat, on the landing board. The four of them, side by side by side.

No one spoke. Helen looked down at her feet. The water distorted and blurred the edges, still it was plain to see that they were not the feet of a young person. Underneath the little toe of her right foot, a bunion had spread sideways. She twisted her leg, to see more clearly. No wonder her shoes hurt so much. And now she looked across at the row of feet in the water. Even Marianne's pedicure couldn't disguise the cracked skin and crooked toes and gnarly joints of middle age. Together these feet had borne the weight of two hundred years, and for a brief moment she thought of her babies' feet, remembering how, when Jack and Libby were tiny, she would hold their toes, so clean, so pink, so uncontaminated by life. 'Kay,' she whispered. 'Caro and I have sorted it all out. I'm so sorry you ever had to hear any of it. It was a stupid misunderstanding. Just stupid.'

'We're both sorry, Kay,' Caro said, leaning to her. 'This was meant to be such a special trip for you.'

Marianne frowned at the water. 'I am too. I should never have introduced you to Tony.'

'It's not Tony,' Kay said as she looked up. She turned first to Helen and then Caro. 'And it's not you, or Caro either.'

No one answered. There was amongst them all the understanding that it wasn't their cue.

And then Kay leaned forward, her chin in her hands and said, 'I came here to look at the stars.'

Over the top of her head, Helen and Caro looked at each other.

Marianne looked straight up at the sky. The ever-blue, ever-starless, painted Venetian sky.

'There are none,' Kay shrugged.

Tenderly, Helen moved to place her hand on Kay's back, but before she could, Kay straightened up and flung herself back against the bridge. 'I'm just a loser!' she cried. 'A failure, and a loser.'

Drawing her hand back, Helen's eyes went blank with astonishment. Never, in all the years they had known each other, had she heard Kay talk like this. *Loser? Failure?* The spectacle those words conjured was ugly, and, used in the same context as the name Kay, ludicrous. Such a clear misfit, she couldn't take them seriously, couldn't even summon up a denial because that would mean allowing that there might, in the smallest quantity, have been a truth to be found. Kay, who, nearly all her life, had pushed ambition and self aside? Who spent her days and energy giving to others? A loser? A failure?

Neither Marianne, nor Caro, offered up a response either, and with their silence, Helen knew they were thinking the same thing. 'Kay,' she said and took Kay's hand, folding it within her own. 'What happened?'

'Tony,' Kay answered, 'said I was a winner.' She began moving her feet up and down, splashing water across the landing board. 'He said I was a winner and I should have believed him. But I didn't.'

'Tony,' Marianne said hoarsely, 'is a liar!'

Kay stared straight ahead. 'I had one chance. I could have won five thousand dollars. The odds were in my favour, and I'm a mathematician, right? I know about odds, it's what I've spent my life teaching and understanding!' A tear rolled down her cheek, followed swiftly by another. 'I didn't take it,' she whispered. 'I could have won five thousand dollars, but I didn't take my chance. It won't come again. If there's one thing I know, it's that chances don't come round a second time so not only am I a loser, I'm a coward too.'

'No. Kay...' Helen started. But she could hardly make her voice heard because Kay had inched in a semblance of truth after all. Chances didn't come round a second time, and so the words... *loser, coward...* had somehow become loaded, or at least were not harmless. And they wounded Helen. Wounded them all. So they sat, silent and flattened and unable to find a way to stop the hurt.

'I could have won that money,' Kay cried. 'I *should* have won it. I could have taken dad and Alex on holiday. I could have begun Alex's fund, given him a real start so he won't be on his own completely. It would have been enough, and I knew that and even though I knew that and I knew what the odds were, I was still too scared! I'm a coward. There's no other explanation. I'm a coward and a loser, and now it's too late... There won't be another chance. It won't come again. I'll die. And it won't ever come again...'

And although the air in the pretend square was as still as the air in a bottle, and there were no stars above, and no insects or birds, animals or humans, a force that was nevertheless alive took Kay's words and shredded them, ripping them into jagged and mutilated pieces, so they became unbearable. Her head dropped onto Helen's shoulder.

And just as she had with every wounded child who had ever crossed her path, Helen scooped Kay in. Wrapped her arm around Kay's back and lifted her chin above Kay's shoulder and held her, as Kay sobbed and her body trembled. And beside them, Caro sat silently and Marianne shook her head, a lone tear spilling down her cheek. And they knew from wisdom that was hard-won not to breach the moment. That these pauses were knots that kept their bracelet of friendship tied. Memories that would always bind them. Because, if in the beginning what they had found in each other was not much more than a sympathetic mirror for a life that hadn't met expectations, it had in these later years transformed into a granite-like awareness that being present was enough. Keeping the thread intact was all that was required. So they sat and they waited and eventually, when they thought she was ready, Helen tried again.

'Kay?'

Kay peeled herself away from Helen's shoulder and looked up. 'I came to look at the stars,' she said. 'I thought if I can't leave Alex anything else, at least I know I'll have left him love... Because I do. I love him so much.' Her voice broke. 'You said it was sad, Caro.'

Caro looked up.

Kay nodded. 'At the ranch, you said it was sad the stars were dead, we could still see their light but they were dead.'

'I didn't mean anything,' Caro said, her voice tight and small.

And again for a long moment no one spoke.

Then Kay whispered. 'I don't think it's sad, you see. In fact, it gives me hope.' Her face glistening with tears, she smiled. 'If it can happen with light, I think it can happen with love. I believe that. I believe that even if I'm dead, Alex will still have my love. He will, won't he?' And the plea in her eyes made it look as if they were breathing. The hope that flared and receded, flared and receded.

Helen nodded, she couldn't speak, the weight of her own grief would not allow it, because what Kay was saying was ringing its truth in her ears, louder than a thousand slot machines could ever hope to. Love didn't die. Didn't she still carry the weight of her love for her lost son with her, every single day?

'He'll still have it, Kay,' Caro managed. She stretched her hand out to grasp Kay's.

Helen looked down at their joined hands. And Caro too carried her own small portion of the kind of love that would never admit defeat.

'He'll always have it, Kay,' Marianne said and now she reached across, her hand on top of Caro's, on top of Kay's.

'And us,' Helen managed, her voice cracking. She added her hand, so now they were joined, the four of them. 'You'll stay with us too, always Kay. Always.'

27

Twenty minutes later, tired and bedraggled, they made a sombre sight as they walked slowly past the deserted bars and shops and cafés. The thin echo of Marianne's sandals slapping the floor was the only sound. Silent and subdued, no one else had bothered to put footwear back on and they walked, swinging shoes by laces or, in Helen's case, laces tied together and hung around her neck. She was exhausted, so many thoughts about the day trying to be heard that she'd given up and concentrated now only upon the floor, which felt smooth and cool, the way the soles of her feet peeled back and pressed down again, peeled and pressed down. The feeling had become a mantra, a rhythm that was carrying her, sure as night followed day, all the way to a more than welcome bed. Even the sharp ridges of the escalator hadn't been enough to penetrate her dream-like state. Down she floated, ever downward.

'Oh, shit!' Caro, leading the way, had stopped.

It didn't take Helen long to see why. The escalator had deposited them at the far end of the slots room. One hundred and twenty thousand square feet, filled with over one thousand slot machines, which they would need to navigate their way across to find the elevators to get back – finally – to their rooms. And nothing to guide them! Not a sun or moon in sight, rather, wave after wave of ceiling-mounted multicoloured neon lighting and a carpet busier than her grandmother's curtains. At least Columbus had had a compass, Odysseus a few friendly gods! The scene ahead, although slightly more muted than it was in daytime hours, had Helen's knees bending like rubber. It was more than she could manage, at the end of this longest of days, too much. If it hadn't been for Caro, striding into the fray, she might have just found the nearest corner and curled up there.

'Where are you going?' Kay called weakly.

Caro stopped and turned to them.

Thank God, Helen thought, because where had she been going? Surely she wasn't going to try and...

'Just follow me,' Caro called. 'Stay close and follow me.'

Helen and Kay looked at each other.

'Does she know where she's going?' Marianne said, close behind.

Helen shrugged. There were, and always had been, some areas of life in which she wouldn't ever have tried to test Caro. Compound interest, or whatever it was. The going rate for a good dry-cleaner. 'Wait!' she called. Because it was clear, from the confident way Caro was moving ahead, they were in that kind of territory now. Or at least Caro thought so.

Caro smiled. 'Don't you trust me?'

'I do,' Helen said, but she was looking at the rows and rows of identikit flashing slot machines. She did trust Caro, she definitely did, but she was also remembering those brief twenty minutes she had been lost in this mega-room. It couldn't have been more than twenty minutes, but it had felt like twenty hundred, and she had been hopelessly lost and the thought of wandering forever, or at least until dawn, had her faint. She was fifty. She needed her bed. 'Just...' And turning the ends of her knotted shoelaces, she lowered her chin and looked down at them, an idea forming that was as silly as it was sensible. She turned to Kay. 'Give me one of your sneakers.'

Wordlessly, Kay handed her sneaker over. She did not ask why, and she looked so tired and so small Helen had the feeling she would have handed tomorrow over, in order to get to a bed. Leaning over, Helen knotted the lace of Kay's sneaker to the lace of one of her own. When she was done she handed Kay her sneaker back so now they were joined. 'I've got you now,' she said and turned to Caro. 'Your turn.'

Offering no resistance, Caro handed her sneaker over.

Helen knotted it with her remaining shoe. Wiping a clump of hair from her forehead, she handed it back, saying, 'And if you tie your other sneaker to Kay's, so Kay and Marianne can use it.'

Caro nodded When she'd finished, Helen dipped forward, checking that they were all joined.

'If the laces were a bit longer we could skip,' she said.

'My relationship with gravity has changed since those days,' Kay said wearily. 'I don't think I'd leave the ground.'

'I haven't skipped since 1969,' Marianne muttered. She looked at Helen. 'This is one of the many things they never tell you about having a baby.'

Helen smiled. 'No skipping. I promise. Right!' And jiggling the laces, she turned to Caro. 'We're ready. At least,' she added cheerily, 'if we perish, we'll perish together.'

'It could take days.' Marianne shook her head. 'I've never seen such an enormous hotel. It makes me miss Cyprus.'

'Well, if it takes days,' Helen said, 'I give you all permission to feast off my body. I've eaten enough since we've been here to keep everyone going at least until morning.' And turning, she was rewarded by the sight of a smile creeping across Kay's face. 'Onward, Caro?'

Caro must have seen Kay's smile too, Helen thought, because she wasn't imagining it. No, it was real. The sense of renewed lightness, of determination and belief that had them – linked as surely as girls with skipping ropes – following on into the mighty labyrinth ahead.

AND CARO DID KNOW the way! Tugging them all along, past slots that Helen had never seen before and would be happy never to see again. Slots depicting women with breasts as round and viciously hard as medicine balls; men with far too much facial hair. Until, quite abruptly, Caro came to a halt, stopping in front of a slot and staring at it, an inscrutable expression on her face.

'What's the hold up,' Marianne called from the rear.

Caro turned. 'You're not a loser, Kay,' she said suddenly.

'Oh... don't—' Kay started weakly.

'No,' Caro interrupted. 'You're not.'

'Caro...' Helen's voice was edged with caution.

But Caro turned to her. 'How much cash have you got on you?'

'I... I don't know.' She was thrown by the question. Thrown by the urgency with which Caro had asked. 'Not much,' she said. 'Maybe twenty dollars.'

'Marianne?'

Marianne, it seemed was quicker. She'd let go of her lifeline to Kay and come closer to the slot they were standing by, the slot that Helen could see now was Titanic.

'Much the same,' Marianne said and looked at Caro.

'It's a random combination,' Kay whispered. 'It's not going—'

'It's going to prove that you are not a loser, Kay,' Caro cut her off. 'Let's play. I want to show you. Five dollars each.' She looked at Helen.

And meeting Caro's eye, Helen did not know what to do. The moment had arrived without warning. A large part of her was scared for Kay's sake, wanted nothing more than to keep them moving forward, to get them all safely into beds, get the night over with... But the assurance in Caro's voice was as real as a roadblock. Caro, she felt, knew how this was going to end. And she wasn't just asking how much cash Helen had, she was also asking Helen to trust her... In a way Helen knew she hadn't done often enough. Silently, she opened her bag and took out her purse, aware of Marianne doing the same.

Caro nodded, turned to the slot and fed in the first note.

Only Kay hadn't moved, her face unreadable.

Golden keys and compasses whizzed past, stopwatches and cellos. One heart of the ocean, then two and then none.

Helen took her turn, one heart, then two and then none.

Marianne stepped forward. Golden keys and a tiny Jack.

'Your turn,' Caro said quietly.

But Kay took a step back, her eyes filling with tears.

And then Helen understood. 'It doesn't matter,' she said. 'Does it?' She looked to Caro, who nodded in agreement.

'Helen's right. That's the point, Kay. It doesn't matter what happens because even if you lose, you haven't lost. Not a single thing that mattered. You'll still have us. You have Alex and your parents—'

'And thousands of kids!' Helen cried. She knew what Caro was doing. 'It must be thousands, probably more. All the kids you've ever taught, Kay. Every time you had them understanding a fraction, you were sending them off to a better life! No one can take that away from you.'

And at this Kay really did smile. 'If only,' she said, 'that was all it took for a better life.'

'It's a good enough start, Kay.' Marianne nodded. 'Better than a lot of kids get.'

'That,' Helen exclaimed, 'is absolutely true!'

'Ok,' Kay breathed. She stepped forward. 'Ok.'

One heart rolled past and then two and then none.

Two hearts rolled past and then none.

On her third roll, three hearts rolled past and stuck, one and then two and three. A burst of golden coins exploded across the screen, blooming over and over again, Hearts of the Ocean pulsating as if they had just been pulled from living breathing bodies. A number flashed up. *1000! 1000! 1000!*

'You've won!' Marianne cried.

Kay stared at the screen.

'You've won a thousand credits!' Helen laughed.

'Ten dollars,' Caro smiled.

Kay nodded. She reached up and pressed the cash button. 'I'll treat you all to coffee,' she said as she bent to collect her winning ticket. And as she stood, carefully folding the ticket in half she said, 'This is what I couldn't afford to lose.' And she looked up. 'This. Us.'

PART IV

28

They never went back to the casino.

The next morning Marianne texted Tony to ask for the return of Kay's chips, which she'd left on the Blackjack table. He hadn't responded, but later that same morning the desk clerk had handed Marianne an envelope with the chips inside. All four thousand dollars' worth. There had also been a handwritten note, which Marianne had read, her face impassive, as she'd slipped it back into the envelope.

THEY'D TAKEN another long stroll along the strip and each bought themselves a new pair of pumps from a shoe vending machine, just because such a thing as a shoe vending machine existed! The money had gone in and a can had rolled out, and when they unpeeled the lids, out had popped a rolled-up pair of gloriously cushioned pumps.

. . .

THEY'D CHEERED at the Cirque du Soleil and sung along with the Elton and Aretha impersonators at Legends in Concert. And finally they had taken a helicopter ride over the Grand Canyon. Where, hovering above that astonishing landscape, the metaphysical enormity of it had silenced them. It would have been impossible not to be humbled by the view, not to feel as if life was bigger and more various than they could ever hope to understand. Transported by the majesty, once again Kay had been left with a feeling of resolute calm. As if she knew she was ready now to face whatever was coming. And it hadn't been a sad feeling. Not at all. Stepping off the helicopter, images of the six-million-year-old landscape still clear in her mind, she had been profoundly light of heart and deeply, deeply, happy. Which was extraordinary. Because hadn't she accepted that happiness was unachievable for her now? That the best she could hope for, going forward, would be calm acceptance? Yes, she was living under a death sentence, but so was every other living creature. Rolling over with calm acceptance wasn't, she had decided, going to be her way forward after all. She'd already talked to Marianne about visiting Cyprus later in the summer.

AND NOW, on this, the last day, she leaned back against the cushioning of her seat, coffee cup in her hands, and smiled. She couldn't wait to get back and see Alex. She'd bought him an artificial orchid from the Botanical Gardens, intending to put it in a pot on the kitchen windowsill and see how long it took for him to notice it wasn't real. About five minutes, she guessed. Orchids were one of Alex's specialist subjects, and she knew too well the breadth and depth of knowledge he was capable of gathering on the things that interested him. Flags, were another example. It was best never to get him talking about flags. Or motorcycles, which to her immense relief he seemed to be turning away from. Again, she smiled. She couldn't wait to see him.

'Ooff!' The noise Helen made was akin to a tyre punctured.

'Are you ok?' Kay said.

Helen grimaced. 'Eaten too much. Again.' She slipped her hand under her waistband to lift it free of her belly.

'Me too,' Caro said and surreptitiously undid the top button of her shorts.

Helen smiled. 'I never thought I'd see the day when you had to do that! Welcome to my world, Caro!'

'It's Vegas,' Caro shrugged. 'You're meant to over-indulge.'

'Has anyone managed to find out what breakfast ham is yet?' Kay said.

'Ham you eat at breakfast would be my guess,' Helen said flatly, and they all laughed.

All around cutlery chinked, pans brimmed, mouths chewed, hash browns fried, waffles popped, and maple syrup hung in the air, cloyingly sweet. And watching her two oldest friends in the world, easy and comfortable in each other's company again, Kay briefly closed her eyes and gave a prayer of thanks to whoever might be listening.

'So what's first? For the last day,' Helen said, mopping the corner of her mouth with a napkin.

'Kay decides,' Caro said. 'Only no more charts?'

Kay laughed. 'I promise. Charts can wait.' Here, she knew, was another explanation for the extraordinary way she felt.

After cashing in her winning chips, Caro had called a conference in her hotel room. And with herself and Helen perched on the edge of the bed, and Marianne and Kay in chairs, she had set her laptop on a table between them and showed Kay where she intended to invest the four thousand dollars. If Kay was honest, the technical talk of tracking errors and exchange privileges had befuddled her, but the figures hadn't. When the time came, if the markets behaved as they had always behaved, Alex, Caro had explained, could expect to retire with a lump sum, that, added to his state pension, would give him a modest degree of comfort. The degree of comfort it gave Kay, when Caro had shown her the chart, was immeasurable. No, she wouldn't be there, but she had managed to put her arms around him in every way she possibly could. And then Helen had leaned forward and said that her uncle, who owned the garden centre where Alex worked and who had given Alex the job in the first place, was adding Alex to the company pension scheme. He'd also asked Helen to assure Kay that, as far as he was concerned, Alex had a job for life. On hearing this, on looking across at Caro and Helen's faces, and feeling the weight of Marianne's arm on her shoulder, Kay had folded in half and sobbed with relief, each heavy tear a rope cut, allowing her to rise again to a lighter state of being.

'Yes,' Helen said now. 'This is your trip, Kay. You choose.' She leaned against the backrest, her cup in her hands. 'Isn't it lovely though? No dishes, no shopping.'

'I'd like a photograph,' Kay said suddenly. 'There's a place that had fancy dress. I'd like a photograph of the four of us together. As whatever it is we choose to be.' She shrugged. 'It's Vegas after all.'

'Sounds fun,' Helen said.

Caro nodded. 'Where is Marianne by the way?'

'She's coming,' Kay said. 'But I think she's probably just

having some quiet time. I expect she's missing the peace of Cyprus.'

Caro nodded. Looking across at the crowded restaurant, she said, 'It is a bit like being stuck in an airport, doomed forever to be queueing for a budget flight. Not that I know too much about budget flights.'

Helen smiled. Looking at Kay, she said, 'Did she ever tell you what Tony had written?'

Kay shook her head. 'No. And I haven't asked.'

'She must be disappointed. Him sweeping in like a knight in shining armour, and then turning out to be nothing of the sort.'

'Oh I don't know,' Kay mused. 'Marianne is the last person to be needing a knight in shining armour.'

'I hope so,' Helen murmured. 'I hope so.'

'I LOVE HOW TALL I AM,' Kay yelped. She was wearing a green leotard, with tasselled edging and an extravagant fringed choker. On her head, a green skull cap, from which sprouted, two feet into the air, a plume of green feathers She put her hands on her hips and looked down at her feet, at the spangly green peep-toe heels that gave her four extra inches.

'We have pinnable bottom pieces,' a slightly-built man in a logo polo shirt said. Denny, the photographer.

'Pinnable bottoms?' Kay said, her lips twitching.

He nodded. 'Would you like to see?'

'Absolutely. When will I ever get the chance again?'

Denny disappeared and Kay moved across to the row of curtained cubicles, behind which Marianne, Helen and Caro were still getting changed. 'Come out!' she called. 'We have pinnable bottoms!'

Helen was first. Along with fishnet tights, she wore a purple diamanté-studded bra top, and a purple diamanté-studded thong bottom. 'My bottom,' she said as she positioned herself to see, 'looks like a sack of oranges. You know? The netted stuff in the supermarket.'

'I know,' Kay laughed. 'Why do you think I chose this?' And she indicated the more modest, fuller cut of her one-piece.

Helen smiled. 'You know me, I'm a show off.' But the truth was, she'd been drawn to this costume the moment they had walked into the shop. *You've never lived,* the angel had said to her on the first day. Well, she was trying to, she was really trying, and a thong seemed as good as place as any to start.

Caro pushed her curtain back. She was in a red one-piece, with a red skull cap and red feathers. Her heels making her even taller and even more slender. She looked fabulous.

'Caro!' Helen clapped her hands together. 'You look fantastic!'

'I feel it,' Caro smiled. 'Moulin Rouge, here I come!'

'Ta dah!' Now Marianne came out. Shortest of all, she was in a yellow two-piece, a defiant slab of midriff spilling over.

Denny reappeared, holding up a brace of multicoloured feathers. 'Anyone for pinnable bottoms!' he grinned.

ONE ARM on Kay's shoulder, Caro towering in her heels behind and Marianne, a drop shorter at the end, Helen could not stop laughing. None of them could. Twenty minutes it had taken them to get into position. Twenty long minutes of uncontrollable hilarity. The kind of non-stop giggling seven-year-olds find so easy. Minutes of outraged shrieks when Marianne, attempting to position the green feathers of Caro's pinnable bottom, onto her real bottom, had stuck the safety pin in too far. Minutes of having to find a chair, quickly, and sit down and catch her breath, when Kay lost several of her tassels. Lost them? *Where could they have gone?* Helen had wheezed with laughter. And, one hand stuck up her crotch, it had taken Kay forever to persuade them back down again; an age of a time with Marianne holding the back of Helen's chair just to stay upright, and Caro walking back and forth, snorting with laughter. Bunions escaping peep-toes and boobs escaping bras, they had, somehow, managed to line themselves up, ready for Denny to take the photo.

'Smile,' he called, but he hadn't needed to. Not at all.

AND NOW THAT it was over, now that Denny was already at the back of the store, behind his screen, getting ready to print the images, an idea had formed in Helen's head that would not leave.

Caro had already changed. Behind the curtains, she could see Marianne's bare feet. Kay's too.

'Cover for me,' she said, as Caro sat to tie her sneakers.

'Cover for you? Why?'

Kay came out. 'Are you staying like that?' she said, because Helen was still in costume.

'I think,' Helen started. 'I am... For the next two minutes anyway.' Again she turned to Caro. 'If Denny comes out, say I'm getting changed.' And grabbing her handbag, she turned and made for the door. 'I'll be back in a moment.'

'Helen?'

Caro's voice fell away. Two strides more and Helen was

out of the photography shop and onto the pavement. She was hustling and jostling her way through the crowds, trying not to notice if anyone had noticed. She was on the strip, walking the boulevard, the sun on her face, a grown woman with half her life still left to live... and a backside that revelled in its newly-found freedom of movement, swinging left to right like a ship un-moored. She made her way to a nearby drugstore, walked straight in and bought a can of coke. Then she walked out, peeled the ring back and stood in thong and feathers, sipping the fizzy sweet drink. *Now I'm living*, she thought as she tipped her head to the cloudless sky. '*Now*,' she cried. '*Now, I'm living!*'

29

My dear Marianne,

The first thing I want to say to you is, sorry. You know now that I have not made a success of my life. In fact it is fair to say I have made quite a mess of it. Sometimes I feel I would like to change. Leave this part of the world and start again. Other times I feel I'm too old. And anyway, the gambling always seems to win. You said it is not a sickness, and I don't mean to compare it to the suffering of others, but I am sick, Marianne. I am sick at heart and I don't know how to cure myself. I have lost everything I ever valued, more than once, and I don't know how to get it back.

The second thing I want you to know is that although I have said things to you over the last few days that have not been true, some were. The time we spent together in Athens has always stayed with me as one of the happiest periods of my life. I want you to know that. You deserve to know it. You never liked your name, but I loved it and whenever the song came on the radio, I can tell you that I would try to find a quiet place to remember you. You were beautiful then, and you are now. We won't see each other again, not in this life anyway. My dearest hope is that, in time, you will be able to forget the lies of today and remember only how we were yesterday.

Always,

Tony.

'Phffh!' Marianne snorted, 'if he thinks I'm going to waste another minute remembering anything about him, he's a bigger idiot than I thought he was!'

Bags packed, flights checked into, they were sitting at a restaurant table, ninety floors above the ground. Hundreds of feet below, Vegas unfolded like a richly embroidered tapestry of gold and silver, white and dazzling violet. The bird's-eye view had the Paris hotel wrapping around the Eiffel tower like origami paper. Opposite, a black semi-circle of water sprouted tiny snakes of fountains. The luminescent high-roller wheel turned slowly, and almost directly below, straight as an arrow, wide as a river, ran the boulevard, with its ever-moving stream of headlights.

'I thought you were quite taken with him,' Caro said, watching Marianne's hands tremble as she folded the letter in half, and then half again.

'I was flattered, Caro,' Marianne said quietly. She looked down at the square of paper in her hands. 'But I was never really fooled. Even as a young man, he made too many promises, so I should have known.' Looking up, she shrugged, her face softening. 'Leopards, as beautiful as they are, can't change their spots, can they?'

'No,' Caro answered. 'I don't think they can.' She turned to Kay. 'Are you ok?'

Next to Caro, Kay was wearing her jacket. She looked tired, her face pale and drawn, dark hollows underneath her eyes. Then again it had been a hectic day and they were all, Caro suspected, reaching their fill of Vegas.

'I'm fine.' Kay nodded. Her hand pressed to her chest, as if she was winded. 'I'm just a little short of breath. She nodded at the letter. 'He wasn't all bad.'

'No one,' Marianne said flatly, 'is all bad.'

'True.' A silence descended that was, momentarily, too difficult to navigate an exit from and so Kay turned to the view. 'Isn't it extraordinary?' she whispered. 'I've never seen anything like it. It makes me think of that poem... *'Had I the heavens' embroidered cloths, Enwrought with golden and silver light...'*

'Yeats?' Caro said.

'I had to learn it at school. I can't remember much.'

Opposite Kay, and next to Marianne, a hitherto silent Helen leaned across the table. *'The blue and the dim and the dark cloths,'* she quoted. *'Of night and light and the half-light, I would spread the cloths under your feet: But I, being poor, have*

only my dreams; I have spread my dreams under your feet...'
Pausing, she turned to Kay.

'*Tread softly,*' Kay finished, '*because you tread on my dreams.*'

'Beautiful,' Marianne nodded.

Helen smiled. 'Some things you never forget I suppose.'

And watching Caro nodded too. No, some things you never forget. Helen was as animated and beautiful, Caro thought, as she had ever seen her. As alive to life, and all that it offered, as she had been that very first day at university, when stunted by inadequacy and stiff with shyness, an eighteen-year-old Caroline Hardcastle had sat herself as close as she dared, hoping that some of the magic from this golden-haired girl would rub off. Remembering that long ago day, a feeling of tremendous wellbeing arose within Caro, swelling her heart. She picked up her wine glass and turned to look out at the cloth of colour that was Vegas, the fantastical city in which any dream might come true. The colour, the glitter, the bright shining possibility of it all was infectious, the beauty of that bit of poetry deeply intoxicating, the warm glow of friendship that surrounded their table, transporting. So much so that she actually felt the reins as they slipped and fell away completely... 'I'm going to accept,' she said, turning back to the table. 'I'm going to accept his proposal.'

A bubble of delight rose up, wrapping the table, encasing them.

Helen gasped. 'Oh, Caro!' she managed, blinking back tears.

Kay's eyes too were unnaturally bright. 'I think he will make you happy. In fact, I know he will. Very happy indeed.'

'I think so too,' Caro whispered.

'Shook?' Marianne said.

'Shook. Yes.'

'A toast,' Helen called, holding up her glass. 'To Caro.'

'To Caro,' Marianne echoed.

'To C—' Kay started, before pressing her hand harder against her chest, digging the next breath out. 'Caro,' she finished.

Caro's smiled faded. 'Are you really ok?' she asked again.

'Fine,' Kay said. 'But let's get a taxi back?'

'Agreed.' Caro picked up her glass. 'To me then.'

'And us,' Helen added.

'Us!' Marianne echoed. She knocked back a large mouthful of wine, the back of her hand at her mouth as it travelled down. 'I almost forgot!' she cried, when she could speak again, and, reaching for her handbag, she pulled out a large envelope. 'Here are your copies of the photo. You can't go home without them.' And she handed out three copies of the same photograph.

'Mmm.' Helen picked up the closest.

'I definitely like how tall I am,' Kay said. She turned her copy around, so they could all see.

And there they were. Showgirls in bejewelled bras and enormous feathers.

'They could at least have altered our faces,' Helen said. 'You know, used the magic eraser, or whatever it is, to rub out a few lines. Except for Caro.' She picked up her reading glasses. 'Caro's forehead looks great.'

'Ah well,' Caro smiled, 'I'm going to stop that.'

'Botox?'

'Shook...' Caro started, and then stopped. She hadn't worked out what she was going to say. Shook had told her it would be nice to see her frown, but that wasn't the reason she'd decided to stop. She was comfortable in her skin. That was the reason. Maybe, for the first time in her entire life she really felt comfortable with herself. 'It's not that he's said anything...'

'You don't have to explain, Caro,' Kay said quietly.

'Well.' She ran her finger around the rim of her glass. 'I have to admit that he said he'd like to see me frown.'

'So would I,' Helen said softly.

Caro nodded.

'But I don't think I will any time soon. Frown that is. You're too happy with him.'

'I am,' she said, turning to Helen. 'I'm very happy.'

'When are you going to tell him?' Kay asked.

'Well...'

Marianne clasped her hands together under her chin. 'Well?' she echoed.

'Well...' Caro took a deep breath in. The atmosphere at the table had turned playfully encouraging. As if they were a bunch of schoolgirls, egging each other on to get her to accept a date. It was silly, and for a moment she felt like an imposter. This wasn't her terrain. She'd never been the schoolgirl who got asked on a date, she'd never even been the schoolgirl, surrounded by a gaggle of girlfriends. The first and only tight group of friends she'd ever had were Helen and Kay. But what did it matter if it was coming a little late in life? If she was fifty-one, not fifteen. Her friends were here, and a new one too, because there was Marianne grinning like a Cheshire cat across the table, every one of these women opening up their hearts to share and amplify the moment. A happy moment in a life that had been a little short on happy moments. She remembered the image of Shook's hand, resting on the ring box. She understood now why he'd done it. Why he'd given her the preview. He'd shown her an image of what it could be like, and then stepped back to let her think it through. And although he'd been right in knowing that she needed time, neither of them had understood that there was another, equally important factor. Courage – to let go, yes, of the reins of life and simply accept there were things that could not be planned for, or predicted. Like this proposal, which had definitely not been planned, just as any subsequent marriage it resulted in could not be predicted. Life wasn't a spreadsheet, it was far more of a gamble. And if she chose to relax and accept it, this belated scene of smiling friends could be exactly where she was supposed to be. 'Well...' she said again, 'I can't tell him now. I mean it's too late... I'll wake him.'

'I don't think he will mind,' Marianne said.

And for a moment Caro sat, frozen with the expectation she had created. *I can't*, she wanted to say, but of course she could. She could just pick up her phone now, press Shook's number and call him. She looked from one to the other.

Marianne winked at her.

Kay nodded.

'Stop thinking,' Helen whispered. 'Just do it. *Do something spontaneous.*'

'I already have,' Caro laughed. 'This trip.'

'So do something else spontaneous!' Kay said.

'Ok... ok.' Caro reached for her phone. Why not? Why not rush headlong into this moment of joy and why not share it, with these women. With Helen, resolutely weaning herself off the crutches upon which she had leaned for too long. With Marianne, stoic as a veteran, in the face of crushing disappointment. And with Kay. Dear Kay, looking at her right now with an expression of happiness that Caro felt she would have done anything to prolong. Anything at all.

· · ·

THE PHONE RANG OUT. Once, twice, three times before Shook's voice, heavy with sleep answered. 'Caro?'

'Yes,' Caro said quietly.

And from the other side of the world, there was silence.

'Yes,' she said again. 'I want to hear the story.'

No one spoke. Helen reached out and grabbed Kay's hand and squeezed it.

'Caro?' Shook's voice was heard across the table.

'He's awake now,' Marianne nodded.

'You mean it?' Shook said.

'I do.'

'Then I will find a time and place to tell you.'

30

'I wonder where Marianne is?' Helen murmured.

'Halfway across the Atlantic, I expect,' Caro murmured.

'Umm.' Pulling back from the window, champagne in hand, Helen stretched her legs out and glanced sideways at Caro, who was sat in the business class seat beside her. She looked well. A sheen of sun on her cheeks, and contentment in her eyes. She had about her an aura of relief, the kind of ease you might display sitting down at the bank of a river and getting your sandwiches out after a long, long hike. It was nice to see. Even the nervous habit of scraping her hair behind her ears seemed to have fallen away and Helen was happy for her. They were, she thought, sharing space more comfortably than they possibly ever had. All the anger and disappointment she'd been carrying had vanished and this was something they both felt. So much so for Helen, that she'd woken up the morning after the ranch trip feeling as if a slate really had been wiped completely clean. And then, just yesterday, watching with admiration the way Marianne had shoved Tony's letter back into its envelope had been a small, but sharp, revelation. Because Marianne was right. Leopards can't change their spots and the lingering suspicion she'd always had regarding Lawrence's behaviour around Caro hadn't been suspicion after all. Something *had* happened. The wonder of it was, the reveal that had finally set her free... was that she didn't care! With every last one of his spots on show now, there was, quite simply, nowhere left to hide from the fact that many years ago she had married an embarrassingly vain man, who had said what he'd said to Caro, not because it was true, but because he thought that Caro might think it was true. Which made it so much worse. If anything, the only feeling Helen was left with, was a sense of frustration at her own inaction. *Why* had she pretended not to notice Lawrence's self-absorption? *Why* had it taken her so long to face up to the deep unhappiness at the heart of her marriage? Marianne had seen through Tony in five minutes and Kay had been right, she certainly did not need any knights in any kind of armour.

Yes, Vegas had been revelatory in so many ways and now, as the wing of the plane cast a lone shadow on the dry lands of the American southwest thousands of feet below, Helen made herself a promise. She would come back. She would fill that rucksack she bought just last year, buy some walking boots and finally, finally set off on the adventure she had for so long yearned for. 'Nine and half hours,' she nodded contentedly, 'with nothing to do but eat, sleep and drink.'

'And a movie or two,' Caro said, unpacking earphones, cashmere socks, a padded sleep mask...

Helen eased her seat back. 'Not too many. We've got things to discuss.'

'We do?'

'Yes.' Helen took a large sip of champagne. 'Weddings need planning, Caro. Where. When. Etcetera etcetera.'

'Oh, the when is easy.' Caro lowered her voice. 'As soon as possible. For Kay.'

'Of course.' Helen looked down at her glass and then levering her seat upright again, twisted to look across the aisle at Kay.

The seat next to Kay was unoccupied, and although business class was fairly spacious, they had decided that Kay should be the one to make use of the extra space an empty seat provided. It looked like she had. Her legs were stretched out and she'd inclined her seat back as far as she could, but her hand was on her chest, again. Caro had mentioned this new mannerism last night, and ever since Helen had been unable to stop seeing it. There was no point in asking. Every time they did, Kay answered that she was fine. And tired. And looking forward to getting back home.

'How are you doing?' she said now.

Lazily, Kay turned her head. 'Fine. A little warm.'

Helen nodded at the jacket Kay still wore. She'd hardly taken it off the last couple of days. 'You can take it off now,' she said. 'It's been worn. You can say you wore it.'

'I can, can't I?' Kay said and smiled. She leaned forward to ease herself out of her Vegas jacket, smoothing her hand across the sequins as she laid it across her knees. 'It was a good trip,' she murmured. 'I'm so glad we made it.'

Caro nodded. 'It was.'

'And now I'm going to try and sleep.' As Kay reached up for the overhead light, her jacket slipped to the floor.

'Here.' Helen unclipped her seatbelt and stood up. Kay would never reach. She moved across, turned the light off, picked up the jacket and spread it over Kay's chest and shoulders. 'Go to sleep,' she whispered.

'Wake me for breakfast?'

'Of course.'

And as Kay closed her eyes, Helen leaned froward to push her fringe back from her brow. Just as she had so many times with her children.

Slipping back into her own seat, she picked up her glass again. 'Right,' she said to Caro. 'Shall we make a start?' She was giggling as she spoke and looking back at her, Caro laughed too.

'It's far too early, Helen.'

'It's not. Are you thinking traditional, or more age-appropriate dress...' She frowned. 'What does age appropriate even mean?'

'Nothing,' Caro answered. 'It means nothing at all.'

THEY DIDN'T GET FAR. A few ideas about dress colour or length that moved quickly onto food and Helen thinking firstly about her appetite and secondly about a recipe she hadn't used in years, for shortcrust pastry and then whether she might take on the food completely, or if Caro would want her to, or if she really could be bothered... And as the peaks of Colorado became the depths of the Great Lakes, and the drawl of Iowa became the French of Quebec City, the Atlantic Ocean began its great three-thousand mile roar. Until hours later the first weak squibs of orange light peeking over a domed horizon were the sign that they were finally catching up with the sun.

Helen was the first to wake. Stirring from under the folds of her blanket, she opened her eyes. The cabin was still mostly in darkness. Her right shoulder ached and her foot was cramping. Sitting up she flexed her toes and looked first at Caro, and then across at Kay. Both were still sleeping.

Pushing her feet into the slippers she'd acquired from the hotel, she made her way to the toilet and, on her return, stood looking along the aisles of sleeping, silent passengers, her eyes moving back to Kay over and again. It was Kay's hand that drew Helen's attention. The way it lay curled across her lap, still and luminously white. Her Vegas jacket was crumpled on the floor, her eyes were closed.

'Kay?' Helen moved to kneel alongside Kay's seat.

Kay didn't stir.

Tentatively she reached her hand to Kay's. It was ice cold. 'Kay?' she managed again and her bladder, although she'd just been to the toilet, loosened in terror, her arms filling warm and heavy with blood. 'Kay...' Helen's voice failed. It failed because now she was close, she could see. Kay's eyes weren't fully closed, a line of white lay exposed, just underneath the lid, lifeless as a statue. And her face was alabaster, the blood gone. Dread balled in Helen's throat, closed it up and pressed it shut as sure as a boot on her windpipe. 'Caro,' she whispered, as she tried to turn, her voice a scrape, her legs wobbly with terror. 'Caro,' she persisted, because something was wrong...

Caro murmured as she opened her eyes, saw the expression on Helen's face and in an instant, sat up and looked across at Kay.

AND FOREVER AFTER, whenever she tried to remember, Helen wouldn't know and could never recall the order of events that followed. How it had started.

Was it the air steward whispering through the slightly open door to the cockpit?

Or the galley lights going on? The white and blue of the crew uniform as they scuttled into life?

Was it the pilot's announcement, asking if there was a doctor on board?

Or the man, in a black tracksuit, two rows back, leaning to the aisle, staring at her?

Or was it the doctor coming forward from economy, a small woman in loose linen trousers and hair in a ponytail, who had pushed Helen aside to bend low over Kay. On her knees, flicking her ponytail back and holding Kay's wrist, pressing fingertips deep into Kay's neck again and again, waggling her fingers impatiently as she reached an arm back for the stethoscope the steward offered... and then, what had seemed an age later, shaking her head sadly, at the red box he held, the tubing of the stethoscope limp around her neck. *No pulse to shock back into rhythm,* she'd explained, and the steward had nodded, his face white, his eyes glassy with shocked tears.

Long after, Caro had told her that this was when she'd screamed. That it had taken two stewards to pull her back from Kay and move her forward to the galley, where they had yanked the curtain across, leaving Caro in the aisle, staring at the doctor. Helen could not remember. At the edge of consciousness, she had a muddled awareness of her hands at her ears, her mouth open, but more than that she could not remember.

She remembered the whispered questions the doctor had asked them both. Questions about medications Kay was taking, about the shortness of breath she'd complained of. How long? How frequent? How severe?

She remembered scattered words of conversation they had had with the pilot, who had stood in the aisle, his white shirt bright against her eyes. *Clot, pulmonary embolism, no pulse.* She remembered the steward, replacing his little red box and closing the overhead compartment in which it lived, that action, like a conductor's final downward sweep of the baton, bringing it all to an end.

And she remembered clutching a tumbler of something, a drink the steward had placed in her hands, and Caro, and the way he had crouched, one hand on the back of Caro's seat as he talked them through what would happen. How, with only a couple of hours left of the flight, they would leave Kay in her seat. There was no one next to her and she would, of course, be covered with a blanket, but as per normal procedures, it was best now to leave her. Would they like to move into first class?

No! Sometimes in her memories, this image came first, the steward indicating the curtain that separated first class from business. But of course, that could not have been the case; it's funny the tricks a mind in turmoil can play. *No!* They had responded together, Caro and herself, equally adamant that *No,* they did not want to move. *No,* they would not leave their friend.

The one memory she was sure of, was that when the cabin lights had been dimmed again, she had slipped out of her seat and had taken Kay's jacket and spread it over her cold shoulders and her cold cold hands. And that, hours later, as the grey light of another London dawn had seeped into the cabin, and the ancient meandering of the Thames had made itself visible, Helen had closed her eyes and reached out for Caro's hand and sat thinking only one thing. Alex. How were they going to tell Alex?

PART V

31

'Cheers,' Caro said and chinked Helen's glass.

'Cheers,' Helen returned.

They were back in Cyprus. In a coffee shop, on the crescent-shaped waterfront that was Kyrenia harbour. On the table between them lay a few crumbled remains of the giant slab of *shamali* cake they'd shared. A few feet away, the sea wall and then the turquoise-blue of the Mediterranean. A thousand sailboats strained at their creaking ropes, masts jiggling, booms humming, canopies fluttering like ribbons. Helen felt the breeze on her face, heard the percussion of the boats and remembered the day she had launched one. Launched it and helped right it after it had capsized. It was only two years ago. It felt like a lifetime.

'To your divorce,' Caro smiled.

'To your wedding,' Helen answered.

She'd done it. She was Helen Winters no longer. A single woman again after two and a half decades, and back to her maiden name of Crossley. She had a small flat, with a spare room and a small balcony that caught the morning sun and had space for a few pots and a hanging basket, in which she had planned to grow strawberries but hadn't yet managed to do so. Libby too had her own place and although Helen wasn't comfortable with the location, she hadn't said a word. Libby had re-taken her finals, had a place for Ben in the nursery, was halfway through her master's degree and nearly all the way back to resuming her role as Number One Giver of Unwanted Advice to her mother. Jack, she never saw. Two thirds of his way through his degree and now a summer in America before his final year. Still, she had his favourite cereal in for the times he did make it back. But she had to face it, the balance of her relationship with her children had changed, because they had changed. Whenever she saw them, it took her breath away. It was as if the dough from which they were made had been re-rolled and thicker, more substantial forms cut. Every time, they were that bit less her children and that bit more their own people. It was a maturity of mind, a switch they were making themselves. It didn't do to dwell on this, so she tried not to and although the first few weeks in her new flat had found her scrolling through her laptop, searching for photographs of children who no longer existed, the habit was loosening its grip. Maybe because she tried hard to remember what Kay had said. The love never dies. And because she knew that she loved her children as much as she ever had, she also knew that, yes, somewhere in this universe, or the next, they were still there.

'Can you ever imagine doing it again?' Caro asked.

Slowly Helen turned to her. 'Marrying?'

'Yes.'

Helen shook her head. 'I don't think so. I suppose I should never say never, but I've changed too much.' She put her glass down and looked out at the water. 'When I was younger,' she said, 'I bought into the fairy-tale hook line and sinker. You know, the soulmate for life idea. Now? Now I wouldn't even buy it if it was half price in Tesco. It's a lie. Unless someone changes in exactly the same ways that you do yourself, how can they possibly be a soulmate?' She shook her head. 'No, it's a lie, and I don't know why it's peddled so hard to young women.'

'Well, I don't think I'd disagree with that.' Caro nodded.

Helen turned to her. 'But I'm so happy for you,' she said. 'I really am, Caro. What you and Shook have is very different to what I once had with Lawrence. You're not going into this making him the foundation on which to build your life. You never hung around waiting for a hero to turn up. You struck your own path, and I always admired you for that.'

Caro leaned forward, her chin resting in the palm of her hand. 'I might have done all that,' she said, with a lop-sided smile, 'if I'd been the girl with the golden hair...'

'Bit grey now,' Helen said, twisting a lock of her hair.

Caro smiled. 'Sometimes it has been a lonely path.'

'I know,' Helen said. 'I might not always have known how lonely you were, but I do now.'

Caro breathed in. 'And you were right,' she said. 'The last time we were here, what you said. You were right, Helen.'

'Oh, Caro,' Helen sighed. 'I'm not sure I've been right about anything.'

'This is difficult but... ' Caro looked down at her hands. 'You said I was having the baby to keep me company. Remember?'

'I said a lot of things... Maybe things I shouldn't have said.'

'What is a friend, Helen?' Caro asked, her smile small but warm. 'If you can't say what you really think?'

'I hurt you.'

'No.' Caro shook her head. 'You challenged me, Helen. And you were right to. I will never be a mother and I've accepted that, but... I will be someone's wife and I am very much looking forward to that.'

Looking up, Helen wiped a tear from her eye. There were speeches and speeches inside her, but none of them could articulate what she wanted to say. The moment was as glorious as it was sad. Caro. Shy Caroline, scared of everything and everyone, in her scrunched-up cardigan and heavy-framed glasses. How far she'd come. How far she still had to go. She put a fist to her mouth, tears brimming. 'Kay should be here,' she managed.

Caro nodded. 'Yes.'

And twisting on her chair, Helen leaned forward to look along the bustling quayside. 'So where the bloody hell is she? Marianne said they were leaving ages ago!'

'I'll text,' Caro said, reaching for her phone. 'Oh! Hang on! She already texted.' And stretching the phone to arm's length, shielding her eyes from the sun, she read from their group WhatsApp chat.

> Sorry. Fell asleep in the sun. Be there as soon as possible. Do not decide anything until we get there. Marianne has a folder of information.

'What time was that?'

'Fifteen minutes ago.'

Helen frowned. 'Kay needs to stop falling asleep in public places. She'll wake up in a morgue one day.'

'She very nearly did!' Caro laughed. 'Remember the

ambulance waiting on the runway?'

'Remember!' Helen snorted. 'I'll never bloody forget it! Never mind Kay, I don't know how I didn't end up in it. The shock when she sat up and asked if she'd missed breakfast!'

'Especially after the doctor—' But Caro couldn't finish. She was shaking her head, tears of laughter streaming.

'Doctor!' Helen cried. 'She had a PhD in podiatry! Anything above the knee and she was clueless! Do you remember that woman on the TV, the one who used to examine people's poo? She called herself a doctor as well.'

Wiping her eyes, Caro nodded. 'Well thank God for real doctors. Otherwise she probably wouldn't be here.'

'True,' Helen said as she picked up her glass. 'People really are living with it now, aren't they?' She smiled, but her eyes were wistful and sad. 'I wish this treatment had been around for my mother.'

Neither of them spoke, and then Caro reached for her own glass, picked it up and raised it. 'Here's to mothers,' she said. 'Yours and mine.'

'And glasses half full,' Helen smiled. 'Oh!' Tilting to look along the pavement, she said, 'Here they come!'

Caro turned.

Kay and Marianne were approaching the table, Marianne carrying a serious-looking folder under her arm.

'Sorry,' Kay breathed as she pulled out a chair. 'I fell asleep...'

'Again?' Helen said.

'No comment,' Kay said. She looked at the glasses and the champagne bottle and the ice bucket. 'Started without us?'

And before anyone could answer, Marianne slapped her folder on the table. 'So! We have a wedding to plan?'

Caro smiled. 'You know we still haven't decided?

England, Poland or here.'

Marianne snorted as she waved a hand at the view before them. 'Why on earth would you choose anywhere *but* here?'

'It is glorious,' Caro admitted. She turned to Kay. 'How about you, have you decided?'

'About work? Yes. I handed in my notice last week. This term will be my last.'

'Really?' Helen gasped.

'Oh.' Caro's mouth stayed open. 'I wasn't at all sure you would.'

Kay nodded. 'Me neither. But life is too short. I want to spend whatever time is left sitting in the sun. Alex is great. He's decided that as he's passed his driving test, he'll do the shopping now. Apparently, he's not keen on lasagne or shepherd's pie anymore and wants to choose himself!' She shrugged. 'It's one less job for me. And with mum gone now, there doesn't seem to be a reason not to.'

'Come and live here?' Helen finished.

'Probably,' Kay smiled. 'I do love it here.'

'Who wouldn't!' Marianne turned her palms to the sky.

'Dad,' Kay smiled, 'is very well. He could go on for another twenty years, he's so sprightly. So...' Reaching across to the ice-bucket, she pulled the champagne bottle out. 'So I think I want to be able to sit in the sun. It's a short flight back if I'm needed and...' As she filled her glass, she turned to Caro. 'You don't regret giving up your job, do you?'

'Nooo.' Caro shook her head. 'Who's going to supply you with tomatoes if I go back to work?'

'True,' Kay laughed. 'They are delicious. How many plants have you got this year?'

'Twenty-four,' Caro said. 'I'm cutting back. My apartment looks like a greenhouse again.'

'You'll be a farmer yet,' Helen smiled.

'Funny you should mention that.' Caro smiled. 'Shook showed me a property just last week, near Gdansk. A farm.'

'You're not!' Putting the bottle down, Kay stared at her.

'A farmer!' Helen was incredulous.

'I must admit I find that hard to imagine,' Marianne said, taking the bottle from Kay.

'So! You're all going off and leaving me!' Helen declared. 'Kay to Cyprus, you to Poland—'

'Whoa!' Caro held her hand up. 'Nothing's decided. It's a decision for another time. And anyway, you're off soon enough, aren't you?'

'Three weeks,' Helen said and took the bottle from Marianne.

'Do you have your itinerary sorted?' Kay asked.

Helen nodded. As the delicate bubbles of champagne fizzed away near the top of her glass, she twisted the bottle to end the flow, and passed it over to Caro. Yes, finally she was going. Six weeks across the States, starting in Washington DC, finishing in Puerto Vallarta, Mexico. Strawberries, in hanging baskets, would have to wait. And this was only the start. Having come to an agreement with her boss, every year she had determined would take her somewhere new on an extended trip. Vegas had re-ignited the flame that Cyprus lit. Her rucksack was half-packed, and she was tramping around with her boots on every night, trying to break them in. She had a subscription to Lonely Planet and had downloaded the app to her phone. Many evenings had passed with her smart new flat looking more like the student flat they had all shared thirty years ago. Planning which campsite to stop at, which stars to sleep under, had turned out to be a lot more interesting than polishing taps.

'So,' Caro said. 'We're looking at September. After Helen

gets back and if you won't be at school, Kay... It could be any time?'

'It could be any time,' Kay echoed.

Eyes narrowing, Caro looked at Marianne's folder. 'Is that *all* wedding info?'

'A little,' Marianne said, one hand firmly on her file. 'But it's also proof!'

'Proof?'

'The door. I've proved that there was room. They've done tests and everything.'

'Door?' Helen looked around the table. 'What on earth are we talking about?'

Caro had her reading glasses on. '*Titanic*,' she muttered as she reached for Marianne's file. 'And I have to say, Marianne, I'm not sure how you can say there is actual proof. I mean short of re-enacting the whole scene—'

'Wait!' Helen raised her glass. '*Titanic* can bloody well wait. We all know how that story ended. First a toast. To friends?'

'And sleeping under stars,' Caro toasted.

'And tomatoes!' Kay laughed.

'And doors that have room for two!' Marianne cried.

'And to not needing any knights in shining armour, ever!' Helen finished.

'*Cheers!*' they echoed, and their glasses made a fairy-tale chink, and the bubbles in the champagne caught the light and passed it on to the silver stars that danced on the waves of an ocean that Helen of Troy, survivor of three husbands and one war, had once crossed, to end her days in the warmth of a setting sun.

THE END

AFTERWORD

Would you like to be a fly on the wall, when Shook tells Caro the story of the ring?

You can do so by ordering *the story of the ring,* a short story that accompanies this series.

ALSO BY CARY J HANSSON

Do you remember the 80s?

The Gen X Series is a brand new collection of women's contemporary fiction, featuring strong female characters who were there in 1985 and have the t-shirt to prove it!

Written by Cary J Hansson, author of the acclaimed and hugely popular Midlife Trilogy these stories merge brutal honesty, with wry wit.

If you like scarred but resilient heroines, nostalgic interludes, and transformative epiphanies, then you'll love *The Gen X Series.*

Start with book one: *Back, to her future*

Postcards from Midlife is a series of short stories, designed to be read and enjoyed in one sitting. Perfect with a coffee and far more satisfying than a pastry!

For more information about my work and books please visit:

https://www.caryjhansson.com/

BACK, TO HER FUTURE.

AN EXTRACT

Sammy's list to live for!
1. Be blonde!
2. Scatter mum's ashes
3. Buy Versace jeans and wear them
4. Renew passport
5. Ride in a DeLorean
6. See George Might-be

Completely bald and wrapped in a fluffy dressing gown that barely knotted across her stomach, Sammy sat at her kitchen table. Round as a snowman, with a pink snooker ball of a head. She pulled the paper closer and read through her pencilled list again.

If it was funny when she'd written it, it was ridiculous now. Now that it wasn't just a list. Now that the DeLorean was parked on the drive and the weekend booked. God knows where Gary had found that car. She'd been too surprised to protest, although she had no idea why she should be. It was on the list, therefore Gary would get it done. The irony was she'd only added it because she couldn't think of anything else. And she'd only added George Michael, because that was impossible. It hadn't stopped him.

She picked up her mug and in an attempt to taste the tea, took a long, determined slurp. Nothing. Only a warm wetness in her mouth. Chemo spoiled everything, and the list was ridiculous! She put her mug down, it left a splodged rim all over the Vers of Versace. Sighing, Sammy rubbed her eyes. What did it matter anyway? Her arse was too huge for Primark jeans, let alone Versace. And blonde? Well she'd fancied trying that since she was sixteen. If she hadn't got around to it by now ...

At the hob Gary banged a pan, sending rashers of sizzling bacon into the air and making Sammy jump. She looked across. How long had she been cooking for him? And the kids? And anyone else who walked through the back door? Thirty years, without ever finding the need to bang a pan so hard the contents jumped. Cooking programmes, she thought as she watched him, had a lot to answer for. She looked down again at her tea-stained list, moving the mug and blotting the paper with the sleeve of her dressing gown.

Is that it? Gary had said when he'd first read it and after he'd left her alone for half an hour to *really* think about it, *because it's important Sammy.* Umm, yeah, that was it. God knows she'd tried hard enough to think, but she really wasn't bothered about swimming with dolphins, or seeing the Northern Lights, or the Great Barrier Reef. And she felt guilty about that. About what? Lack of ambition was the answer she'd eventually come to. That, and a complete inability to see through the little ambition she did have.

Because why for example hadn't she ever dyed her hair blonde? Or renewed her passport? When had her world grown so small? She picked up her mug and took another slurp of tea and it burned her throat. Renewing the passport now, like Gary had suggested, was plain ridiculous. Ten years? It could last longer than she did. Probably would.

'You Ok?' Gary turned, the spatula he held pointing heavenward.

'Fine,' she muttered. '*Fine.*' And she put her head to one side and feigned an interested, expression, as she pretended to the study this list she knew so well. Are you Ok? He was *always* asking her that. And what was she supposed to say? No, I'm not Ok? I'm terrified. I'm mutilated. I'm struggling to find a way to carry on? *Re-new passport,* she read three times, waiting for him to turn back to the bacon.

Finally, he did.

Her eyes followed the numbers down, reaching number five. *Ride in a De Lorean,* and suddenly no pretence was needed. Her smile was natural and real. Oh yes. Enfield Odeon. January 1986. *Back to the Future.* Her first ever date with Gary. Sitting in the dark of the cinema, butterflies raging in her stomach like bulls with wings. Those first fledgling stirrings of romance had produced feelings so rare and wondrous, she'd remembered them all her life. That's why it was on the list. The car was a time machine wasn't it? And if she'd like to go back to anything, she'd like to go back to that.

'You look happy.' Gary plonked a plate of bacon and eggs on the table.

Startled Sammy looked from the plate, to her husband. She hadn't even smelt it cooking. How the hell was she going to eat it? 'Thanks, darling,' she said, the smile nailed down. 'Looks lovely.'

He grinned back and Sammy thought what she'd been thinking a lot recently. If she ever won the lottery, the first thing she'd do was get his teeth fixed.

She picked up her knife and fork. Get his teeth fixed? She hadn't been thinking that back in the dark of the Odean but ... well things change. Thirty years this year they would be married, and every time the anniversary was mentioned Gary made the same joke. *You get less for murder.* Every single time. She gave him a reassuring smile and took a mouthful and waited for him to turn away before she began the laborious process of chewing. From day one, the entire family had approached her illness with such a *Can Do!* positive attitude, she'd felt she had zero choice but to make merry and get on board, when sometimes, like right now, she craved a little space to just be miserable. To be left to chew her tasteless food in peace.

And chew ...

And chew ...

God, it was tasteless.

Gary started whistling, elbows wide, scrubbing the frying pan.

Sammy put her hand across her mouth and forced the bacon down. Sighed. Readied herself and scooped another forkful in. Desperate for distraction, she picked up her list again.

Scatter mum's ashes

This ... She shook her head as she swallowed. This was a hard one. Why in five years hadn't she managed to fulfil the promise she'd made to her mother and scatter her ashes. Fleetwood wasn't the North Pole for Gods sake. Why had it taken cancer to move her? And it had. She was under no illusions about that. A cancer-free Sammy, she knew, would have shrugged and said, *I'll get round to it*. But this new

Sammy was different. A significant part of her body had been removed. If she felt less solid now, so did life itself. One more day gone and now she knew ... Those left were countable after all. None of the old excuses worked anymore.

'Right.' Gary was wiping his hands on a tea towel. 'Are you going to be ok?' he said. 'I can still drive you there?'

'In the DeLorean?' Sammy glanced out to the driveway. (Yesterday, she'd peeked inside. It was so low!) 'I'm fine,' she said. 'I'll take the tube.'

'Ok.' He took his anorak from the peg and pulled it on.

That was another thing ... if she won the lottery, she'd throw that old thing away and buy a Calvin Klein. If Calvin Klein did anoraks.

'I'm going to check the oil and the tyres. Alma knows we have to leave at two?'

Sammy nodded. Alma knew. Everyone knew. Gary had told them at least 756 times. Pointing her fork at a small bottle of clear water that stood by the drainer, she smiled. 'Aren't you forgetting something?'

Gary picked up the bottle. It was labelled *Holy Water*. 'Don't, Sammy,' he said warningly. 'Just don't.' And with a last look of reproach he was gone.

She looked at the empty space where his anorak had been. Funny. The boy she'd fallen in love with had been the rogue of the class. Her handsome carefree Irish rover. Now? She blamed parenthood. He took it all so seriously.

She waited until he was in the car, had backed out the drive and disappeared around the corner before she reached for her cigarettes then, tipping the remains of her breakfast into the bin, she took a satisfying drag, leaned against the kitchen door and watched the street go about its business. The kid from three doors down walking the dog. The tail-less cat from No 37, sitting on the bonnet of No. 45's car. It was a favourite past time. She was after all, a natural by-stander. And she'd been watching for so long, that the new faces were now the old faces, and the kid from three doors down was actually a lanky teenager and she could remember when the cat from No 37 had a tail. They should sell. The house was far too big for just the two of them and a century had passed over since they were the new kids on the block. She brought her thumb to her mouth and bit free a thread of loose skin, smoke stinging her eyes. What did Gary say when he came home yesterday in that car? It would take her back to her youth? Take her back! The idea had her tipping her bald head to the sky and laughing, which had her coughing. Fist at her mouth, folded over, cough-laughing. Youth? She never had a youth! Sean was born the month before her eighteenth, for which Sammy had always partly blamed Madonna and all that *Keeping my Baby* stuff. Oh, but hadn't they been happy? In their little house with their little baby? Not once, not really, had she ever thought she'd missed out and, for the longest time she'd blithely assumed Gary had thought the same. But ... she looked down at her fingers, the half smoked cigarette. But what? She knew what. Along with that *Less for murder* quip, Gary had starting saying other stuff. Just last week, she'd heard him on the phone to an old friend. Same house, same job, *same old, same old*. And the row they'd had when she'd gotten cold feet about Australia! Yes, she missed, Sean but she preferred to wait until he came back home, thank you. Which she was sure he would. Gary hadn't been happy. And so she'd stopped assuming some things, and started assuming other things. Perhaps he hadn't ever really been happy? Perhaps it hadn't been enough? She looked at the cigarette again, went into the kitchen, drowned it under the tap and buried it deep in the bin. Then she ran her hand over her smooth bald head and looked at the clock.

Ten-thirty already.

Thank God, Alma had put their meeting back an hour! Imagine if she hadn't? Alone in her kitchen, Sammy laughed. *You'll be late for your own funeral,* her mother used to say ... which was a bit too close to the mark these days. Still, she was glad to have this little bit of extra time and because this was the new Sammy, she remembered to be thankful that she was glad. A fleeting victory. And then she remembered! And her hand flew to her mouth in delayed shock. Alma had re-arranged their meeting because she was meeting Meryem Saylan first.

'Meryem Saylan,' Sammy said, shaping each syllable as if she were re-discovering the sound. Brilliant, funny, loud Meryem who just disappeared one day, never to be seen again. In the quiet of her kitchen, Sammy snapped her head up to the kitchen door, 'Gary, you'll never guess ... '

But of course, he was long gone.

A NOTE FROM THE AUTHOR

Thank you for reading, *A Midlife Gamble*

Gaining exposure as an independent author relies mostly upon word-of-mouth, so if you have the time and inclination, please consider leaving a short review or rating wherever you can.

Your local amazon platform

Goodreads

If you interested in having me participate in your reading group, do get in touch via my social media.

(Don't worry, I'll bring my own wine!)

To keep up with new releases and all my book news you can join my mailing list Here

And for a more regular fix of my writing try following my blog:

https://postcardsfrommidlife.blog/

Thank you for helping to spread the word,

Cary